BEST ACTRESS

BEST ACTRESS

JOHN KANE

BALLANTINE BOOKS · NEW YORK

A Ballantine Book
Published by The Ballantine Publishing Group
Copyright © 1998 by John Kane

All rights reserved under International and Pan-American Copyright Conventions.
Published in the United States by The Ballantine Publishing Group,
a division of Random House, Inc., New York,
and simultaneously in Canada by
Random House of Canada Limited, Toronto.

http://www.randomhouse.com

Library of Congress Cataloging-in-Publication Data

Kane, John
Best actress / John Kane. — 1st ed.
p.   cm.
ISBN 0-345-42071-3
I. Title.
PS3561.A4675B47   1998
813'.54—dc21   97-38568
CIP

Cover design by Heather Kern
Cover illustration by Steven Salerno

Manufactured in the United States of America

First Edition: February 1998

10   9   8   7   6   5   4   3   2

THIS BOOK IS FOR MY PARENTS

AUTHOR'S NOTE

Best Actress is a work of fiction. Certain public figures, publications and television shows make cameo appearances in these pages, but only for purposes of verisimilitude and window dressing. Their appearances are the work of my imagination and not intended to be taken as fact or as a negative reflection upon them. To repeat, this is a work of fiction.

"There's no deodorant like success."
—Elizabeth Taylor

BEST ACTRESS

OSCAR NIGHT, 4:00 P.M.

She opened her small Chanel purse and examined its contents: a bejeweled lipstick case, some Maybelline eye shadow (cheap as hell, but it worked for her; she always knew what worked for her), a box of wintergreen Tic-Tacs, a small vibrator (after all, you never know) and, of course, the pearl-handled revolver.

She slid her hand into the purse and began to massage the revolver, rubbing the handle, fingering the barrel. A small sexual frisson shot through her as she did so, causing her to moan softly.

Lucky the driver couldn't hear her. But even if he had, he wouldn't talk. Limo drivers in Los Angeles knew better than to trade stories on their movie-star clients. Unless it was the kind of really juicy dirt the tabloids would pay top dollar for. A sexy little sigh in the backseat was nothing. Hell, it could have been the unseasonably hot weather that made her do it. How could the aspiring actor in the front seat, separated from her by a pane of tinted glass and several million dollars per year in earned income, ever know that it was the possibility of murder that was sending a shiver of sexual ecstasy through the loins of his world-famous client?

And she was famous. She'd fought hard for that fame; it was

her most valued possession, the one that allowed her to acquire all her other possessions. Like the glittering, ice-white Bulgari diamond bracelets that adorned her wrists.

They're all mine, she thought, looking at the bracelets, bought and paid for.

She inspected her body with pleasure. Her legs were long and supple. They peeked out from a slit in the stunning dress she had persuaded an internationally known designer to loan her for the night. Her breasts swelled magnificently from her small waist, their nipples now hard with the thought of violence.

They're all mine too, she chuckled to herself. Bought and paid for just like the diamond bracelets.

So what if they were fake? So were everybody else's. A year ago when she'd had them done her plastic surgeon told her there hadn't been a real set of tits in Hollywood since Jane Russell. And that was forty years ago.

These things—her breasts, her diamonds, her fame—helped to calm her as the car climbed the winding roads of the canyon to pick up her escort. And she needed to remain calm: she was, after all, a nominee for the Academy Award for Best Actress of the year.

She saw him standing in the doorway of the house as the driver swung the car into the driveway. Lucky man, she thought, he's in for quite an evening. He's going to be either the escort of the recipient of the Best Actress Oscar or the unwitting accomplice of a cold-blooded murderess.

Because if she didn't hear her name called out tonight, she knew what she would do. She would reach into her Chanel purse, pull out the pearl-handled revolver, point it at the stage of the Shrine Auditorium and shoot the bitch who had been named Best Actress right between the eyes.

Of that much she was sure.

4

GOOD MORNING: Oscar nominees were announced this morning, 5 ayem, by two-time winner Sally Field and Academy President Arthur Hiller in a pre-dawn broadcast from the Academy headquarters on Wilshire. Our congratulations to all the happy nominees.

—Army Archerd
Daily Variety
February 6

1

Fiona Covington snuggled under the floral Laura Ashley sheets in the Santa Monica bedroom of the house she and her husband Colin were renting. The owners of the house, a television comedy writing team whose show had been canceled last season, had been under the sway of the Santa Fe decorating craze that swept the west side of Los Angeles in the mid-eighties. Thus the room was complete with bleached floors, Indian baskets, a dull pink and aqua rope rug and a Mission-style bed. But Fiona, who had never been away from London for more than a week or two, found herself terribly homesick in the mornings. So she had gone out and bought yards of homey Laura Ashley fabric, lovely purple and russet, and draped it over the windows. A collection of pewter mugs was arranged on the bedside table, accompanied by Colin's pipe collection. And on the dresser stood a triptych frame containing photos of Prince Phillip, Queen Elizabeth and the Queen Mum. The total effect of the room could best be described as Royal Family Navajo.

Fiona couldn't have cared less. At thirty-two she was married to the brilliant young actor/director Colin Tromans, the man most often referred to as the next Laurence Olivier, and had become a star in her own right. She and Colin had met during a production of *Titus Andronicus* at the National Theatre in London while they were both students at the Royal Academy of Dramatic Arts. Though the play mystified Fiona (who could possibly care about these horrible people, she wondered, as she took the underground back to her flat in Earl's Court), there was no mistaking the gleam in Colin's eye when he spotted her on the first day of rehearsal.

"One lump or two?" he asked as he passed her a cup of tea during a break.

"One and just a little cream," responded Fiona breathlessly.

In England this is what passes for foreplay, and by opening night Fiona and Colin were lovers. Six months later Colin's avant-garde production of *Hamlet*, in which he portrayed both Hamlet and the Ghost, opened to raves at the Chichester Festival and his career was launched. For her part, Fiona became the darling of the Merchant-Ivory set when she made her film debut a year later in *A Private Chamber*, based on a little-known E. M. Forster short story, portraying a sexually repressed librarian who experiences her first orgasm while gazing out her Florence hotel room window at the Ponte Vecchio. Her pale English schoolgirl looks—button nose, red hair and large brown eyes—were soon decorating the pages of English *Vogue* and *Tatler* on a regular basis.

After their triumphant West End revival of *The Sound of Music* (Fiona's Maria won the *Evening Standard* award, as did Colin's direction), the duo embarked on separate film projects. He directed and starred in a remake of *Blithe Spirit* with Maggie Smith as Madame Arcati, while Fiona took on the challenge of the lead role in *Mary*. A revisionist telling of the Mary Poppins story, *Mary* featured Fiona as a repressed lesbian nanny who took out her hatred of the ruling class by terrorizing the little children she had been hired to care for. Burt, the chimney sweep, became a middle-aged drag queen, and at the film's conclusion Fiona is seen drunk in a Soho pub muttering, "God save the Queen. No one else fucking will!"

The film stirred enormous controversy in England, with Margaret Thatcher even announcing that she planned to run for Prime Minister again so that she could ban it. But the controversy translated into great box-office and *Mary* quickly became the highest-grossing English film since *Goldfinger*. The United States reception was even more overwhelming, with *Time* magazine praising Fiona for "fearlessly revealing the dark side of Victorian London."

And so last month Fiona and Colin had departed their Chelsea flat for a Santa Fe–style bungalow in Santa Monica. He was to direct a film version of *Macbeth* for TriStar in which Fiona and Richard Gere would portray the dreadfully ambitious Scottish couple. Fiona was also scheduled to meet with Robert De Niro to discuss the female lead in his new film. And, best of all, this morning she would learn if she had been nominated for the Academy Award for *Mary*.

Fiona pulled the Laura Ashley sheets closer, closed her eyes and imagined that she was back in London, listening to a BBC Radio broadcast of the speeches of Sir Harold McMillan while chewing on an overpriced chocolate biscuit. Her reverie came to an abrupt end as Colin swept into the bedroom bearing a large tray laden with food.

"Morning, dearest," he said as he placed the tray before her, being careful not to muss her bedsheets or his maroon silk bathrobe.

"Oh," sighed Fiona, "you've brought me brekky." Brekky was Fiona's affectionate nickname for breakfast. Like so many educated, upper-class English people, Fiona had the lamentable habit of lapsing into a cloying childspeak at almost any moment.

She referred to her pocketbook as "my pocky" and used to call her breasts "my bosies" until Colin forbade her to do so.

The breakfast Colin had served up was certainly not fit for a child. There were three fried eggs surrounded by rings of sausages and bacon, all dripping in grease. A large bowl of porridge and a pot of cream sat next to the teapot. A stack of toast, heavily buttered, was accompanied by three kinds of marmalade—orange, grapefruit and prune. As a special treat there was a plate of fried blood sausage, made from pig's intestines, cornmeal and spices. The entire meal probably would have killed a child, much less a cow, but it was the traditional English breakfast and Fiona adored Colin for making it for her.

"Hungry are we now, dear?" queried Colin as he settled in next to Fiona.

"I'm so nervous I'm not sure what I can get down."

"Why not eat it all? Then if you're not nominated you can throw it all up."

"You're a cruel one," laughed Fiona as she grabbed a piece of toast, dipped it in the grease from the blood sausage and spread prune marmalade on it. "Now switch on the telly."

Colin hit the remote control and Sally Field's smiling face filled the television screen. She hadn't made a film this past year and was therefore a safe choice to announce the nominees. Academy president Arthur Hiller stood stiffly by her side. "And Robert De Niro for *Blood Roses*," said Field as the sound came on.

"Oh, De Niro," crooned Fiona. "What a meeting we'll have if I get one too."

"And now the nominees for best actress," said Hiller. Fiona grabbed Colin's arm with her left hand while shoving the greasy toast in her mouth with her right.

Sally Field looked straight into the camera. "The nominees for Best Actress are Fiona Covington for *Mary . . .*"

Fiona's scream drowned out the names of the other four nominees. She hugged Colin, rocking him back and forth. "I made it! I made it!" she cried as she hugged him, dropping the greasy toast on the Laura Ashley sheets, creating a large stain that resembled an oil spill.

"Oh I'm just so excited, for both of us, my darling, for both of us," she heaved breathlessly into his shoulder.

"I'm quite happy for you," said Colin, pulling away and holding her at arm's length. "And now I've something to tell you."

"What is it, my love?" she asked, pushing a strand of her auburn hair away from her face and inadvertently smearing some of the prune marmalade on her cheek.

"I want a divorce," said Colin.

Fiona reared back in amazement. Had she heard him correctly? Was this a joke? Some perverse English schoolboy prank? And yet Colin looked so deadly serious as he adjusted the sash of his robe and continued.

"You heard me, I want a divorce. You got your bloody nomination, now I want out of this marriage."

Fiona's second scream eclipsed the first one by several hundred decibels. As she howled in pain she moved toward Colin, upsetting the elaborate breakfast tray. The greasy eggs flew onto the Laura Ashley drapes, their sunshine yellow yolks clashing horribly with the purple and russet. The porridge landed on the dresser, splattering Queen Elizabeth's face in the photo triptych and landing in a puddle at her feet.

"There's no use in getting hysterical," said Colin as he bolted to the doorway. "This charade of a marriage is over."

2

The face in the mirror was perfect.

Two thick, bee-stung lips were outlined in a thin trail of rust and colored in with a vibrant, almost ruby red. They contrasted perfectly with the porcelain white skin, which was creamed twice daily and never exposed to the sun. The impossibly high cheekbones led to the piercing eyes, which were either violet or cobalt blue, depending on how they caught the light.

"Not bad for a kid from Bascom, Florida," said Karen Kroll as she turned her eyes from the mirror to her hairdresser Lars.

"Not bad at all," he agreed as he combed out her lustrous white blond hair. They had chosen white blond as her color with the knowledge that it was one step beyond Lana Turner. Lana had been platinum blond, so Karen was white. Karen liked thinking of herself as one step beyond Lana, although she had never taken a Mafia lover, not yet anyway.

Karen and Lars had been inseparable since they met on the set of a *Playboy After Dark* nudie entitled *Jacuzzi Madness*. It had been her first feature and Lars was doing hair and makeup. All Karen had to do was take her clothes off and utter the immortal line, "The decoder has been stolen by a transsexual." Nonetheless, she noticed in the scene where the girls were nude by the pool and talking on their cellular phones that everyone

11

got a full body shot but her. Sulking over lunch, she looked up to find Lars sitting across from her.

"No body shot, huh?" he inquired.

"Do I look that bad?" she asked. "I've been on a liquid diet for five days. I can't figure out why they don't like me."

"I can tell you why," smiled Lars. Karen leaned forward to hear the reason. "It's your foliage."

"My foliage?"

"Your bush. Only it's not a bush, it's an overgrown Canadian fur tree."

"You're talking about my pubic hair?" she asked in amazement.

"It's so thick you could hide Roseanne in it," chided Lars.

"But I've always been . . . bushy down there," Karen said, blushing.

"Would you like me to take care of it for you?" asked Lars.

And so they repaired to the makeup trailer where Lars trimmed Karen's overgrown pubic hairs and tinted them a light golden. Looking in the mirror when he had finished, Karen felt as if she'd just gotten a five-hundred-dollar cut and blow-dry from Jose Eber. That afternoon she got her full body shot.

"You're a genius," she gushed as she kissed him.

"All in a day's work, really," he replied shyly.

"Promise you'll do this for me for the rest of my life."

"My dear," he responded, "I'll cut it, comb it out and blow-dry it for you anytime you want. Just don't ask me to kiss it."

They were fast friends from that day forward, but it had taken Karen less than five years to graduate from made-for-cable tits 'n' tubs epics to starring roles in thirty-million-dollar features. And as she moved up, Lars moved up, from her pubic hair to the bleached roots that grew on her head.

Not that it had been easy. Realizing that *Playboy After Dark* was nothing more than the nineties version of Miss Rheingold, Karen embarked on a career as a serious actress. A friend got her an audition for the West Coast branch of the Actors Studio, and Karen, giddy with the thought of studying where Brando, Newman and Pacino had honed their craft, scrambled desperately to get ready.

For her audition she had chosen Maggie's opening monologue in *Cat on a Hot Tin Roof*, the one where she enters the bedroom in a slip and strips off her stockings while complaining about "no-neck monsters" and "hot buttered biscuits." Karen bought a cassette of the film version and studied Elizabeth Taylor's performance with the fervor of a Druid scholar. She taped Taylor's rendition of the monologue and then listened to it on her Walkman while she did the StairMaster at the gym, talking out the dialogue, trying to emulate the legendary actress's petulant, sexy delivery. To study Taylor's facial mannerisms she constantly hit freeze-frame while the cassette was playing, looked into a mirror and mimicked what she saw on her television screen.

When the big day came, Karen arrived ten minutes early. The older Jewish couple who were to evaluate her, Broadway veterans who had met in a William Inge play and moved to Los Angeles for a seventies television series, were surprised to see their applicant clad in a quilted pink housecoat and mules.

"Were you planning to clean house?" joked the husband.

"No," Karen replied, "I just wanted to dress the part." Then she shed the housecoat to reveal her stunningly sculpted body clad only in a white slip and sheer nylon stockings. The man moaned audibly.

Unfortunately it was the last favorable comment she got that afternoon. Launching into the monologue Karen found herself unnerved by performing in front of two highly esteemed professional actors. Her attempts to duplicate Taylor's petulant tones came out shrill and abrasive and her jerky body language was merely clumsy. As for her stab at matching the Oscar-winning actress's facial repertoire, it was forced and desperate, a sort of amateur Kabuki minus the white face paint. When she was finished, she knew she was finished.

"Thank you very much," said the wife.

As she was leaving the stage, Karen heard the man mutter, "She's Tori Spelling, only without the talent."

A comment like that might have stopped any aspiring actress, but Karen Kroll had decided a long time ago she wasn't just any aspiring actress. She promptly had an affair with a married casting director who helped her get a two-scene part as a hooker in a direct-to-video erotic thriller. That led to an affair with a Paramount executive who promoted her for a role in a Jean-Claude Van Damme film. She wound up making two films with Van Damme, *Steel Army* and *Hot Fury*, doing a one-page interview in *Movieline* magazine to promote the second film.

That's where she got lucky. Karen had grown tired of Van Damme's constantly trying to hit on her; not because she wasn't attracted to him, but because he refused to do anything for her. (Karen would have fucked Nixon's corpse if she thought it would have helped her career.) And so she blasted him in the interview. "Nobody's as awful as the Belgian waffle," she cracked, and people were taken by her audacity in knocking a major star. Liz Smith picked up the comment and referred to Karen as "the feisty, curvy blond who's not afraid to speak her mind." The next week she got a $750,000 offer to appear opposite Jeff Bridges in a robbery film.

After that she made five movies in two years: *Purple Moon* with Richard Gere (his eyes actually showed some animation during their sex scene), *Seven Come Eleven* with Luke Perry (who had a great ass; he could have been a superstar, she thought, if he could only recite dialogue through it), *Deadlier Than the Male* with Michael Caine (he fell asleep during the big love scene), *Hangman's Luck* with John Travolta (he ate two bowls of pasta puttanesca, a calzone, an order of fried peppers and half a cheesecake for lunch the first day; the resulting farts almost set off an earthquake alert) and *Apocalypse* with Sylvester Stallone (she could never get over the feeling that he had learned his lines phonetically). In all these films she played the same role: the girl. And she always played the same scene: a sequence in which she emerged completely nude from a shower, tub, pool or Jacuzzi to make passionate, animalistic love to the leading man. Lars tried changing her pubic hair styles from film to film, but boredom soon set in.

Until last year, when she snagged the role of an American nun who is raped and tortured in El Salvador in Costa-Gavras's *Sacrilege*. The famed director, who hadn't had a hit in over a decade, had cast Jeremy Irons as a diplomat, but Warner Bros. wanted a female name to ensure the box office. With Michelle Pfeiffer, Geena Davis, Sharon Stone and Demi Moore all committed to other projects, Karen got the role four days before shooting began. Having been cast for the first time in her career in a film that required no nudity, she wisely brought an acting coach to location and worked on her scenes every night after the day's shooting wrapped. It all paid off when Roger Ebert gave *Sacrilege* a thumbs-up and added that "for the first time in her career Karen Kroll has gone beyond her breasts and into her heart."

"I think we're almost there," said Lars as he began to spray and shape her hair into place.

"Can you be an angel and just fluff it out a little more," Karen pleaded. "I've got to look good, especially if I don't get nominated." At the urging of her publicist, Susan Sakowitz, Karen had consented to allow Leonard Maltin and a crew from *ET* to film her as she watched the predawn announcement of the nominations. If she got nominated it would be a public feather in her cap; if not, Susan assured her, she'd come off as a good sport.

"You'll be nominated, my darling," cooed Lars. "They can't deny you."

Yeah, thought Karen, or I'll wind up like Susan Lucci does every year: smiling through a public humiliation while vowing to kill all the pricks who didn't vote for me.

The phone rang as Lars worked his comb through Karen's hair. "Will you see who that is?" she asked.

Karen lit up a Marlboro Light as Lars picked up the receiver. Then, pressing it to his chest, he turned to her.

"It's a Mrs. Ida Gunkndiferson from Bascom. She says she knows you."

"Oh Christ," moaned Karen. "I've been dodging her for weeks."

"Who is she?"

"Just a pain in the ass I can't get rid of. I hate the bitch. Tell her I'm sick."

Lars put the receiver back to his chin. "Mrs. Gunkndiferson, I'm afraid Miss Kroll is not well right now. She's, I guess you'd have to say it's that time of the month. . . . Yes, I was sure you'd understand and . . . My what a vivid term for it. Miss Kroll simply refers to it as the curse. . . . Yes, I'll be sure to tell her."

Lars hung up as Karen began to laugh. "The curse," she chortled. "I haven't heard that one in decades."

"Well," giggled Lars as he returned to Karen's hair, "it was good enough for good old Mrs. Gunkndiferson."

"Guess it was," agreed Karen.

"You know, aside from being a name, it means something in Swedish," said Lars.

"Really? Gunkndiferson?"

"Yes, it means one who bites the balls of the reindeer."

Karen shrieked with laughter at Lars's joke; it was the kind of thing he always did to loosen her up before she had to face a big moment, like a heavy scene or a movie premiere.

"Lars, honey," she said, grasping his hand, "if I get nominated, I'm taking you to the Oscars."

Downstairs Susan Sakowitz was in an absolute frenzy. Anorexically thin, a veteran of collagen lip injections, hair extensions and laser surgery for crow's-feet, Susan lived in a state of constant panic that A: her clients would leave her and B: she wouldn't be able to find a second husband at thirty-seven. (Her first one had expired while she was performing oral sex on him, leading her friends to speculate that he had died of boredom.) As with so many female publicists in Hollywood, Susan had two distinct personalities: ass-kissing supplicant or screaming bitch. Like the Middle East, she was either at your feet or at your throat.

Right now she was trying to assert herself by getting the crew to rearrange the lighting. "I'm not sure Karen will want it this strong," she pleaded to Leonard Maltin. "It's so early in the morning. What about throwing some shadows on her?"

"This is the same lighting we used for Raquel Welch, who is twenty years older than your client," explained Leonard cheerfully. After ten years on the job he had learned how to deal with hysterical control freaks like Susan.

"I just think Karen will want some shadows," whined Susan.

"This is an interview, Susan," replied Leonard patiently, "not a film noir. Why not lighten up?"

The disagreement could have gone on forever, given Susan's terrier-like tenacity, but at that moment Karen and Lars emerged from her bedroom. Susan grabbed Leonard's elbow and whispered frantically, "Don't forget about her college drama coach."

Leonard smiled as he disengaged himself. "Our affiliate in Florida taped an interview with her yesterday," he said as he turned and put his hand out. "Karen, you look great."

"Thank you. I'm so nervous I could faint," Karen said, feigning anxiety by clasping her hands.

"This'll be great," said Leonard as he guided Karen to a seat on the couch. "Let's turn on the set and see what Sally Field has to say."

I can't believe my fate is in the hands of the fucking Flying Nun, thought Karen, wondering if it would be possible for Field to substitute Meryl Streep's name for hers, leaving the Academy none the wiser.

By the time Sally Field got to the female nominees Karen and Leonard were sitting together on the couch. It was a nice visual, thought Susan, who worried that Karen might fire her if she didn't get nominated.

"The nominess for Best Actress," said Field as she read from the TelePrompTer, "are Fiona Covington for *Mary*, Karen Kroll for *Sacrilege*..."

Karen whooped with joy and hugged Leonard so hard his face began to turn purple.

"You did it! Congratulations!" said Leonard, readjusting his body mike and trying to regain his breath.

"This is so ... so emotional," gulped Karen, wiping away a tear.

"I know that it is," replied Leonard, the cameras rolling. "For you it's been a long journey to a dream come true, hasn't it?"

"Oh yes, a very long journey," agreed Karen.

"But you've had help along the way from lots of wonderful people," continued Leonard, as Karen nodded. "And yesterday we got to talk to one of those people. Do you remember your college drama coach from Seminole State University?"

"How could I forget her?" replied Karen, shaking her head in wonder as she wiped away a tear. "She was always so encouraging to me. I'll always have a special place in my heart for Mrs. Gunkndiferson."

It was as good a performance as she'd given in *Sacrilege*.

3

Amber Lyons watched the daddy longlegs spider as it crawled slowly up the putty-green living room drapes of her West Hollywood condo. Moving delicately, the insect navigated the folds of the fabric and moved to the top of the drape where a thin string from his web was connected to the ceiling. As the spider moved onto the string Amber hurled her frozen Milky Way bar at it, snapping the string and crushing the spider against the wall.

"Way to go," exclaimed Amber's pal, Tatianna.

"Show 'em no mercy," chimed in her other chum, Brianna.

Tatianna Finkleman and Brianna Schwartkopf were a pair of twin Beverly Hills horrors, twenty-year-old USC dropouts whose fathers were top-level studio executives. They had latched onto Amber at the Beverly Hills Adopt-a-Pet Luau (all the dogs were required to wear leis) last July, convinced that the young redheaded actress was going to be a "major, major star."

The three women had started their evening at a coffeehouse on Melrose, proceeding to the Sky Bar where they met a stunt-man who invited them to a party in the Hollywood Hills. After flirting with all the available men they went to Kate Mantilini's for cheeseburgers and then headed over to Amber's. They had intended to get stoned and watch old episodes of *The Brady*

Bunch, but Amber had misplaced her *Brady* tape and Brianna, in a rare moment of compassion, had given her stash to the valet parker at the restaurant. So, instead, they stayed up for hours and indulged in their favorite pastime: gossiping and dishing about all the men they met.

"I thought that writer from *Frasier* was too cute," offered Tatianna, an ash-blond who had recently had collagen injections in her earlobes to make them appear more suckable.

"Ugh," said Brianna, "it's no bigger than an acorn."

"How do you know?"

"Jennifer Reilly slept with him."

"Isn't she a dyke?" said Amber.

"No, she's just outdoorsy," replied Brianna whose nose had been reconstructed more times than the ceiling of the Sistine Chapel.

Of the three young women, Amber was the only one who hadn't had facial surgery. But then she didn't need it: Tatianna and Brianna spent hours applying makeup, crimping their hair and dressing like rich sluts in a vain attempt to look like the women in a Guess? jeans ad; Amber had merely to slip on a tank top and slap on some lip gloss to achieve the same effect. Her lightly freckled complexion and her mane of disheveled red hair effortlessly emitted that famous siren's call: come to Mama.

And as much as Amber enjoyed hanging out with Tatianna and Brianna, she was aware that they were just a pit stop on her way to the top. Even as a child in Sandusky, Ohio, Amber had been certain she was destined for great things. At the age of seven she stared for hours into her mother's vanity mirror, making faces and imagining how those faces would make people laugh, cry and swoon. I've got "it," she thought to herself, I know I do.

That "it," a sullen, Lolita-like frankness, broken by a shy smile that implied that underneath it all she just wanted to be loved, was recognized by a talent agent only two weeks after Amber arrived in Hollywood. She got the first part she auditioned for—a recurring role as a psychotic baby-sitter on *Picket Fences*—and caused a sensation when her character slept with seventy-year-old actor Ray Walston. Her fan mail soared, but Amber grew bored and began showing up late for shooting. When the producer fired her she thought her career might be over.

That's why she agreed to star in a low-budget independent feature for nothing more than her expenses and a promise that she could keep her wardrobe. The movie, *As if . . . Chillin'*, cast Amber as a spoiled brat from Beverly Hills who takes a job as a substitute teacher in Watts. After turning the homeboys on to the joys of shopping at the Beverly Center, Amber's character is wounded in a drive-by shooting. At her assailant's trial, she rises to denounce the LA justice system and is borne out of the courtroom on the shoulders of black nationalists.

A ludicrous amalgam of *To Sir with Love* and *Do the Right Thing*, *As if . . . Chillin'* was nonetheless a huge sleeper hit. It won the Audience Prize at the Sundance Festival and was picked up by Miramax, which hyped both the film and Amber. By November, *As if . . . Chillin'*, filmed at a cost of one million, had grossed over thirty million, and Amber was declared "find of the year" by *Entertainment Weekly*.

"My father says Julia Roberts is going to have everything done within the next two years," said Brianna.

"She is such an oxygen thief," muttered Amber, who was jealous of anyone who managed to rise faster than she had.

"Yawn, yawn, it's almost dawn," whined Tatianna.

"Oh chill," snapped Brianna. "What have you got to do tomorrow?"

"I have to take my Jeep in to be serviced. Ugh. Maybe I'll ask Consuela to do it for me."

"Your maid is named Lydia," chided Brianna. "Consuela is your chihuahua."

"Whatever," said Tatianna, rolling over onto her stomach and dipping her frozen Milky Way into the bowl of Marshmallow Fluff that sat on top of the coffee table. "I still think that writer from *Frasier* was cute."

"I've heard he's got a bisexual side," warned Brianna.

"Yeah, so which side of him do you think I should fuck?"

In the midst of this deathless discussion the phone rang. Amber picked it up and was surprised to hear her agent's voice.

"You've gotta be careful with all the freaks out there," continued Brianna. "Joni Chagollan slept with an agent from CAA and got a yeast infection."

"Joni Chagollan *is* a yeast infection," laughed Tatianna.

"Hey, guys," exclaimed Amber.

"But then I heard she videotaped it for a one-woman performance piece she's doing Friday night at Starbucks in Santa Monica," said Brianna.

"If Joni Chagollan's a performance artist, I'm Madonna," parried Tatianna. "I just hope Lydia can take my Jeep . . ."

"Guys!" barked Amber. Tatianna and Brianna, not used to being shouted at except by their therapists, looked up at her in unison.

"Are you ready for this? My agent just told me I got nominated for the Best Actress Oscar for *As if . . . Chillin'*!" The two youngest patrons of the most expensive plastic surgeon in Beverly Hills squealed with delight and rushed over to embrace Amber.

"Let's turn on the TV," said Amber. "Maybe they'll show an update."

"This is so cool," exclaimed Brianna. But Tatianna looked depressed.

"Is something the matter?" asked Amber.

"I just remembered. Lydia moved back to Costa Rica last month," replied Tatianna.

4

"**O**h baby," moaned the brunette as she spread her legs open wider, "lick me some more."

"Yes, lover," responded the blond who had been resting on the black-haired woman's inner thigh. She quickly moved her head back into the woman's crotch, flicking her tongue back and forth at a frenzied pace.

"Oh baby, that's it. Don't stop," sighed the brunette.

The two women had been making love for over an hour now, never tiring of each other's bodies, perusing them with each other's tongues like pigs in search of an elusive truffle. The scented candles on the nightstand filled the air with the warm smell of vanilla, while the raw silk curtains stirred fitfully in the early morning breeze. This was their favorite time to make love, just as dawn was breaking over their Hollywood Hills cottage. While the other residents of Beachwood Canyon rose to breakfasts of muesli and fruit juice and bagels, the two women preferred to devour each other for their first meal of the day.

"Harder, baby, harder," pleaded the brunette. "Push it all the way in."

Any further, thought the blond, and I'll be licking Egypt. Still she pushed forward.

"Oh yes, yes, yes," moaned the brunette.

The television on the bureau droned on in the background, the newscaster's scripted patter creating a surreal commentary to the couple's feverish lovemaking. "Late news on the invasion of Algeria," said the man as the blond's tongue delved deeper. "High winds causing turbulence off the Carolinas," advised the weatherman as the black-haired woman exhaled a stream of "baby, baby, baby."

The blond kept up her oral aerobics, a dutiful sentry at the gates of Xanadu. The brunette's body heaved and bucked like a bronco with a cattle prod up its ass.

"Oh more, more," she pleaded. "Don't stop, don't ever stop."

The voice from the television was now a female's. "The nominees for Best Actress are Fiona Covington for *Mary*, Karen Kroll for *Sacrilege*, Amber Lyons for *As if . . . Chillin'*, Lori Seefer for *Losing Sofia . . .*"

The blond lifted her head from her lover's crotch. "Hey," she said, "I just got nominated for the Oscar."

The brunette writhed in response, emitting a low, soft moan.

"Unbelievable. After all this time those bastards finally nominated me. I made it, I finally made it. I'm a nominee for Best Actress of the year!"

"That's beautiful, baby," said the brunette as she guided the blond's head back to her crotch. "Now go back down and finish me off."

5

"**H**arder, harder ... that's right, push in ... now softer ... keeping pushing in ... more, more ... Oh God, do I ever need this ... harder, harder ..."

The instructions Connie Travatano barked out to her Swedish masseuse were the same as those she gave to the producers, directors and sound engineers she worked with: direct, to the point and weighted with the suggestion that you either do it Connie's way or you could leave. After thirty years in the business, Connie was used to getting what she wanted.

Helga, who had been Connie's masseuse for three years now, worked her way up and down the superstar's thighs. "Would you like an herbal face mask when I'm finished?" she asked.

"You've given me one two days in a row now," protested Connie.

"They're good for you, Madam. Invigorates the skin."

"No," said Connie, "one more herbal face mask and I'm gonna wind up growing tarragon out my nose. Besides, I have to go watch the nominations in a minute."

"Bjork and I said a prayer for you last night," said Helga. Bjork was Helga's husband, a man who claimed to have once been Ingmar Bergman's bootblack.

Connie sat up and slipped into her robe. "Thank you,

27

Helga," she said. "And thank you for coming so early for the massage."

"My pleasure, Madam. Bjork wanted to get up early anyway to continue working on his book."

"He's still writing that tell-all?" asked Connie.

"Oh yes. *Icy Feet, Icy Heart: The Shoes of Ingmar Bergman.* It's a good title, don't you think?"

"Beats the hell out of *The Eyes of Laura Mars.*" Connie was not going to destroy Helga's dreams of being the wife of a best-selling author. In show business there were big people and little people. Connie learned a long time ago that you could get what you needed from the little people if you didn't destroy their dreams.

Leaving Helga to pack up her oils, Connie left her spa and entered the corridor that connected it to the rest of her Bel Air mansion. As she walked down the hallway she passed by row after row of gold records. Taken in sequence, they formed a precise history of changing tastes in American popular music over the past three decades: *Connie Travatano: The First Album, Connie Travatano's Sicilian Serenades, Broadway's Baby, Connie Goes Liverpool, Connie Travatano: The Fifth Album, Love, Peace and Connie Travatano, Where Am I Now That I Need Me?/The Soundtrack, Under the Glittering Disco Ball, Oliver II/The Soundtrack, Connie's Greatest Hits, My Sharona/My Connie, Country Connie, Pillow Fights/The Soundtrack, Connie: Live at the Sands, Connie Travatano: Broadway Is My Life, Just a Slice of Sondheim, Connie and Julio: The Mirage of Love, Connie Travatano: The Ultimate Collection,* and, finally, *Simply Connie.*

The most interesting fact about the albums was that they represented the only way to hear Connie sing. A pop diva whose fifty million in sales rivaled both Barbra Streisand and Diana Ross, Connie had chosen ten years ago to stop singing in public. The decision was a practical one; she wanted to concentrate on reviving her film career. But as her next few albums outsold her previous ones, the Newark-born singer became aware that her lack of concert and television vocal appearances was only increasing her popularity. Though her next few films flopped, Connie stood by her no-singing-in-public decision. When the time's right, I'll do it again, she thought. Until then, it's my ace in the hole.

She had almost played that ace when she found the script for *Tomatoes and Diamonds*, a comedy-drama about an Italian widow from Brooklyn who wins the lottery and returns to Naples. Putting up half the financing herself, Connie convinced Sidney Lumet to direct and got Andy Garcia to star opposite her. After three flops in a row, the film emerged as a modest hit, winning acclaim for Connie's portrayal of a flighty, love-hungry woman. Now if she could only cop an Oscar nomination—and go on to win!—she'd be a bona fide movie star again.

But the odds against her were enormous. There were over two hundred eligible performances by lead actresses this year. Only five would be nominated. And of those, only one would be declared the best. The other four nominees would be consigned to a plate of gristly chateaubriand and a pasted-on smile at the dreary, dreary Governor's Ball. The thought of it sent a chill through Connie's freshly massaged flesh.

Maybe that's why she reached into the planter of the ficus tree at the end of the hallway and pulled out a fifth of vodka. She had many secret hiding places in her mansion where she had stashed bottles, small vessels of comfort that helped her navigate the rough seas of stardom. There was a bottle of Southern Comfort secreted in the toilet tank of her private bathroom, some tequila hidden behind the rakes in the toolshed and, in her cleverest move, she had substituted gin for the white wine vinegar in the kitchen closet. (The night she forgot about that and had the cook serve a chef salad with an oil and vinegar dressing, everybody went home happy.) Whenever Connie felt nervous or agitated, she just reached into one of her secret stashes and took an instant dose of relaxation. It's not as if I'm an alcoholic, she reasoned, it's just my little secret. In truth, Connie was such a controlling, type-A personality that she didn't want anyone to know she drank, not even her staff.

She sucked down three greedy gulps of vodka before putting the bottle back. A warm glow soon enveloped her as she entered her Tudor-style den. (A student of architecture and design, Connie had decorated the twenty-four rooms of her house in a variety of styles: the den and living room were Tudor, the dining room Art Deco, her bedroom Moroccan and the main bathroom Byzantine, complete with stone columns and miniature gargoyles decorating the walls. Director Sydney Pollack, on using the bathroom for the first time, was heard to exclaim, "It's like taking a shit in Notre Dame.")

Erika, her assistant for over fifteen years, was waiting for Connie with a cup of tea. The television was already on.

"My fingers are crossed," said Erika.

"For what?" asked Connie as she settled next to her on the huge brown velvet sofa, "my nomination or a new man in your life?"

The two women, both divorced, laughed over their mutual loveless state. Both in their early fifties, both still trim and attractive, they had long since given up on the idea of a permanent mate in a city where all the eligible, decent men seemed to only want a woman with the body of Pamela Anderson and the intelligence of a houseplant. Actually, mused Connie, Pamela Anderson would do nicely on both counts.

"The nominees for best actress are," began Sally Field. Connie's heart beat faster as Erika reached over and squeezed her hand.

"Fiona Covington for *Mary* . . ."

"They're a sucker for accents," offered Erika as moral support.

"Karen Kroll for *Sacrilege* . . ."

"I heard she fucked everyone but the accountant on that picture," hissed Connie.

"Amber Lyons for *As if . . . Chillin'* . . ."

"Amber Lyons!" screeched Connie. "What is this, MTV?" Her nails dug into Erika's palm as they both leaned forward to hear the last two nominees.

"Lori Seefer for *Losing Sofia* . . ."

"There goes the dyke vote," moaned Connie.

"And Connie Travatano for *Tomatoes and Diamonds*," finished Sally Field with a smile. "Congratulations to all five actresses."

"Hallelujah," cried Erika, jumping up and down with glee. "Hallelujah! Hallelujah!"

Connie, however, relieved as she was, wasn't overcome with joy. Instead, she stared straight ahead and smiled. She'd known for two weeks now what she would do if she were nominated, what, in fact, she would do that could help her turn her nomination into a Best Actress Oscar. It was time to play her ace.

"Call the White House," she said coolly to Erika.

"The White House?" asked Erika.

"Yes. The press secretary's office. Tell him I've accepted the President's offer to sing 'God Bless America' on the *Tribute to Vietnam Veterans Special* he's hosting next week on ABC."

Connie sat back and smiled. Who needed vodka when you had a voice that the world was dying to hear?

"Good evening, it's February fifth, the day of the Oscar nominations. I'm Bob Goen and this is *Entertainment Tonight*."

"And I'm Mary Hart. It was Oscar madness this morning at the Academy headquarters on Wilshire Boulevard where a phalanx of photographers, journalists and TV crews crowded together to learn who had been nominated for Hollywood's highest honor. There were some old favorites, some newcomers and a few surprises."

"And high on that list of surprises, Mary, would have to be twenty-two-year-old Amber Lyons, who just three years ago was a sweater saleswoman at The Gap in Sandusky, Ohio. She got a Best Actress nomination for her portrayal of a rich girl who embraces black rights in *As if . . . Chillin'*."

"Maybe not a surprise, Bob, but certainly an old favorite was Connie Travatano, who got her Best Actress nomination for *Tomatoes and Diamonds*, a movie that asked, Can a fifty-year-old widow find happiness with Andy Garcia? In fact, Connie was so thrilled by her nomination that she told us late today in an *ET* exclusive that she's accepted the President's offer to sing on the upcoming *Vietnam Veterans Special* on ABC. This marks Connie's first public singing appearance in over ten years."

"And speaking of years, Mary, it's time to take out the calendars as we take you on an exclusive supermodel shoot in Australia for the Mobil Oil Service Station Calendar. Yes, the supermodels get greasy down under when *ET* returns in just . . ."

6

Lori Seefer's Jeep barreled down Sunset, headed toward Beverly Hills, a Garth Brooks tape booming out of the stereo. Her blond hair whipped back and forth in the breeze as she cut off a Toyota at Crescent Heights and sped forward down the Strip. This was Lori's favorite way to drive, the wind whooshing past her while the music blared. It was just so butch.

It was also one of the few ways she felt comfortable expressing her lesbianism. A child actress who had grown into a genuine movie star, Lori learned early how to play the Hollywood game.

Her first lesson came when she guest-starred on *The Brady Bunch* as Greg's date for the annual Halloween dance. Her girlfriends in the San Fernando Valley public school she attended had been eager to get the scoop on how dreamy it had been to dance cheek to cheek with Greg, and Lori dutifully supplied them with all the juicy details. She never mentioned the fact that she had spent the whole time on the set dreaming about making out with Marcia.

She had her first recurring role on a series when she played an orphan adopted by Tom Selleck on *Magnum, P.I.* for a season. Selleck was every woman's dream, and Lori made sure to tell friends how cool it was to stare into his deep blue eyes during filming. When not filming, however, she found time to have her first lesbian affair with the show's female makeup artist. The woman liked to take the tiny brush she used to comb out Selleck's moustache, brush it between Lori's legs and bring her to climax.

While other young television actors fell into drink and drugs, Lori wisely went to London and enrolled in the Royal Academy of Dramatic Arts. After four years of Shakespeare, Shaw and Ibsen, she returned to Hollywood to pursue a serious acting career. She had no sympathy for her former cohorts who now had trouble finding work. On hearing that Dana Plato of *Diff'rent Strokes* had been arrested for holding up a dry cleaning store in Las Vegas, Lori shocked her friends by confiding that "it was probably a good career move for her."

Her breakout role came in 1985 when she played a young welfare mother in the HBO Picture *Carolina on My Mind.* That led to features opposite Keifer Sutherland (when he tried to hit on her, she pretended to have scurvy), Robert Downey Jr. (she told him she was experimenting with celibacy) and Tom Cruise (thank God for Nicole). Her performances in a wide variety of roles were marked by the same qualities: each one was meticulous, well conceived and, ultimately, cold. In *Losing Sofia* she portrayed a scientist who injects herself with a serum that robs people of their senses. The role allowed Lori to go deaf, dumb and blind, and she did so in a brilliant, albeit mechanical, manner. Reviewing the film in *New York* magazine, David Denby commented, "Lori Seefer makes Meryl Streep look spontaneous."

Big deal, thought Lori as she careened onto Rodeo Drive and headed into the heart of Beverly Hills. I got the Oscar nomination anyway.

There was just one problem: Lori was petrified that her lesbianism would blow it for her with the Academy voters who were old and unsympathetic to alternative lifestyles. Much less the public, who could erase her career in an instant. That's why she paid Melissa Crawley, head of Crawley/Perkins/Rowan public relations (or CPR, as it was known in the industry), two thousand dollars a month to keep the lid on her little secret. And although most people in the business and the press had suspicions, no one had dared to air them publicly since Lori put Melissa on the case five years ago. As one insider commented, "Lori Seefer's lesbianism is the best-kept secret since David Hasselhoff's talent."

"But Andrew, if you go ahead and put Meg Ryan on your cover instead of my client, I may be forced to cancel that photo shoot you're so desperate to have with Demi."

Melissa Crawley was seated behind her Mission-style desk doing one of her favorite things: playing hardball with the press. At sixty-two, impeccably attired in a black wool skirt and cream blouse, her graying hair twisted into a French knot, Melissa looked to be nothing more than a well turned-out schoolmarm. But this schoolmarm wielded a mean ruler; journalists and photographers cowered when she wheeled out her heavy equipment.

"That was not part of our agreement and you know it," said Melissa tartly to the British editor of *Elle* at the other end of the line. Her constant stream of honey-coated death threats was suddenly interrupted by the buzzing of her intercom.

"What is it?" she barked, switching lines.

"Lori Seefer is here to see you and Tina Brown is on line two," said her assistant Phillip from his cubicle.

"Send Lori in and tell Tina I'm vomiting blood and can't speak to her until I'm finished," snapped Melissa, irritated that she had been interrupted just as the sniveling Brit was about to cave in.

"Andrew," she said, switching back to line one, "I think you have to learn to look at this reasonably." Melissa's gaze fell on the embroidered plaque on her wall that read:

FREEDOM OF THE PRESS? BULLSHIT!

"It's a question of authority," she continued. "I mean, where is it written that you get to choose who goes on the cover of the magazine just because you're the editor?"

Phillip ushered Lori in as Melissa was finishing up. "Think about it, dear," she chided. "Demi may not want to do that nude layout if she hears you've been mean to me."

Melissa motioned to Lori to sit down. "Of course you can take some time. Just do it my way or get the fuck out of Dodge City." She slammed down the receiver triumphantly and went over to greet her client.

"Congratulations," said Melissa as she hugged Lori. "What a great day this is for you. Now come sit on the couch and let's make a plan." Melissa making a plan was akin to Attila the Hun scheduling an invasion; at the end of the day there were guaranteed to be no survivors.

"We're going to use this to help your career and get you the Oscar," said the fearsome flack. "The first thing I think we should do is to contact *Personality* and tell them we're ready to go ahead with that profile they've been begging to do for three years now."

"*Personality,*" shuddered Lori. "But they get so . . . personal." Up until now Melissa had let Lori be interviewed only by soft magazines like *InStyle* and *Redbook.* A reference to the star's "bachelor girl lifestyle" was as close as the articles ever got to her private life.

"Don't worry," chortled Melissa. "I've got that all covered too."

Just then a strapping six-foot-two Brazilian man entered the room and dropped a sheaf of papers on Melissa's desk. It was Claudio, the new mailboy. Since he'd started at CPR all the women and gay men at the agency had been victims of endless sexual fantasies. With his high cheekbones, shoulder-length black hair and muscular frame, he looked like a refugee from a Calvin Klein underwear ad.

"Thank you, Claudio," nodded Melissa. Even at her age she was not impervious to his charms.

"Yes, Miss Crawley," he said as he left, flashing a smile that could best be described as a freshly opened pack of Chiclets.

"But *Personality*," protested Lori, "they'll ask me who I'm dating, why I'm not married."

"And you will have an answer for that," reassured Melissa. "But what I'm most excited about is Barbara Walters. She told me this morning she'll interview you for her annual Oscar broadcast."

"Barbara Walters!" exclaimed Lori. "You know I don't know how to cry."

"You won't have to," replied Melissa, taking Lori's hand in hers. "Barbara will be talking to you about the exciting new development in your life."

"What," said Lori, "that I'm the new poster girl for Birkenstock sandals? Melissa, this is going to blow everything!"

"The exciting new development," continued Melissa unfazed, "is the man in your life."

"Man?" said Lori incredulously. She pronounced the word as if it were in an ancient foreign dialect she barely understood.

"Yes, we're going to use the media to show off the man you've begun to date. You'll start by showing up on his arm for the premiere of Meryl Streep's new film, *Foreign Accents*, in Westwood next week."

"Where am I going to find a man by next week?" pleaded Lori. "The only two men I know are my agent and my gynecologist and they're both fags."

"Don't worry, dear," cooed Melissa. "I've picked the perfect match for you. He's very excited about going out with you and he's going to say all the right things."

"Who is he?"

"Claudio," replied Melissa.

"Claudio?" said Lori.

"That gorgeous Brazilian stud who brought the mail into this office not two minutes ago," said Melissa. "I'm adding one hundred dollars a week to his paycheck just for taking you to some premieres and posing with you for the *Personality* story. Claudio will be perfect. You'll see."

"Oh," said Lori feebly.

She hadn't even noticed him.

7

Connie Travatano lay on the chaise by her pool, softly singing one of her signature numbers, the theme to her first film, *Where Am I Now That I Need Me?*

> *Tell me, where am I now that I need me?*
> *Why does your heart always bleed me?*
> *When will your love come and feed me?*
> *Tell me, where am I now that I need me?*

The song was vintage seventies Connie: lush, melodramatic and absurdly over the top. Forget singing in public; Connie, whose sophisticated taste in music ran to Sondheim, Cole Porter and Lennon and McCartney, had sworn to herself years ago that she'd never sing this bar-mitzah special anywhere, anytime for the rest of her life. But today was different. She'd gotten her Oscar nomination, and with it a major shot at renewed film stardom. Today Connie was happy enough to sing the greatest hits of Barry Manilow.

The portable phone by her side rang. She picked it up to be greeted by the guttural tones of Morty Saltman, her manager for over twenty-five years. As Morty was fond of saying, he not only knew where all the bodies were buried, Connie had ordered him to shovel the dirt on them himself.

"Connie," rasped Morty, "I've been talking to the White House."

"How's the President?" Connie asked, loving the fact that heads of state and journalists now routinely included her in their circles.

"Still troubled by his prostate," said Morty. Whether it was show business or politics, Morty's entire frame of reference was below the waist. "Everything's set at Ford's Theatre for the special," he continued. "There's no set; you'll be singing in front of the curtain at the close of the show. You'll just have to fly in two days in advance for the rehearsal."

"Great. You've told them I'm bringing my own arrangement and my own conductor?"

"Of course, my darling," replied Morty, belching softly. Connie always dictated the rules when it came to a performance.

"Thanks, Morty." Connie was about to put down the phone when a sudden thought occurred to her. "Morty, what color are the curtains at Ford's Theatre?"

"Green," he said.

"Green!" shrieked Connie. "You know I can't sing in front of a green curtain. It doesn't go with my Italian complexion, there's not enough contrast. Besides, I was planning on wearing a blue dress. It'll clash!"

"I don't know what I can do," said Morty. "They've got to keep the curtain closed because the veterans are all behind it. When it goes up, that's the end of the show."

"Morty, I am not singing in front of a green curtain. Get me a silver one."

"Connie, please, it's Ford's Theatre in Washington, D.C."

"Yeah, I know," she snapped. "Lincoln died there. But I don't intend to. I want a silver curtain."

"But this is a national landmark," pleaded Morty.

"I'm not asking you to blow up the fucking Grand Canyon," she said in her steeliest voice. "Now why aren't you doing exactly what I asked?"

"I'll get back to you," sighed Morty, stifling a second belch. Nothing was ever easy with Connie.

Why did they always fight her, wondered Connie as she returned to her sunbathing. Her requirements in any situation were so simple: she just wanted things done exactly the way she demanded, with no mistakes and no complaints. Was that so hard to do? After all, she was always right.

And, to a large degree, Connie Travatano *was* always right, at least about her career. She'd always known what she wanted: to be a famous singer and actress. And she'd always known how to get it: aim for perfection, work as hard as you can and never give up.

Her perfectionist streak started back in her hometown of Newark, New Jersey, where she was raised by her mother Rose after her father had been killed in the Korean War. Money was tight and Rose, a court stenographer, took a second job as a cashier in an Italian deli on weekends. Because she couldn't afford a baby-sitter, Rose brought Connie to work with her, and soon the youngster was helping out behind the counter. The first day she went to the deli Connie, as if by instinct, lined up all the salamis by size. When the owner, Mr. Pepaloni, saw her handiwork, he was delighted.

"Little girl," he said, "someday you're going to own your own deli."

But Connie knew differently. In 1955, at the age of ten, she went to the Newark Albee five times in one week to see Doris

Day in the musical drama *Love Me or Leave Me.* That Sunday morning, while her mother was at church, Connie dyed her hair blond and practiced singing all of Doris Day's songs from the movie while she stood in front of the full-length mirror in her bedroom. When Rose came home she was horrified by her daughter's cheap dye job and prayed to Saint Xavier, the saint of hair diseases, so that Connie wouldn't turn into a scarlet woman.

Instead, she turned into the best employee at Mr. Pepaloni's deli, working nights and weekends, sweeping the floors and never hesitating to battle her way through the jungle of giant salamis that hung from the ceiling of the meat freezer as she searched out a customer's order. More than once the twenty- and thirty-pound salamis hit her in the head, but Connie never complained. After all, how else could she pay for the singing lessons that would turn her into the Italian Doris Day?

Those singing lessons paid off when Connie began to sing on what was affectionately known as the pasta fasoul circuit, wedding receptions held in the rec rooms of local Catholic churches. An A and R man heard her and offered her the chance to cut a demo at Decca Records. Connie was thrilled; she was only fifteen and already on her way to becoming Doris Day.

Not for nothing had she knocked into those salamis for all those years.

But Rose, a woman whose religion bordered on hysteria, forbade her daughter to enter the world of show business and prayed to Saint Sadie, the saint of the performing arts, to help her see the light. In retaliation Connie ran away and joined Ringling Bros. Barnum and Bailey Circus as a dancing girl. She had a torrid affair with Ernesto, a swarthy sword-swallower who helped her lose her virginity and regain her self-confidence. Connie even studied Ernesto's sword-swallowing technique and remarkable control of his throat muscles to help her with her singing.

When Connie was returned to her mother by the police, the beleaguered woman took out her life savings to send her daughter to a private Catholic girls' boarding school, Our Lady of the Immaculate Vestments. Connie hated the regimented lifestyle, but found a mentor in Sister Agnes-Mabel, an older nun who secretly smoked Lucky Strikes and also ran the drama club. For a pack of Luckies a week, which Connie swiped from the local soda shop, the good sister introduced Connie to the works of Eugene O'Neill, Tennesse Williams and, most of all, the great Russian dramatist Anton Chekhov. Chekhov, said Sister Agnes-Mabel, understood more about human nature and human failings than any other writer. Eager to learn, Connie kept stealing the Luckies.

After graduation, and in spite of her mother's pleas, Connie skipped college and moved to New York where she found a cold-water flat in Hell's Kitchen. She auditioned for everything, worked as a waitress at Howard Johnson's and waited for something to happen. Two years later it did when she was cast in an off-Broadway play entitled *Moscow or Bust!*, a musical version of Chekhov's *The Three Sisters*. The show closed the night it opened, but the second-string critic of the *New York Times* wrote that "Connie Travatano is the only person onstage worth watching. She sings Chekhov the way Chekhov should be sung."

Not for nothing had she stolen all those packs of Luckies.

Morty Saltman was also in the audience on opening and closing nights, his presence a favor to the producer whose second cousin had operated on his gall bladder the previous spring at Mount Sinai. When Connie launched into her big second act number, "The Samovar Strut," Morty was so impressed that he stopped belching. Later that night, over chow fon and a Pepto-Bismol at an all-night Chinese restaurant in the Village, Morty signed Connie to a management contract.

The next few years passed in a blur of success after success. Connie's first album went gold over the course of a year and led to her first television special, *Call Me Connie.* Her fan club grew with each album, peaking with the release of the late sixties classic *Love, Peace and Connie Travatano*, on which she reinterpreted the psychedelic classic "In-A-Gadda-Da-Vida" as a torch song. When she moved to Hollywood in the early seventies it was to star in *Where Am I Now That I Need Me?*, in which she portrayed a drug-addicted rock star who learns the meaning of life when she goes blind. Shrewdly combining the life stories of Janis Joplin and Helen Keller, the role offered a perfect showcase for Connie's talents and won her an Oscar nomination.

There had been hills and valleys since those days—three years ago Connie bombed ignominiously in *Divorce Me Darling*, an ill-advised updating of *How to Marry a Millionaire* in which she, Meryl Streep and Liza Minnelli portrayed corporate wives trying to fleece their husbands out of their 401(k) plans—but none of that mattered today. Today Connie Travatano had been nominated for the second time for an Oscar and announced that she would sing in public for the first time in ten years. In front of the President of the United States, no less. Today was a good day, she thought as she rolled over to get some sun on her back.

It was then that she saw the pool boy who was slowly gliding his net through the pale aqua water that she loved to swim in. Connie had never seen him before. He was dark, probably Mexican, and he wasn't dressed the way the regular pool boy was. That kid wore khakis and a shirt, but this boy was clad only in a pair of red Speedo trunks. They cut across his buttocks, offering just the tiniest view of the crack of his ass. God, thought Connie, I'd love to be the tag on those trunks.

The boy saw Connie looking at him and smiled shyly. "Buenos días, señora," he said to her.

Good, chuckled Connie to herself, he doesn't speak English. That made the chance of his talking to the tabloids next to nil. It had been six months since Connie had been with a man, and she knew exactly what she was going to do now. She'd done it before and would probably do it again.

Rising quickly, Connie gestured for the boy to follow her to the pool house. When he entered the small dark chamber lined with canisters of chlorine, she was waiting for him. Unhooking the top of her suit, Connie proudly displayed the breasts she had had done just a few years ago. The boy didn't move toward her, but he couldn't take his eyes off the Travatano twin peaks. Connie reached for his hand and guided it to her left breast. She moaned softly as he first massaged it, then began to kiss it.

Now it was her turn. Connie stuck the two middle fingers of each hand into the elastic trim of the boy's red Speedo and pulled down sharply. She gasped at what she saw.

Hanging between the boy's legs was the biggest, thickest cock Connie had ever seen. It measured at least nine inches in length and was as thick as a fist. She thought of the giant salamis that had hit her on the head back at Mr. Pepaloni's deli.

The boy cupped his enormous cock and looked pleadingly at Connie. She got on her knees and began to take it in her mouth. God, this thing is gigantic, she thought, I feel like I'm going down on the Empire State Building. At first she gagged, but slowly, opening her throat bit by bit, breathing through her nose, pushing onward like one of Caesar's armies crossing the Rubicon, she got the whole thing down her throat.

Not for nothing had she studied sword-swallowing in the circus.

8

Fiona sat in the office of her agent, Lionel Latham, and sobbed into a Kleenex. She had been sobbing for three hours now, leaving a trail of wet, crumpled tissues all the way from Santa Monica to her rented BMW and now into Lionel's office. Johnny Appleseed had nothing on her.

"It's just so appalling," she gulped, bursting into another round of sobs.

"Jeffrey," cried out Lionel to his assistant in the next office, "bring in a fresh pot of tea and another box of Kleenex." He surveyed the fifty or so tissues that littered his immaculately carpeted floor. "On second thought," he added, "better make that a roll of paper towels instead."

A transplant from London, Lionel had a small office that specialized in handling English stars. A precise, unruffled man in his late sixties, most people assumed he was gay. This was not the case, although he had been observed fondling a cocker spaniel's genitals in Sir John Gielgud's rose garden during a tea party in the 1960s. The sad truth was that Lionel had slept with neither men nor women for the past forty-five years, having been frightened by a wild boar while masturbating to a copy of *Lady Chatterley's Lover* during a safari in South Africa.

"There we go, ducks," said Lionel as his assistant poured

Fiona some fresh tea. "Just have yourself another cuppa and it will all begin to fall into place. After all, you were nominated for the Oscar today."

"And yet it all seems so meaningless now," moaned Fiona, her tears plunking into the cup of Earl Grey she raised shakily to her lips. "It's as if the best day of my life has become the worst day of my life!"

"Now see here," said Lionel sharply, "you wouldn't recite that kind of maudlin pap in a movie; please don't do so in real life. This is not some sort of Joan Crawford melodrama. Now let's get on with it."

Fiona took a deep breath and put down her teacup. She fished into her purse for a Tic-Tac and calmly contemplated Lionel's criticism. Like most Englishwomen, her stiff upper lip was only a grimace away.

"Nothing in life is irrevocable," continued Lionel. "There's every chance that Colin will be back by this afternoon."

"Not very likely," responded Fiona. "He took his pipes, his condoms and the complete works of Chaucer."

"That does sound final. Do you think it's another woman?"

"I'd never thought of that."

"Or another man?"

"Lionel!"

"After all, he is an Englishman, ducks."

"No," sighed Fiona. "I suspect it's our sex life."

"Unsatisfactory?"

"Nonexistent, I'm afraid."

"Nothing at all?" queried Lionel, secretly fascinated.

"Not for over a year, I'm afraid," blushed Fiona, popping another Tic-Tac. Since coming to America Fiona had become practically addicted to the tiny candies.

"Well, darling, you can't expect the fox to stay in the

henhouse if you don't ruffle your feathers," said Lionel, who was fond of unwieldy metaphors.

"It all started when we were doing *The Sound of Music* last year in the West End," admitted Fiona. "Mind you, I'd never really enjoyed sex. I don't think any proper Englishwoman does, except for Joan Collins and that horsey tart Camilla Parker Bowles. But I did my duty, lay back and thought of England, just like my mum taught me to. I'd practically worked my way through the entire countryside by the time I took on the role of Maria. So then I lay back and thought of Austria. But the strangest thing began to happen during rehearsals. The more I got into the role of Maria, the less I wanted Colin to touch me. By opening night we were sleeping in separate beds. We haven't had sex since."

"Oh dear, dear, dear," clucked Lionel. "I don't think this is what Rodgers and Hammerstein had in mind at all."

"I'm afraid I carried my identification with Maria Von Trapp one step too far," confessed Fiona. "The role turned me off sex completely. But you know me. When I'm attacking a part I feel I must climb every mountain."

"And yet now it appears you've managed to throw away one of your favorite things," observed Lionel.

"Perhaps you're right," offered Fiona. "There may be another woman. Greener pastures, and all that."

"Forget the greener, ducks, he was probably just looking for any old pasture. I mean . . . for over a year," said Lionel.

"So what am I to do?" asked Fiona.

"Leave that to me," responded Lionel. "I know someone who may be able to help."

"A sex therapist?"

"No, ducks, a private detective."

"A private detective. But what could he do?"

"Find out if there's another woman, for one thing," said Lionel. "And if there is, we go to the media with the news."

"But that's so common," protested Fiona.

"Common and quite effective. If word gets out that Colin's been two-timing you, you'll get sympathy votes. And don't forget the *Macbeth* you're scheduled to do with Richard Gere. Do you really think Colin will give you the part of Lady Macbeth if he's divorcing you?"

"I should venture not," replied Fiona.

"Not at all," said Lionel vigorously. "But if you win the Oscar and he's seen in the press as a cad, well it should be quite easy to convince TriStar to replace him with Bertolucci or Scorsese."

"It's quite the plan you've worked out for me, Lionel," said Fiona, popping a final Tic-Tac.

"A private detective," he concluded. "It's your best option."

"Do you think that awful little man who works for Michael Jackson would be available?" she inquired.

9

Colin Tromans lay back on his motel bed and listened to the Wagner CD he had just bought at Tower Records. Though he'd left Fiona in haste, he'd been wise enough to take along his portable CD player. Stopping at the record store on his way to the exclusive Shangri-La Motel, he'd picked up a few CDs as an alternative to the radio. Nothing filled Colin with a greater sense of passion and life's possibilities than the surging, primal melodies of Wagner's Ring Cycle. And the CD had been on sale, only $9.99.

Extraordinary how cheap potent music could be, mused Colin.

Passion, potency, these were the things he needed to get back in touch with now that he'd made the break with Fiona. Good Christ, how could he have gone without sex for so long? He should have known something was wrong on their wedding night when Fiona began to hum "God Save the Queen" as he entered her.

At least that was over with now. Especially since he'd found this new playmate. Colin's penis stiffened instantly into a rigid baton capable of conducting the entire eight-hour Ring Cycle at the mere thought of the woman he'd been having sex with for the past two weeks. I need a shower, he thought. Perhaps I'll even wank it off while I'm in there.

The warm water beat down upon him, releasing him from the stress of the ugly early morning confrontation he'd had with Fiona. At thirty-five, Colin still retained the youthful good looks that had turned heads when he was a British schoolboy. But school days were far from his thoughts just now: Eros reigned supreme. He reached for his cock, which was the size of a hearty English kipper, and began to massage it. Suddenly the shower door slid open.

Karen Kroll, clad only in her panties and a bra, was standing in front of him.

"Did you think you could start without me?" she taunted him, slipping out of her underclothes and stepping into the shower. Slowly she pushed her magnificent breasts against him, feeling his cock throb and pulse with life like the needle of a lie detector during an interview with O. J. Simpson.

"Actually, I'd been thinking of Wagner's Ring Cycle," gulped Colin.

"Are you ready for the final movement," teased Karen as she grabbed his cock and slid it inside her. Pulling her legs up around his, she wrapped herself around him and began to squeeze in a manner that recalled the death grip a boa constrictor applies to its prey.

Colin reached his climax ten minutes before Wagner's.

They had met only twelve days ago at the Ivy in Beverly Hills. Colin had been lunching with a TriStar production executive to discuss his upcoming filming of *Macbeth*. Only the savory crunch of the Ivy's fabled crab cakes made the asinine suggestions of the executive ("What about Bruce Willis as Banquo? Can we make the ending a little more upbeat? I can call Quentin Tarantino.") even remotely bearable. After considering, but never quite consenting to, the executive's requests, Colin made his way to the coat check where he had the good fortune to run into Karen.

"Karen Kroll," she said, extending her hand. "I'm a great admirer of your work."

"Why yes," replied Colin, flustered. "And I of yours." He wondered if she had a clue as to how many times he had rented the cassette of *Hangman's Luck* to jerk off to her nude love scene.

"I understand you're doing *Macbeth*," she said, handing her coat to the attendant. The top three buttons of her blouse were open; there was no bra underneath.

"Well, a bit of Shakespeare, you know."

"It's every actor's dream," purred Karen.

"Actually, Shakespeare was an actor himself, you know," said Colin, hoping that his knowledge of that mundane fact might have the effect of making him seem simultaneously erudite and a plausible sex partner.

"I'll bet he was a big ham," teased Karen.

"Actually there are many people who think he was Bacon," offered Colin, referring to the well-known theory that Sir Francis Bacon was the actual author of many of Shakespeare's plays.

"Bacon," cooed Karen. "I'm from the South and I just adore bacon. I think I'll have a BLT for lunch." The reference had gone completely over her head, but Colin didn't care. He was too busy staring at her nipples, which appeared to be harder than diamonds. Tastier too, I'll bet, he thought to himself.

"Listen," she said as the maître d' beckoned her to a table, "I'd love to talk some more with you. Why not call my agent, Bill Wyman at ICM, and we can get together for coffee? After Ralph Fiennes, Shakespeare is my favorite Englishman."

They met for coffee at eleven the next morning, and by half

past noon Karen had him in bed. Colin was amazed by her knowledge and prodigious sexual technique; fucking her was like reading the entire Kama Sutra in one sitting. After five years with Fiona, Colin couldn't get enough of Karen. He felt like a starving man who'd been let loose in the food shoppes at Harrod's.

"I've been thinking," said Karen as they sprawled together on the bed at the Shangri-La.

"What's that, my dear?" said Colin, lighting up a Player's Club cigarette.

"Maybe we should go to the Golden Globes together," she said. As she spoke the words Golden Globes she massaged her breasts, never missing an opportunity to remind Colin that he was her sex slave.

This woman is every adolescent sex fantasy I've ever had, he thought. "But do you think that's a good idea?" he asked. "I thought we agreed to be discreet. I just left Fiona this morning."

"She's got to know sometime," smiled Karen, her thumbnail idly flicking at her nipple.

Jesus God, I can't believe the things she does, Colin thought. "Let me think about it," he gulped.

"All right, lover," said Karen, now brushing her other nipple. "I don't want you to think I'm too ambitious, like Lady Macbeth."

"No, we don't want that, now do we," he said, exhaling.

"I've been thinking about Lady Macbeth a lot lately," said Karen.

Colin steeled himself.

"I've got lots and lots of ideas about how to play her," she added. There was a price for everything in the world, he reminded himself. "I mean, that whole thing about 'out damned spot'? Last night I flashed on the fact that she's not only concerned about her dirty hands, she also has a guilty conscience!"

"Spot on," lied Colin. Maybe he had made a horrible mistake by promising her the part. He'd been impressed with her work in contemporary parts, but the classics were a much greater challenge.

"You'll see, baby," she purred, rubbing her breasts against him. "I'm gonna be the most fabulous Lady Macbeth you've ever seen." With that Karen sank down and took Colin's turgid cock in her mouth.

Lady Macbeth, Lady Madonna, what difference did it make, he thought. Karen's blow jobs were classics and that's all he cared about for now.

10

Amber put the Milky Ways back in the freezer and washed the rest of the Marshmallow Fluff down the garbage disposal. Tatianna and Brianna had soon tired of talking about her Oscar nomination and turned to a more fascinating topic: the current theory that hair extensions could cause brain cancer. Tatianna was terrified for Fabio's health until Brianna reminded her that, in this particular case, there was nowhere for the cancer to grow.

They were fun, thought Amber as she lit up a Marlboro Light, but they were headed in different directions. One night, under the influence of hashish and Heath bars, the three had confided their ultimate goals in life. Brianna wanted to never gain weight and wear only natural fibers; Tatianna settled for sleeping with the entire male cast of *Melrose Place*. Only Amber, a refugee from a lower-middle-class background in Ohio, wanted a career and the fulfillment that went with it.

She was secretly glad they'd gone; now she could chill and maybe do ... But just then the doorbell rang. Had Tatianna forgotten her retainer?

It was Billy Walsh, lead singer for the alternative rock band Toxic Naomi whose debut album, *Vomit for the People*, had sold over three million copies. Amber had met him two months ago at Bar Marmont and they had gone out on a few dates. Right now he was holding a magnum of Cristal champagne and a huge bouquet of white roses.

"Amber, babe," he exclaimed. "You're nominated. It's too cool." Billy's denim vest revealed a skinny, hairless chest that Amber's tongue had wiped clean more than once.

"Billy, you're sweet," she said, accepting his gifts. Which meant, despite her reluctance, she had to invite him in. "I was just about to wash my hair," she lied.

"I won't stay long," he said. "Hey, how about we play a little sushi?" Sushi was a game Billy had devised. He put a slab of raw tuna between Amber's legs and then ate it until she reached orgasm.

"It's too early for that," she replied.

"Okay, then how about Aunt Jemima?" he asked. This was another one of Billy's homemade diversions, one in which the girl made pancakes, cut out the middle and then played ring toss with them, using Billy's erect penis as the pole. Amber had no idea why all of Billy's childish amusements revolved around food and sex; perhaps he imagined he'd been molested at a young age by Julia Child.

"I don't think I'm up for any games right now, Billy," she smiled. "But thanks for the flowers and the champagne."

"Hey, no sweat," he replied, tugging on his nose ring. "I wanted to ask you if you'd come to the MTV Video Awards with me next week. I'm giving out an honorary award and we could do it together."

So this was his game, riding on the coattails of her nomination by bringing her to the biggest rock/media event of the year. Well, it wouldn't hurt her to be seen at the Awards. In fact, they'd both benefit from the exposure. Just like Madonna turning up on the arm of Michael Jackson at the Grammys.

"That'd be great," said Amber as she gave him a kiss on the cheek. "I'll call you over the weekend for the details. Now would you hate me if I washed my hair?"

"Not if you let me come in it first," he grinned.

"Beast," replied Amber as she kissed him again and closed the door. She'd heard better pick-up lines when she was folding sweaters for a living back at The Gap in Sandusky. But Billy was cute and the Awards would be fun. And now she could relax and . . .

The phone rang. Amber picked it up grimly.

"Yes?" she said.

"Amber, it's Kenny." Kenny Blairman, her agent. Hadn't she already talked to him?

"Yes, Kenny? What is it? You already told me I'm nominated for the Oscar."

"Hey, forget that. I just got a call from Disney. They want to talk to you about a picture."

"How many weeks' work?" Amber's sole goal in life was to work as little as possible for as much money as she could get.

"Two weeks. It's an animated version of *To Kill a Mockingbird* and they want you for the voice of the little girl. Ten days in a sound studio and I can get you a quarter of a million."

Now Amber was interested. "Who else is in it?"

"Richard Thomas is doing the father and Mark Hamill will be Boo Radley." The thought of working with a couple of decent, clean-living people like John Boy and Luke Skywalker repulsed Amber, but the money was tempting.

"Can you give me until this weekend? I think I'd like to," she said.

"Sure, kiddo," said Kenny. "Leave it to me."

Amber hung up, praying there'd be no further interruptions. It had been a busy morning and she really needed to restore herself. Moving into her bedroom, she pulled open the drawer of her nightstand and reached into the very back of it. There she found what she had wanted all morning: a little silver foil packet. Undoing it carefully, Amber tapped two lines from the white powder that lay inside. Taking a straw she snorted both of them, then lay back on her bed and waited for the drug to kick in.

Five minutes later the heroin had taken hold and Amber was dreamily contemplating the speckled texture of her terra-cotta ceiling. It was all such a gas. First Hollywood, and all these cool boys who lusted after her and now an Oscar nomination. She was thinking what the other salespeople at The Gap, poor saps, must be feeling, when the doorbell rang again.

"Hold on," she cried out, "I'm coming."

Amber floated into the living room, the heroin having taken the edge off her bad mood. It was probably just a telegram or some other friend who had come by to wish her well. Other people's adoration, she could deal with that.

But when she opened the door she was confronted by a pathetic sight. A bedraggled-looking woman in her early fifties, her clothes torn and filthy, her hair ratted into little snakes, her lips cracked and caked with grime, stood in the doorway, her palm extended.

"Do you think you could possibly spare some change?" asked the poor woman.

"Hello, Mother," said Amber after a pause.

═══

"I've been told that one of this year's Best Actress nominees is home alone with nothing but her nomination to keep her warm. The lady's spouse has taken a powder—and a room at the Shangri-La Motel in Santa Monica, where he's been seen in the company of another Best Actress nominee. Does this subject of the Queen think he was fooling anyone by pretending to be a tractor salesman from the Midwest and registering under the name of Biff Wellington? Just asking."

—Mitchell Fink
People Magazine
February 13

11

Ted Gavin stared at the words on his computer screen: "Heather Locklear walks through Bijan in Beverly Hills, credit card in hand, while talking on her cellular phone and munching on a taco. The blond vamp is doing her three favorite things in the whole world: gossiping, shopping and eating junk food."

No, he thought, that will never do. Makes her sound too superficial. They want to know what makes her tick, what's human about her. His fingers returned to the keyboard. "Heather Locklear stares at the five-thousand-dollar emerald pin in the display case at Bijan in Beverly Hills. Suddenly her eyes fill with tears. The delicate blond actress is thinking about all the poor children in Bosnia who will never get to wear this expensive piece of jewelry."

Too limousine liberal, sighed Ted to himself. That might fly for Streisand, but it'll never work for Heather. What was so charming about Heather was that she never took herself seriously.

Why, he wondered, couldn't he do the same?

Ted turned off his computer and stared out the window at the haze that hung over the Santa Monica mountain range. As the Los Angeles correspondent for *Personality*, the country's largest-selling weekly magazine, he was assigned to cover Hollywood. He was supposed to pierce the veil of celebrity and reveal the funny, touching, real-life human beings that lay behind the glossy facades of the likes of Brat Pitt, Sharon Stone and Michael Douglas. "Bring them down to earth," his editor, Fatima Bulox, instructed. "Tell us of their hopes, their fears, their petite disappointments." And all for the same sick reason, thought Ted in disgust: to convince the magazine's readers that their idols were "just folks," people no different from themselves.

Ted hated his job, telling his friends that *Personality Magazine* was airplane reading for people who took buses. The reason for his animus was a familiar one amongst celebrity journalists: he didn't want to report on the lives of the stars; he wanted to be one himself.

Tall, lanky and with a shock of blond hair that hung over one eye like an errant awning, Ted could have had his pick of beautiful young Los Angeles women since he was straight, itself a rarity among celebrity journalists. But his ambition was such that he only wanted to sleep with stars. Even starlets failed to arouse him; Ted couldn't get hard for anyone whose name was below the title. But a night with Cameron Diaz or Jennifer Aniston was rarely bestowed on a man unless the title of producer, writer or director preceded his name. And so Ted burned with the desire to become a player.

That was the plan when he arrived in Los Angeles five years ago, tan, fit and with a masters in creative writing from Tulane. He figured he'd write a screenplay, sell it for a couple hundred thousand and then move into producing.

There was just one catch: Ted suffered from a case of writer's block that made Truman Capote in his final years look like a whirlwind of creativity. He would turn on his computer, take a deep breath and then stare at the blank screen for hours in the hope that inspiration would arrive.

Alas, it rarely did. He was amazed, and then bitterly resentful, at writers who seemed to be able to switch their muse on and off at will. He came to dread reading the *New York Times Book Review* which, almost monthly it seemed, had a review of a novel, essay or poem that Joyce Carol Oates had just whipped off. How could she be so productive? He began to hate her and pray that her hands would be torn off in an industrial accident. Then one day he realized it would make no difference: Ms. Oates would probably just lean forward toward her keyboard and peck out her next opus with her nose.

It took him almost two years to write his screenplay, *Heavy Artillery*, a comedy action film about an overweight suburban husband who goes to a fat farm, uncovers a terrorist plot and saves the free world. "It's *Die Hard* in a girdle," he said to his agent, who saw it as the perfect John Candy vehicle. But when Candy died, so did the script's chances of getting picked up.

Ted's agent pleaded with him for a rewrite. "Change the sex and switch it from obesity to bulimia. Maybe Kate Moss will be interested." But rewriting proved too great a task for Ted. Close to broke, he signed on at *Personality* and finally began to draw a regular paycheck. For money, and a deadline, Ted found he could crank it out.

"Staring at the Santa Monica mountains again?" asked a familiar voice, disturbing Ted's reverie. It was Fatima Bulox. "You'll never find Heather Locklear out there. You'll find her in here and in here," she chided, striking her head and her heart with her tiny Islamic fist. Fatima was a former novelist who had moved to Los Angeles and married a Beverly Hills divorce lawyer. That put an end to her novels about tortured, neurotic Middle Eastern women, though she still referred to herself as "the Joan Didion of Mecca."

"I was just trying to come up with a fresh angle on her," replied Ted weakly.

"Forget Heather," snapped Fatima. "We've pushed that story back for another JFK Jr. piece."

"Again?"

"There's a rumor going around New York that he's got a third testicle. It's next week's cover."

Ted sighed, secretly relieved at his reprieve. But Fatima was far from finished.

"New York's decided we should do a roundup piece on the nominees for this year's Best Actress Oscar," she continued. "Call the library and get the files on Lori Seefer, Fiona Covington, Karen Kroll, Amber Lyons and Connie Travatano. I'll make the calls to their representatives so you can talk to each of them."

"But what's the angle?" asked Ted.

"Tell us about their hopes, their fears, their petite disappointments," barked Fatima as she strode away down the corridor.

Ted lay sprawled on the sofa in his one-bedroom Brentwood apartment, sucking on a joint while he watched *Melrose Place.* Heather Locklear was planning to take over a printing firm by having its president, her former lover, declared legally insane.

"Heather," muttered Ted, inhaling deeply on the joint, "I hardly knew ye."

In truth, Ted hardly knew any of the celebrities he profiled. They and their publicists spewed glossy lies and Ted wrote them down dutifully. The magazine then printed them, and at the end of the day everybody went home with a paycheck. What a life.

Of course, Ted would have liked to know Heather. Or Drew Barrymore or Cindy Crawford. He'd interviewed them all, to say nothing of Burt Reynolds and Elton John. But celebrities always kept the press at bay. The women would never date you and the men would never have a drink with you. Which left Ted on his sofa with a joint and the video image of a woman he had lusted after ever since he saw her in *Dynasty* wearing a pair of cutoff shorts.

Well, if he couldn't have them in the flesh, he had the next best thing. Ted got up and wobbled over to his bedroom closet. Pushing the clothes aside, he pulled out a large wooden trunk. Flipping the lock, he opened it and gazed at the treasures it held.

There, spread out before him, was the booty from the celebrity interviews he had conducted since working for *Personality*. Whenever Ted was admitted to a star's home, he made it a point to steal some object or article of clothing. He figured it was payback for having to sit at their knee and take down all their self-serving quotes. But it also made Ted feel he had bonded with the star, that he now possessed some mysterious part of them. It made Ted, a failed writer who begged for crumbs from the star's table, feel important.

In a trance he picked up the panties he had swiped from Heather Locklear's boudoir and sniffed them. Sadly, the maid had washed them just before Ted's big heist, but the scent of Tide still gave him a roaring hard-on. With the panties draped over his face like a veil, Ted surveyed some of his other prized possessions: here was Drew Barrymore's navel ring, sitting next to the eyebrow pencil that Cindy Crawford used to color in her mole. Glenn Close's pitch pipe was perched on Faye Dunaway's sheet music for *Sunset Boulevard*. Elton John's cock ring lay nestled atop one of Burt Reynolds's finest toupees.

What, Ted wondered, his brain muddled by marijuana, his vision blurred by the lace trim of Heather Locklear's panties, would he be able to steal from the homes of this year's Best Actress nominees?

12

Connie Travatano sat in the doctor's office doing one of the things she hated most: waiting. In a recording studio or on a soundstage other people had to wait for Connie; but in the office of a Beverly Hills specialist even a diva had to take a number. Zealous about every aspect of her being, Connie was a borderline hypochondriac, a trait she had inherited from her mother Rose who once asked for general anesthesia for a hangnail. Fighting boredom, she studied the pretty young receptionist who was pointedly trying to act nonchalant in her presence. You know you want to talk to me, thought Connie smugly, you just don't have the guts.

Well, thank God for that. One thing Connie hated was chatting with the little people. It was fine if you had to tell them to adjust a sound level or move an arc light. That was work. But this was real life and time was too short to waste it by telling everyone to have a nice day. You didn't have a nice day, thought Connie, you made a nice day by working hard at it. That's what the little people didn't seem to understand. That's why they were little.

The scare this morning was probably nothing, but it was enough for Connie to cancel a rehearsal with the musicians and head into Dr. Mayerwitz's office. She wasn't taking any chances, not with her appearance in Washington only five days away. She'd already gotten a note from the President telling her he was looking forward to hearing her "legendary vocal technique." Connie liked the President. Too bad he was married and his wife kept him on such a short leash. She'd show him vocal technique.

"It shouldn't be too much longer, Miss Travatano," said the receptionist.

"I hope not. I've been here fifteen minutes."

"The doctor is in with Kenny Rogers right now."

"Oh," replied Connie. Like that explained everything.

"He's one of his favorite patients."

"Ah ha," smiled Connie. Kenny Rogers one of his favorites? Maybe she had been wrong about Dr. Mayerwitz. As far as Connie was concerned Kenny Rogers was not even a logical patient for a veterinarian, much less one of Beverly Hills's leading eye, ear, nose and throat doctors.

"Would you like a magazine?" asked the receptionist.

"What have you got?"

"*People*, *Personality*, *Time* and *Vanity Fair*."

"I think I'll pass." Connie had been on the cover of all four and had been unhappy with the stories they'd written about her. Lots of emphasis on her perfectionism, her unrelenting drive, not nearly enough on her talent and beauty. What was wrong with these magazines anyway? Why couldn't they write what she wanted them to write?

Connie's mind drifted back to the kindly old general practitioner Rose had taken her to when she was a little girl in Newark. The waiting room was filled with children, there was a big jar of lollipops on the receptionist's desk and a pile of *Reader's Digest*s on the coffee table for the adults. Connie always grabbed a copy of the magazine and flipped to her favorite feature, The Most Fascinating Person I Ever Met. Each month someone would tell of a memorable teacher, lawyer or carpenter who had changed their life through a simple human interaction. Connie used the stories as a measuring stick: if this is what made people fascinating, then this is what she would have to do when she grew up. Because deep in her heart Connie Travatano was sure of one thing: she was the most fascinating person she had ever met and always would be.

Karen stretched out under the voluminous sheets that adorned her bed, her nipples hardening as they scraped against the pale silk fabric. It was 10:30 and she should have been up hours ago. But for what? *Regis and Kathie Lee* and a bran muffin? She'd rather sleep in.

The phone on her bedside table rang.

"Hello," she said, picking up the receiver.

"Dearest heart." It was Colin.

"Hi hon."

"I was just wondering what you were up to?"

"I'm just sleeping late. Where are you?"

"At my place. I mean Fiona's, the house we rented."

"You cheating on me?"

"God no. I'm just here to pick up my clothes. Fiona is at the hairdresser."

"Just checking."

"All I do all day is think of fucking you," blurted out Colin, who had been rendered priapic by Karen's charms.

"That's sweet," she murmured, moving softly under the sheets.

"In fact, I was wondering if you'd mind if I stopped by for a spot of the old in and out in a little while."

"I'd love that, but I have to meet with my agent at noon."

"But I haven't seen you in over four days," whined Colin.

"We'll get together soon," said Karen. "Besides, we're going to the Davises' party next week."

"This waiting is killing me."

"Me too. But think what fun it will be when we start filming *Macbeth*."

"Ah yes, *Macbeth*," said Colin weakly.

"We can do Shakespeare all day and each other all night."

"So I've got to wait until the party?"

"We'll get together sooner than that," said Karen. "Call me tomorrow."

"Bye, love."

"Bye."

Karen put down the phone just as the man entered her bedroom from the shower. He was six-foot-two, with dark hair, a long, lean frame and slate-blue eyes. His cock was so large that it hung down below the towel he had wrapped around his waist.

"Who was that?" he asked.

"Telemarketing," replied Karen. "Sprint wanted to know if I was interested in a better long-distance rate. Now why don't you come back to bed and fuck me again?"

Colin put down the phone and looked at his reflection in the bedroom mirror. His skin was white and his hands were shaking. He was a mess and he knew it. Like an alcoholic who not only falls off the wagon but goes on to roll down to the bottom of the hill, Colin had left a sexless marriage to become a drooling, eros-obsessed fiend. He was so sexually besotted by the mere thought of Karen Kroll that it was beginning to affect the thing he had always taken the most pride in, his work. Just yesterday at a meeting at TriStar for *Macbeth* he had inadvertently referred to the role Karen so desperately wanted to play as Lady MacMuff.

And he shuddered at the thought of her attempting one of Shakespeare's most challenging female characters. Karen Kroll as Lady Macbeth? It could bring back Mel Gibson as Hamlet.

Perhaps therapy was the answer, he thought, as he moved into the bathroom to collect the rest of his toiletries. Ah, bugger that, it was an American thing. He and Fiona had tried couple therapy back in London; it hadn't brought her back to the marriage bed. Gathering up his prescriptions, skin creams and toothpaste from the bathroom cabinet, his eye fell on Fiona's diaphragm case sitting on top of the toilet tank. Grimly Colin noted that there was a layer of dust on it.

It was as he reentered the bedroom that Colin saw Fiona standing in the doorway.

"Collie dearest," she murmured, noting the plethora of tubes and bottles he was carrying. "Cleaning out the lavvy are we?"

"I thought you were at the hairdresser," stammered Colin.

"I decided I wanted to be with the man I love," said Fiona, moving to embrace him.

"Please," said Colin, backing away from her. "I've made my decision."

"And a very hasty one it was, I might add," replied Fiona. "Five years of marriage and suddenly you bolt off one morning like one of the Queen's corgis in pursuit of a rabbit. Regardless, I've brought you a prezzy." Fiona thrust a small, wrapped package into Colin's hands. "Unwrap it. Please."

Sheepishly Colin tore the white paper and silver ribbon off the package to discover a briarwood pipe. On its stem the words "From Fiona, all my love" were engraved.

"It's quite lovely," murmured Colin.

"It completes your pipe collection."

"Yes, I suppose it does."

"Something for you to suck on," she added.

"Puff on," he replied hastily.

"Whatever, my dearest, whatever."

"Fiona, what's done is done," said Colin softly, laying the pipe on the bedside table. "As Alan Bates said to Julie Christie in *The Go-Between*, 'the past is a foreign country.' "

"As Julie Christie said to Warren Beatty in *Shampoo*, 'Who's the best little cocksucker in the whole wide world?' " countered Fiona, grinning provocatively.

"Fiona, we haven't had sex in over a year!"

"Forget that, my dearest," she urged. "That was then. This is now."

"How can I forget all the frustration and embarrassment. You've had me feeling like a randy teenager."

"Collie, that is all in the past. You must believe me."

"Believe you? I must fuck you! That's been the problem."

"Not anymore, my pet," said Fiona, lowering the left shoulder strap of the shapeless floral smock she was wearing. "Now come and make passionate love to me."

"Fiona!" barked Colin. "Stop this at once. Stripping off that little schoolgirl frock. You look like Shirley Temple with a hot flash."

"Do I now?" she replied coolly, undoing a button and letting the dress fall to the floor. She stood before him nude.

Colin fell speechless. To be confronted in the nude by his estranged wife, a brilliant classical actress, while he was secretly lusting for a smarmy Hollywood sexpot: how mortifying.

Fiona stood her ground. Ignoring Lionel's advice, she had decided to forgo a private detective and see if a display of wicked sexual behavior could rescue her marriage. Five years of wedded bliss was worth five minutes of naughty behavior, she reasoned.

"Fiona," pleaded Colin, "put your clothes back on."

"Only when we've finished mating like two doves in heat," she replied, running her tongue over her lower lip and then biting it with the top row of her teeth.

It was the bite that caused Colin to buckle. As a lad in Islington he had achieved his first erection while watching Farrah Fawcett do the very same thing on the premiere episode of *Charlie's Angels*. Subsequently he had never missed an episode, or an erection. A beautiful woman biting her lower lip, inviting one into eros; that's all it took for Colin.

How strange, he mused: you study at the Royal Academy, marry well, move to Hollywood to become a millionaire, and in the end it all comes down to an Aaron Spelling t&a show from the seventies.

Colin leaned forward and kissed Fiona. "My darling," she murmured.

"Do you truly want to make love?" he asked.

"As never before," she cooed.

"Then let us begin."

Fiona broke away from him and moved to the bathroom. "Just one second, dearest Collie."

Colin lay back on the bed, awaiting Fiona's return. "You're quite sure of this now," he said. "No doubts? No second thoughts?"

Fiona picked up her diaphragm case and blew the dust off the top of it. "My darling," she replied, "I'm looking forward to the biggest invasion since D day."

13

Lori threw back her second shot of Cuervo Gold and gazed out the living room window. The long, thin shadows of the palm trees were fading into darkness. Soon it would be night. Soon Maria would be home. She needed all the tequila she had on hand to steady her nerves.

"Claudio will be over in a limo to pick you up for the Meryl Streep premiere at six-thirty tomorrow," Melissa Crawley had informed her over the phone that afternoon.

"I'll be ready," responded Lori.

"There's a big party afterward at the Armand Hammer Museum and tons of photographers and camera crews will be available to take a picture of you together. This is very dressy, so please don't try to be cute by wearing a man-tailored jacket or sneakers. I want to see high heels and cleavage."

"Yes, Madame Chanel," joked Lori.

"Chanel is exactly right. Do you have a Chanel purse?"

There was a silence. Lori didn't know what Melissa was talking about.

"I guess not," hazarded Melissa, "what with your predilection for backpacks and hiking boots. Not to worry, dear. I'll have Claudio pick one up for you at Nordstrom's. He'll bring it over with his résumé."

"His résumé?"

"I want you to study all about him so that you can speak freely with the press. Details make anything sound true."

"All right," agreed Lori.

"Oh, and one more thing."

"What's that?"

"Are you still living with that little Mexican girl?"

"Well, yes," said Lori.

"I'm afraid she'll have to go for the time being," said Melissa smoothly. "The reporter from *Personality* is coming to the house to interview you on Thursday. I need to have your little friend out and Claudio installed in residence."

"He's moving in here?" asked Lori incredulously.

"He doesn't have to move in actually. But I want him present during the interview. It's important that we create the inference that he has complete access to your house."

"How am I supposed to pull that off?"

"Oh, I don't know, dear. Be creative. Hang a jockstrap on the bedroom doorknob. Something casual."

Great, thought Lori, Maria's going to love all this. Lori had met her almost a year ago when, coming home from an aerobics class, tired and hungry, she pulled into the drive-thru lane at a family-style Mexican restaurant on Santa Monica Boulevard. As Lori spoke into the microphone and ordered the El Grande burrito, she looked up to see a striking black-haired Mexican woman taking down her order. The waitress's almond-shaped eyes flickered with interest, and Lori felt her heart beat faster. When the burrito was almost ready, stuffed with beans, cheese and rice, the black-haired woman lifted it to her lips and licked the flap of it to seal it. That made Lori's heart beat even faster. When she unwrapped her food, quaking with desire as she drove toward her home in the Hollywood Hills, a piece of paper fell out. It had Maria Caldone's phone number on it.

Lori called the very next day. Within two weeks Maria had moved most of her belongings, really just a few clothes and a CD player, from her parents' house into Lori's. Their affair proceeded feverishly, although it hit a few speed bumps along the way.

The primary one was political. Maria, a student at USC and a member of the Gay Students League, felt no shame over her lesbianism and proudly trumpeted it at any occasion. Lori, deep in the Hollywood closet, tried to avoid the issue at all times, petrified of the impact it might have on her career. Aware that she was a potential target of gay protesters who resented her closeted lifestyle, Lori always brought an extra dress to the Oscars in the event that members of the AIDS activist group ACT-UP splattered her with paint, as they had threatened to do ever since 1991.

The differences in their outlooks led to constant friction. Just last month they had argued for two days straight over whether or not to go to Chastity Bono's birthday party in separate cars. Their solution—Maria rode up on a motorcycle, Lori snuck in the back door dressed as a Sparklett's deliveryman—pleased neither of them.

And then there had been the time they were stopped by a zealous young female fan at the meat counter of Gelson's on Franklin Avenue. The girl, an aspiring actress, was lost in her admiration for Lori.

"Miss Seefer," she gushed, "I loved you in *A Bridge to the River* with Matt Dillon."

"Thanks," smiled Lori.

"That scene where you and he made love during the flood, I thought that was great acting on your part."

You bet it was, thought Lori, who flinched at the memory of Dillon's snakelike tongue down her throat. But she kept smiling and said, "We had fun with that one."

"I mean, you're just so lucky," continued the girl. "Matt Dillon is beyond cute."

"He's a nice guy," responded Lori, wishing the conversation were over.

"Too bad it wasn't a nude scene," said the girl.

Maria, who had grown weary of this adolescent ardor and her lover's tolerance of it, inched closer to Lori.

"Imagine getting paid to make love to Matt Dillon!" exclaimed the girl.

"Imagine doing this for free!" countered Maria, who grabbed Lori and kissed her passionately on the lips.

Lori broke free of Maria's embrace as the girl gasped and stepped back in shock. Maria smiled at her in triumph.

Lori couldn't believe it. A scene in a public supermarket! Didn't Maria care anything about decorum? But then, Lori knew she didn't. Passion was everything to her; that's why Lori couldn't resist her.

"Let's go," urged Lori, grabbing Maria's hand.

"Remember, sweetheart," said Maria to the girl. "This is the way it's supposed to be. Not Adam and Eve, but Madam and Eve."

After that, Lori shopped alone. But she never stopped loving Maria. She even pulled strings to get her a job with a top Hollywood catering firm. Now, instead of rolling burritos on Santa Monica Boulevard, Maria spooned caviar and crème fraîche onto tiny English crackers at parties held in palatial Bel Air estates. It was a nice job and left Maria plenty of time to study and putter around the house.

But it wouldn't be a happy homecoming tonight. Not with Lori telling Maria she had to move out temporarily. Maybe the fact that it was for the Oscar would make a difference, thought Lori. Maybe Maria would be amused by the whole charade. Maybe . . .

Lori reached for the Cuervo and poured herself another shot. It was going to be a long night, no maybes about it.

"**M**other, please!" screeched Amber as she contemplated the spectacle before her.

Shana Lyons was soaking in Amber's tub and doing three of her favorite things: smoking, drinking and her nails. A freshly lit Winston smoldered in Amber's faux marble soap dish, while the shower caddy, once reserved for shampoo and conditioner, now held a bottle of vodka and several limes. At fifty-two Shana had the sneering B-girl looks of such fifties screen icons as Gloria Grahame and Jo Van Fleet.

"What's your problem, kid?" she said.

"You've turned my home into a zoo," wailed Amber. "I can't even go the bathroom without tripping over one of your bottles!"

"You got something against the lived-in look?" shot back Shana, taking a deep drag on her Winston.

"I can't live this way."

"Yeah? Well I couldn't live the way you left me in Sandusky. Homeless and with no money."

"You wouldn't have been homeless if you hadn't married that jerk Cal Roberts," snapped Amber.

"Every woman's entitled to marry a thief for her fourth husband," countered Shana. "Besides, Cal gave me some very good head before he defaulted on the mortgage."

"You've been here a week, Mother," said Amber. "You've got to make some plans to move on."

"You gonna give me the money for that?"

It always came down to the money, thought Amber bitterly. She'd left her mother and her worthless stepfather three years ago, determined to sever all ties. But Shana had seen Amber on *Picket Fences* right about the time she lost her house. A series of embarrassing phone calls to the studio followed, which Amber tried to cover up by complaining of being stalked by an older woman from the Midwest. She'd ignored all the letters Shana sent her, but to no avail. The drunken bitch had panhandled money for a bus ticket to Hollywood and now Amber was stuck with her own personal version of *Mommie Dearest*.

"You've got to be reasonable," sighed Amber, trying another tack. "I can't have you living here with me being an Academy Award nominee and all."

"Why?" asked Shana. "You afraid Jack Valenti wouldn't approve?"

"I've got my own life now, Mother. You have to get on with yours."

"Your poor old mom is broke and homeless. You really think it's right to turn her out into the cold?"

"We have an average temperature of sixty-five here in Los Angeles," said Amber frostily.

"I'm not hitting the streets when I can live in a condo with a Jacuzzi and a gas fireplace."

"You don't fit in with the way I live," said Amber. "I have a life filled with wealthy friends and big producers. What do you do all day? Drink vodka tonics and watch the talk shows."

"There was a very good Sally Jessy this afternoon," snapped Shana. "Ungrateful daughters."

"You've got to make plans to move," said Amber, grabbing the vodka bottle from the shower caddy and washing the ashes out of the soap dish. "I'll give you till the end of the week."

"And I'll give you a counteroffer," sneered Shana. "Two hundred and fifty thousand bucks. Or otherwise, it's Mother's Day for the rest of your life."

14

"I don't know any easy way to say this," said Dr. Mayerwitz, sitting down next to Connie, "so I'm just going to say it. You're not going to be able to sing at the President's gala next week."

Connie felt as if she'd been hit in the face by one of Mr. Pepaloni's salamis. "That's not possible," she said, trying to remain calm.

"I'm afraid it's a fact," said the doctor gently.

"But I've given my word. The publicity is out there. I've got to do it."

"If you do, I can't be responsible for the consequences."

"Which are?"

"Permanent damage to your vocal chords."

"It can't be that bad," wailed Connie.

"It's very serious, Miss Travatano," replied Dr. Mayerwitz. "You need a recuperation period of three to four weeks at the very least."

"You don't understand," she pleaded. "I haven't sung in public for ten years. My fans, the public, the whole goddamned world is waiting to hear me sing 'God Bless America' in front of the President of the United States and the Vietnam veterans. If I cancel now, I'll look like a backslider." Connie didn't mention the fact that it would also rob her of brownie points toward the Oscar.

"Couldn't you lip-synch it?" asked the doctor.

"Lip-synch it?" replied Connie incredulously. "I've never recorded 'God Bless America.' Who do you think I am, Kate Smith?"

"I think you're a very great singer, and I want you to stay that way," replied the doctor evenly. "That's why I'm telling you not to sing next week in Washington."

"Look," she continued, "what is it, a cold, a sore throat? Can't you give me some antibiotics? I'll take them all week and save my voice until the day of the performance."

"It's more serious than that. Your throat has suffered trauma damage."

"But how is that possible?" said Connie, mystified.

"I don't know," replied Dr. Mayerwitz. "All I do know is that your throat and vocal chords appear to have been stretched far beyond their capacity. Normal singing, even screaming, shouldn't do this. As odd as it sounds, it's almost as if someone tried to push a large battering ram down your throat."

The Mexican pool boy's cock! Connie writhed with humiliation and self-loathing.

"Is it possible," continued Dr. Mayerwitz, "that you attempted to swallow a large cucumber or a banana whole? That might account for the trauma."

Connie's face flushed redder than after any herbal mask that Helga had ever given her. "I'll have to try to remember," she stammered.

"I'm not just talking about swallowing something," said the doctor. "It would have had to be lodged there for a good fifteen or twenty minutes. Surely you'd remember that?"

"Maybe in my sleep," she offered lamely.

"Whatever," said Dr. Mayerwitz, seeing Connie to the door. "The important thing is not to further stress your vocal chords. Speak in a soft voice, gargle with warm water twice a day and come back to see me in two weeks. You should be fine by then. And as for Washington, if you need me to make a statement in a press release about your health, I'll be glad to do it."

"**P**enny for your thoughts, babe."

Karen exhaled a long, thin stream of smoke and looked over at the dark-haired man in bed with her. She had been engaging in a ritual—postcoital tristesse and a cigarette—well-known to all blond starlets who had fucked their way to the top, and now he had interrupted it.

"Oh, I was just thinking about being nominated for the Academy Award," she said.

"Must feel pretty good," said the man.

"It doesn't feel bad," she said as she got out of bed and went into the bathroom to freshen up.

"When's the ceremony?"

"Monday, March twenty-sixth," she replied as she drew a brush briskly back and forth across her teeth.

"Got a big gown all picked out?"

"I think so," said Karen, gargling with Listerine and then rinsing her mouth out. "Valentino is supposed to send over something for me to look at next week." Feeling fresh and clean, she left the bathroom and slid back into bed next to the man.

"Know who you're going with?" he asked casually.

Karen drew the man closer and kissed him hard on the lips. "I want to go with you," she said, lying through her freshly brushed teeth. "But my agent may have some different plans. Let me talk to him."

"Hey, babe, what's to talk about?" said the man, returning the kiss and savoring the tingle of Listerine which, oddly enough, never failed to excite him. "You wanna go with me, you go with me."

"That's what I like about you," purred Karen. "You're so decisive."

Actually, what Karen liked about Johnny Dante was that he could fuck her for three and four hours at a time without even pausing for so much as a cigarette. Lean, hard-bodied and sexually inexhaustible, Johnny was as reliable as a vibrator and required no cleaning or changing of batteries. They had met on the set of *Sacrilege*; she was the star, he was the second assistant electrician. That didn't bother Karen, who had long harbored a hankering for the blue-collar types who lived in the San Fernando Valley, drove four-wheel pick-ups and made a living doing the grunt work on movie sets. She learned early on in her career that whenever she was tense or nervous before a scene nothing relaxed her like a good fuck with a member of the crew. Karen was one uptight actress who took the advice "get a grip" quite literally.

Their romance had continued after filming, with Karen inviting Johnny to spend one or two nights a week at her place. The only problem was that Johnny sometimes wanted to go out in public. For Karen to be seen on the arm of an Italian roughneck who favored gold chains and Brut for Men was simply unacceptable. And so she pretended an interest in indulging in Johnny's lifestyle.

"I'm so tired of Morton's," she had said just last week. "Why can't we go to that Red Lobster near your place in Reseda? Nobody ever takes me there."

"I love these fried clams," she said an hour later, burping softly on the combination of grease, salt and bread crumbs that passed itself off as fish. "Oh and look, they bring the bottled salad dressings right to the table. How clever."

Then there was the time Johnny wanted to go to Wolfgang Puck's new Spago, in Beverly Hills. Karen told him she had booked a table for Friday night, knowing full well that the restaurant was closed to the public for a private party in honor of Barry Diller. When they arrived and were turned away at the door, Karen quickly steered them to a Kentucky Fried Chicken in Hollywood before anyone could notice Johnny's pistachio-colored shirt and his pinkie ring of St. Sebastian complete with miniature arrows. To make up for his disappointment, Karen treated to a large order of extra crispy fried chicken livers.

In four months with Johnny Dante Karen had had some of the best fucking, and the worst food, of her life.

"I've got a tux, you know, babe," said Johnny.

"I'll just bet you do," said Karen, feeding him another taste of her antiseptic tongue. Now he wanted to go to the Oscars with her. Well, she'd really have to maneuver to get out of this one. For now, at least, there was a way to distract him. Karen took her tongue from Johnny's mouth and began to trace a trail down his chest, leading to the place that she had affectionately nicknamed Dante's Inferno.

I've passed my orals, thought Fiona triumphantly.

Fellatio was hardly her favorite sport. Learning about it as a British schoolgirl she had registered only disbelief. Who had invented such a nasty thing? And what sort of people practiced it? Americans, I'll bet, she sniffed. No sensible people would indulge in such primitive behavior. Why lick the Maypole when you could affix a ribbon and dance around it in a circle?

Regardless, she had attacked Colin's privates with the succulent vigor of a Dustbuster switched on high, and the rosy glow in his normally pasty cheeks was proof that it had been worth the effort.

"Dearest, that was memorable," he whispered.

Memorable. How typical of Collie, she thought. Everything was a performance to him, even sex. Just as well; she could play that game. If Colin needed to believe he was in bed with a lusty Renaissance tart, then a full-throated wench she'd be. Fiona desperately wanted to return to the connubial bliss she had known with him in their early years. The days of cuddling naked together and reciting passages from "Beowulf" to each other as foreplay. She missed that.

Their love life and their work had meshed together perfectly until *The Sound of* . . .

No, thought Fiona firmly, I'm not even going to think about that. I went too far with that role and look at the price I've paid.

"Dearest, I want to mount you," said Colin.

How like an actor, thought Fiona, always ready to make an entrance.

"Then do so, my love," she cooed back.

Colin positioned himself above Fiona. She closed her eyes and contemplated a lovely damask pattern she'd seen just the other day at Laura Ashley's. The lacy interweaving of flowers and vines helped distract her from the heaving weight her body bore.

"Yes, my love," she murmured, "yes."

"Is it good, my darling?" inquired Colin.

"Not good," said Fiona. "Great."

"Ah yes," he chuckled. "Some are born great, some have greatness thrust into them." He pounded away at her.

Fiona bore the relentless jabs dutifully, feeling like a small craft in a rough and choppy sea. Colin's breath became quick and labored, rather like the third act of *Camille*. It was going well, thought Fiona, punishing, but well. She closed her eyes tighter, trying to reconjure the lovely floral damask.

But it wouldn't appear. Instead she saw a hillside, verdant and green, dappled with early morning sunshine. A distant melody hovered in the background. Then a figure appeared, dressed in black, rushing over the crest of the hillside. It was Maria Von Trapp!

"No!" screamed Fiona.

"What is it?" asked Colin, withdrawing immediately.

"Not you, dear," said Fiona. "It's just . . ." Fiona drew her legs closed.

"Not the bloody *Sound of Music* again!" wailed Colin, his erection collapsing as quickly as an umbrella after a brief summer storm.

"My darling, please," pleaded Fiona, as she gathered the sheets around her protectively. "Give me a little more time!"

"Fiona, dearest, you've had more than a year to get over that role," said Colin softly. "Clearly some part of you wants to cling to it." He rose from the bed and began to assemble his clothes.

"No, Collie, no!"

"I'm afraid it is so, my love. This was foolish of both of us. We can't recapture what Rodgers and Hammerstein have destroyed."

"I don't want you to leave me, Collie," said Fiona. "I don't want to go on without you."

"I fear you must."

"But what shall I do?"

"Get thee to a nunnery," replied Colin tenderly as he zipped up his pants.

━━━━
━━━━

SONGBIRD SILENCED: Connie Travatano, known as the Sicilian Songbird early on in her career, will not sing "God Bless America" on the upcoming ABC-TV special in honor of the Vietnam veterans as previously announced. Travatano, who has been battling a viral infection, has withdrawn from the show on the advice of her physician. The announcement is sure to cause disappointment for the vocalist's fans who had been looking forward to her first public singing appearance in over a decade. "Connie will sing in public again," commented her longtime manager Morty Saltman, "this is just not the right time." Saltman would not comment on rumors that his client may make good on that promise by singing the Oscar-nominated song from the Disney animated film version of *The Scarlet Letter*, "Gimme an A," on the upcoming Awards show.

—*Los Angeles Times*
Morning Report, Calendar section
February 15

15

"**Y**ou're leaving me for a man?!" shrieked Maria as she threw the ceramic teapot across the kitchen. It sailed into the distressed Southwestern hutch, distressing it even further, and shattered into pieces. They fell to the floor, joining the fragments of the Steuben glass vase, the Italian china platter and the Mr. Coffee that were already lying there. Lori's kitchen was beginning to resemble a Pottery Barn outlet the day after an earthquake.

"I'm not leaving you," pleaded Lori, dodging a metallic iced tea glass that barely grazed her left ear. "I just need you to lay low until the Oscars are over."

"Lay low?" hissed Maria, tossing a frozen can of concentrated orange juice into the microwave and switching it on to high. "Baby, I have never laid low, and I never will. I'm proud of who I am! I am the world's biggest Mexi-dyke and you know it."

Lori did know it, and that was the problem. Maria's fiery nature could not countenance, much less understand, why anybody would want to lie about who they were. There was a soft pop as the orange juice can exploded in the microwave. Lori would clean it up later; for now she decided to try another tack with Maria.

"Don't you understand what it would mean to me to win an Oscar?" she said. "It could make my career."

"You've already got a career," said Maria, tossing the salt and pepper shakers down the garbage disposal. "What's so special about the lousy Oscar?"

"It's the biggest prize an actor can win," snapped Lori as she grabbed the shakers, nearly mangling her hand in the process. "And stop ruining my kitchen."

"Don't worry about your fucking kitchen. Worry about our love!" screamed Maria, empty-handed but still as dangerous in the kitchen as Betty Crocker on a bad acid trip.

"Damn it, Maria, not everybody is a radical dyke," barked Lori. "Some of us have careers and public images. Our lives have to be private."

"That didn't stop Ellen DeGeneres," shot back Maria.

"I don't do sitcoms!"

"Good. Because you won't be doing me for a while either!" Maria turned to leave but Lori grabbed her wrist.

"It's the Oscar, Maria," she said softly. "I've dreamed about winning one my entire life. Just imagine what it'll be like for me. I'll be in an auditorium with the most important people in Hollywood. My name will be called out and I'll go to the podium. And everyone there will give a big cheer."

"Everyone there will have moved here!" sang Maria as she threw back her head, laughed and clicked her heels. She kept on doing a mean Rita Moreno as she tore into the bedroom, dragged out a suitcase and began hurling her clothes into it.

"You can move back in next week," countered Lori. "Just as soon as I finish the *Personality* interview."

"I'm outta here for good," said Maria. "I'd rather move in with my family than stay with a woman who's ashamed of our love."

"I am not ashamed," insisted Lori. "I just can't be out to something like *Personality Magazine*. I mean, this interview will go straight to the heartland of America."

"You forget I'm in America!" blazed Maria, snapping the suitcase shut and heading for the front door. I never should have bought her that *West Side Story* CD, thought Lori, cursing herself as she rushed after Maria.

"It's publicity for God's sake. My publicist has arranged for this guy in her office to take me out on a couple of dates. It's just a big sham."

Maria put down her suitcase and addressed Lori with a new-found calm. "And because of what your publicist says you're going to have me sneak around in back alleys while you go out and let this stud paw you in public?"

"He's supposed to be a very nice boy," protested Lori weakly.

"You know what your problem is?" said Maria coldly. "You've been in the movies so long you've begun to believe your own publicity. So tonight, when you're lonely for me, why don't you wrap a copy of *People* around your vibrator and fuck yourself with the lies you live on!"

She slammed the door behind her and was gone.

Amber stared into the refrigerator in shock. All the Häagen-Dazs bars were gone, to say nothing of the Milky Ways and Marshmallow Fluff. Yesterday it had been the Kool-Aid and the Lucky Charms. This woman is eating everything but the mail, she thought to herself.

From the living room came the sounds of an old Doobie Brothers album. Shana loved them and the rest of the long-haired, walrus-mustached rock musicians of the early seventies on whom she had misspent her youth. "Whoa, whoa, whoa, listen to the music," she croaked through her cocktail glass.

Do I have any choice, thought Amber as she went into her

bedroom, shutting the door behind her. After their last fight Amber had retreated into silence, hoping that her mother would tire of the cold shoulder treatment and move on. Fat chance. Shana seemed determined to stay on and leech off Amber until she got the money she wanted. Amber, for her part, had given some thought to a hit man.

It was no use, she concluded. Even if she did pay off her mother she'd only come back in a few months and demand more. Best to just ride it out, let her get tired and leave. Until then . . .

Well until then there were other ways to feel good. Amber opened the drawer in her bedroom table and reached into the back of it. Her hand was searching for the secret silver foil packet she craved so desperately, but all it kept coming up with were bobby pins and nail polish remover.

Panicking, she pulled the drawer out of the table and dumped its contents on the bed. Three condoms, a half-crushed pack of Marlboro Lights, matches, a pack of Tic-Tacs and an audiocassette of *The Bridges of Madison County*. No heroin anywhere.

Amber rushed into the living room and accosted Shana, who was weaving back and forth to *Boston's Greatest Hits*, a vodka tonic in one hand, a joint in the other.

"Have you been snooping in my bedroom?"

"Why daughter dear, whatever do you mean?"

"You know what I mean. My heroin is gone."

"Now see here, missy," said Shana, taking a long, deep drag on the joint. "No daughter of mine is going to get caught up in a drug habit."

"Oh cut the Nancy Reagan crap," said Amber.

"I'm serious dear. You don't know what you're playing with."

JOHN KANE

Shana exhaled the marijuana smoke in one long whoosh as a buzz crept down her spine, making her toes feel like they were cemented into the carpet.

"Where did you put it?" demanded Amber.

"On the Lucky Charms I had for breakfast yesterday," giggled Shana. "I don't think I've ever enjoyed Matt Lauer as much as I did after that."

This was it! Her own mother breaking into her private stash—was nothing sacred?

"All right, Mother," screeched Amber. "I'm going out to score some more dope and I want you out by the time I get back."

"You wouldn't . . ."

"Oh yes I would," snapped Amber. "In fact, if you're not gone when I return I'm calling my lawyer and getting a court order to have you evicted!"

Like Maria before her, Amber slammed the door behind her.

And Shana wobbled over to the phone and started to dial a number she had memorized long ago: 1-800-ENQUIRE.

16

Fiona sat stiffly on the Naugahyde sofa, her buttocks feeling as if they had been fused to it with Krazy Glue. She stared straight ahead at the bronzed Uzi and the framed *Soldier of Fortune* magazine cover that adorned the far wall of the tiny, airless office on Hollywood Boulevard. The hulking man who sat in front of her, whose most prominent features appeared to be a ponytail and an eye patch, was telling her things she didn't wish to know.

"For five thousand dollars," said Ralph Spivak, "you get the complete range of services. Twenty-four-hour surveillance, tapping of all cellular phone calls and video coverage of any activities that may benefit you in court. As an added bonus, I should point out that I have an exclusive arrangement with *Hard Copy*. If I get public drunkenness, an arrest or exposed genitalia on tape, we get the lead story on the show that night."

Lionel, I'm a fool to have let you talk me into this, thought Fiona, as she glanced over at her agent on the other end of the sofa. But Lionel was as unflappable now as he had been on the phone this morning. "If we're to announce this breakup, you need to be positioned as the injured party," he insisted. "It will help win you sympathy votes. After all, you haven't got a husband; you might as well try to get an Oscar."

"My operatives and I will be fully briefed on your husband's modus operandi," continued Ralph, who favored CIA jargon when talking with a client. "We will return to you with a full list of his proclivities. Who he drinks with, fights with, sleeps with."

How utterly dreadful, shuddered Fiona.

"You can learn some very interesting things from an investigation like this," continued Ralph as he picked up a silver toothpick on which the salutation "Love ya babe, Tony's Steak Hut" was engraved. He began to pick his teeth with it as he told his story. "Just last month I handled a tail for a very wealthy woman from Beverly Hills who thought her husband might be stepping out on her. Three weeks later, after following him five times to a veterinarian's office in Westwood, I caught him with his pants down making love to a German shepherd. Seems like this little piggy liked to go to market."

Fiona's insides twisted into a double knot. She felt as if she had descended into the sewer and was now being flushed into another universe.

"Lionel," she said, rising, "I feel a bit faint and should like to use the lavvy. Would you be so kind as to finish the arrangements with Mr. Spivak?"

"Certainly," he replied.

"Thanks ever so," she said, grabbing her Chanel purse and heading to the door.

What a squalid little man he was with his guns and his ponytail and his toothpick! Fiona spotted a cockroach slowly crossing the floor as she moved to the door. That's right, dear little bug, she thought, let's both flee from this awful man before we expire from his complete and utter ghastliness. Her hand was on the doorknob when Ralph spoke.

"Uh, Miss Covington?"

"Yes?"

"You're an actress, right?"

"Well, yes I am."

"Ever work with Steven Seagal?" asked Ralph.

"That was the most appalling experience," said Fiona as she took a sip from her Bloody Mary. She and Lionel were seated in a booth at Le Dome awaiting the arrival of Robert De Niro and the producer of his next film. "That awful man picking his teeth whilst he regaled us with a tale of bestiality."

"When we spoke of your career at this time last year, you told me that you wanted the same kind of American popularity that Julie Christie and Emma Thompson had achieved," responded Lionel. "Both those ladies won Oscars. I'm trying to do the same for you."

"I daresay Julie Christie didn't win her award by hiring a private detective to tail Warren Beatty and report back to her on his sexual peccadilloes," said Fiona.

"She'd have needed the entire Los Angeles Police Department to help her out on that one, my dear," observed Lionel tartly.

Their brief spat was ended by the arrival of Robert De Niro and his producer, Brian Cosgrave. Smiling shyly and extending his hand, Robert De Niro seemed to possess a humility that was foreign to most movie stars.

"Fiona, I loved your work in *Mary*," he said.

"Oh Mr. De Niro . . ."

"Robert, please."

"Robert, this is such a pleasure," said Fiona. Brian Cosgrave ordered a bottle of wine and asked for menus as they seated themselves. He was used to playing the producer.

"*Mortal Coil* is going to be a big movie for Bob," he enthused. "Big like *Raging Bull* or *Godfather II*. Francis is considering directing and if he falls out we've got Rob Reiner very interested. Bill Goldman has given us a wonderful story. A corrupt politician and a female scientist battling over the fate of a new antiviral drug. With his adopted Chicano daughter for comic relief. It's both sad and funny. Like life itself."

There was a moment of silence and then De Niro spoke in a soft, even voice. "I like this bread," he said, chewing on one of the rolls from the breadbasket. "It's salty, but still sweet."

"Like life itself," observed Fiona. The foursome broke into shared laughter. Oh good, she thought, he likes me. Perhaps he'll cast me. Fiona could almost taste the role of Helen LeVek, lady scientist.

"That's very funny," said Brian, who had sucked more ass in Hollywood than all of Heidi Fleiss's girls combined. "And Helen needs to be funny. It's a funny role."

"And yet written with such depth," said Lionel, jumping in to join the brownnosing brigade.

A young waiter approached the table. "Is everything all right, Mr. De Niro?" he inquired.

"Yes, fine," he responded. "Maybe we should order now." The young man wrote down everyone's choices and then turned back to Robert De Niro. An aspiring actor, he had been waiting to say the following sentence for fifteen years.

"I just want you to know that your performance as Jake LaMotta in *Raging Bull* is the single greatest piece of acting I've ever seen in my life."

"Thank you," stammered De Niro, staring in embarrassment at the tablecloth. "That makes me feel very proud."

He's so dear, thought Fiona. Such a dear, dear, modest man!

"Now I'll be right back with four Chinese Chicken Salads," said the waiter, who had just given a pretty fair performance himself.

"The whole world loves Bobby," gushed Brian. "He's the King!"

"It's nice to be King," said Lionel, raising his wineglass. Robert De Niro blushed a deeper shade of crimson than the merlot they were drinking. Outward displays of enthusiasm or emotion always embarrassed him.

How sensitive, despite his brutish exterior, pondered Fiona. I must be very careful not to crowd him if I want to get this role. None of the toadying that Lionel and this producer are trafficking in so heavily. Remain cool and collected.

"Have you tried the breadsticks?" she asked Robert De Niro, extending one to him. "They taste oddly of anise."

De Niro took the breadstick and smiled humbly at Fiona in return. But Brian was not to be deterred.

"Hey, what's your favorite Bobby performance? For me, it's got to be *Taxi Driver*. 'You talkin' to me? You talkin' . . .'" As he prattled on Fiona's gaze fell on a smartly tailored middle-aged woman who had just been seated at the adjoining table. She was impeccably groomed and seemed oddly familiar, even though her back was to Fiona.

"I mean when you picked up that gun and sprayed Harvey Keitel's brains all over the wall, that's what I call interior decorating," continued Brian.

"It was just a movie," murmured De Niro, almost choking on the words.

"Just a movie!" exclaimed Brian. "It's a classic. They teach it in film school now. God's lonely man, who can forget it?"

Suddenly the middle-aged woman turned and Fiona could see her face: it was Julie Andrews! Thoughts of her abortive reconciliation with Colin flooded her mind; their carnal reunion cut short by the image of Julie Andrews running through the Alps. Fiona's heart began to beat madly as she thought of all the sorrow and loss this fellow British thespian had brought, however inadvertently, into her life. Her eyes filled with tears and a lump the size of a grapefruit formed in her throat.

"And the mohawk!" said Brian. "That mohawk nailed the performance. Nailed it."

Fiona felt a huge, primal sadness surge through her being. Would she and Collie ever be together again? Would she ever have sex again? Would she ever be free of *The Sound of Music* and the starched, sexless, clean-as-a-whistle, sunny-as-a-summer's-day performance that first Julie Andrews and then she had given as Maria Von Trapp? Her misery spiraled into woe and then deeper into lamentation. A marriage, a theatrical union to rival Laurence Olivier and Vivien Leigh, Richard Burton and Elizabeth Taylor, and it had been ruined by a goody-two-shoes nun running over a mountain. Fiona's loss seemed incalculable; her pain infinite. Surely no actress before her had suffered as she had.

It was at that moment that Julie Andrews noticed Fiona staring at her. Smiling brightly, she nodded and mouthed the words "God bless you" to her.

Fiona burst into huge, racking sobs that shook her whole body. They seemed to come from the very depths of her soul, as Mercedes McCambridge's voice had come from Linda Blair's mouth in *The Exorcist*. Lionel, Brian and Robert De Niro stared at her in shock.

"Fiona," cried Lionel in alarm, "what's wrong?"

But Fiona could not speak, her breath coming in short, sharp spasms, her tears coursing down her Devonshire cream cheeks. She reached out in agony, spilling a glass of merlot across Robert De Niro's Armani jacket. He jumped back as Fiona tried vainly to blot her tears with a breadstick, the salt from her eyes combining deliciously with the anise from the pastry.

"Please, have some water," urged Lionel. But Fiona waved him away, her sobs having brought on a case of the hiccups. She was now alternately emitting low, wailing moans or short gasps of breath.

Robert De Niro rose and regarded the scene dispassionately. His face, as it had in so many films, betrayed no overt emotion. But inside he was feeling only one thing: this woman is insane. I could never act with someone so emotionally unhinged.

"Is there something I can do?"

Fiona looked up to see Julie Andrews's beatific face smiling at her. "No! No! No!" she wailed.

The former Mary Poppins retreated in haste. Lionel was left to try and console the truly inconsolable Fiona.

Robert De Niro took Brian by the arm and nudged him to the exit. "Is Sharon Stone still available?" he asked.

17

Connie adjusted the cheap blond wig and looked at herself in the hallway mirror. Perfect, she thought; I look just like any other Beverly Hills yenta.

She had been depressed ever since learning that she would not be able to sing at the Washington gala. It had seemed like such a perfect parlay: an Oscar nomination and a return to public performance. Show business was all about momentum, riding the wave, and she had been convinced that singing in front of the President on national TV would give her the momentum to go on and win the Oscar. And now it was all over, with lots of nasty sniping in the press about how disappointed all her fans were. If she wasn't careful she was going to wind up in diva limbo with Diana Ross and Liza Minnelli: unable to get a film deal and forced to do concerts to meet the mortgage.

When Connie was depressed she bypassed psychotherapy and went directly to one of her three primal pleasures: eating, fucking or shopping. Eating was out if she wanted to fit into her Oscar gown and the thought of sex, after her fateful escapade with the pool boy, was repellent to her. That left shopping, and this afternoon she was determined to do some real damage at the posh new Barneys on Wilshire Boulevard. She always wore a blond wig and sunglasses on these expeditions so she wouldn't be bothered by autograph hounds.

Tossing her keys to the valet parker, she walked through the entrance to Barneys and headed to the elevator to the second-floor woman's department. Two young Beverly Hills matrons, serene, blond and married to entertainment attorneys, squeezed in with her just as the doors closed. Nothing better to do with their lives than shop, snorted Connie. Then again, who was she to criticize?

The slow-moving elevator lurched upward and then stopped.

"Oh my," said blond number one, "something's wrong."

"Just be calm," said her companion. "If anything happens we can always sue."

Connie remained silent behind her sunglasses, not wanting to be recognized. Then a voice issued forth from the speaker box in the elevator's control panel. "Please don't be alarmed. Our elevator is activated by a timer that has inadvertently shut down. We'll have you on the second floor in less than two minutes."

"There goes your court case," giggled blond number one.

Blond number two swept her hair behind her ears and stifled a yawn. "Did you read about Connie Travatano the other day?"

"You mean about her backing out of singing in front of the President?"

"Yeah. Some nerve, huh?"

"But it said she was sick."

"Artie told me the rumor is she's scared. She hasn't sung in public in so long she's afraid she's lost it."

Connie flushed with embarrassment and looked down at the floor.

"I never liked her that much anyway," said blond number one.

"She'll never touch Streisand in my book," agreed blond number two.

"Or Diana Ross or Liza Minnelli. Those are real singers."

Connie looked up at the two women, sheer hatred coursing through every particle of her being.

"Another thing," said blond number two, "I hated her in that movie. What was it? *Lasagna and Rubies?*"

"*Tomatoes and Diamonds.*"

"I was close."

"I agree with you about the movie. Who could believe that Andy Garcia would make love to an old woman like that?"

May your hearts be torn out by vultures while wild jackals devour your innards, thought Connie.

"I was shocked when she was nominated for the Oscar," continued blond number one. "If that's what passes for acting out here, Mickey Rourke may have a chance after all."

"You know this town," said blond number two dismissively, "hang around long enough and they start taking you seriously. It worked for Pia Zadora."

The elevator shifted and began to rise. Just before its doors opened, blond number one turned back to blond number two.

"I'll tell you this much," she said, "Connie Travatano has about as much chance of winning the Oscar this year as Lana Turner does."

"But Lana Turner's dead."

"Exactly."

The blonds sailed out of the elevator, leaving Connie shaking with rage and mortification. She had become a laughingstock by canceling on the President. People were probably talking about her right now in coffee shops and hair salons. Dishing her career and mocking her dreams of Oscar glory. She felt helpless and out of control.

Moving in a daze, she walked over to the leather goods counter. There was no salesperson to be found in the area, so she began to examine the merchandise by herself. Sitting on top of the counter was a row of Chanel purses. Connie usually resisted buying high-ticket items, preferring to keep her wardrobe after every film. But these purses were so beautiful, and she needed so badly to revive her spirits. Cautiously she turned over the price tag.

Three hundred dollars! What an outrage. She had paid less than a hundred five years ago in New York for a Chanel purse that she still used. How could Barneys get away with such highway robbery? This store was as bad as its customers: arrogant, high-handed and uncaring.

Well she'd show them, the bastards. Picking up the first purse in the row, she noticed that the theft protection tag was loose. Pulling it out with one quick tug Connie took the purse and thrust it into the large handbag she was carrying.

It was when she looked up that she saw the tall, handsome blond man staring at her. Connie froze for a second, but she knew what to do. She had shoplifted before and had always managed to get away with it, even if someone saw her.

Reaching up to her head she pulled off the cheap blond wig and the sunglasses. Then she shot the man her most dazzling smile.

"How are you?" she asked, cool as iced tea on an August day.

"Connie Travatano?" he stammered.

"Thanks for being such a fan," she said, squeezing his arm as she swept past him and back into the elevator. The man was staring at her with a big grin on his face as the door closed.

It worked every time, she thought triumphantly. People were too starstruck by her to do anything in such a situation. And if that man had known what she'd gone through, how she'd had to listen to those two blond bitches dissect her entire career, he'd have probably helped her pocket the Chanel purse. Control freak Connie always felt a wonderful surge of power whenever she shoplifted to relieve her anxieties.

She was waiting for the valet parker to bring her the car when she felt a hand on her elbow.

"Miss Travatano?" It was the handsome blond man.

"Would you like an autograph?" she asked casually. Surely he wasn't going to cause her any trouble.

"That's not why I'm here."

"They're worth money, you know. I don't give them to everybody."

"I'm afraid you've taken something that doesn't belong to you," said the man.

"Now look," retorted Connie, her eyes narrowing to two steely Sicilian slits, "this is nothing more than your word against mine. And my word goes pretty far in this town."

"Not with me it doesn't," he countered.

"And just who are you?" challenged Connie.

"Eric Collins," he responded evenly, reaching into his jacket and pulling out a badge. "I'm a sergeant with the Beverly Hills Police force. Right now I'm off-duty. I was shopping for a birthday present for my sister when I happened to see you steal that purse."

Connie saw her Oscar receding into a dark, impenetrable twilight.

"Good evening, this is Ann Martin with Channel Two Action News. Harvey Levin is standing by in Beverly Hills with late-breaking news on a scandal involving one of Hollywood's most famous stars. Harvey, can you hear me?"

"Yes I can, Ann. I'm standing here in front of Barneys department store where early this afternoon superstar singer and Oscar nominee Connie Travatano was arrested on a charge of shoplifting."

"Can you tell us where Connie is now, Harvey?"

"Ann, it's my understanding that, after fingerprints and a mug shot at the Beverly Hills Police Station, Connie Travatano is now in seclusion in her Bel Air mansion."

"Any reports on what she's accused of stealing, Harvey?"

"No information on that yet, but I do have an exclusive comment from Ernesto Felipe, a janitor at the store who's here with me now. Mr. Felipe?"

"Yes."

"Mr. Felipe, can you tell us what Connie Travatano is accused of stealing from the store?"

"Is that Ann Martin at the other end?"

"Yes it is, Mr. Felipe, now if you could . . ."

"Miss Martin, I would love to fuck you."

"Thanks, Harvey, we'll be getting right back to you in a second. But first, killer bees on a rampage. A Glendale woman finds a nest of killers in her Wonderbra. We're live from Glendale with Michelle Williams. Hello, Michelle? . . ."

18

I *am* Scarlett O'Hara, repeated Phillip Castleman to himself as he drove his 1983 Toyota Tercel down Santa Monica Boulevard to the offices of CPR. I am Scarlett O'Hara and nobody's ever going to make me eat radishes again.

An émigré from Clinton, South Carolina, Phillip had seen *Gone with the Wind* forty-seven times, most recently last night on the VCR he still owed two payments on. The film never failed to move him to tears, but last night it held a special meaning for him. Munching on a box of Polly's Pralines, the sticky, sweet Southern candy his mother sent him monthly, he had seen a vision of his future in Scarlett's struggle to hold on to Tara and Rhett Butler.

Phillip had moved to Los Angeles four years ago and spent the past two working as the personal assistant to Melissa Crawley of CPR. He fielded over two hundred calls daily, ran Melissa's personal errands and put up with her demanding, bitchy behavior. And all the while he told himself it would pay off, that someday Melissa would reward him with a big, fat job handling some of her beautiful, skinny clients. He'd believed it too, until he learned the other day of the deal that Claudio had cut for himself. Well if that Brazilian bombshell could get something out of the spooky Melissa Crawley, so could he.

Scarlett had saved Tara yet again last night; this morning he would save his career.

Phillip parked his Tercel in its assigned space in the underground parking garage, locked it carefully and headed into the offices of CPR feeling as if he were wearing a ball gown made out of old curtains.

"**N**ow listen, Melissa," said Fatima Bulox over the phone, "I'm not going to have you tell me how we cover a story here at *Personality Magazine*. You can save those strong-arm tactics for those little old Ukrainian ladies who vote for the Golden Globes."

"But Fatima," protested Melissa Crawley at the other end, "I'm just trying to tell you how we see the story running. An exclusive interview with Lori Seefer should stand alone; most magazines would kill for it."

"Most magazines don't have our circulation," snapped Fatima, who had grown weary of Melissa's manipulative ways over the years. "New York has decided that we're doing a roundup piece on all five nominees for this year's Best Actress Oscar. If Lori wants to be a part of that, fine. If she wants to remain discreetly silent, that's fine too. Lord knows, she's been doing that for years now."

The two women fell into silence, a tacit acknowledgment on both their parts that they were now discussing Lori's raging lesbianism. The tiny Islamic witch, thought Melissa bitterly, she's got me cornered.

"Lori has an exciting new angle to offer you," said Melissa, hoping her soon-to-be-public "romance" with Claudio could sway Fatima.

"We got one of those from Connie Travatano at Barneys yesterday," countered Fatima. "It'll all be part of the piece, just like your client's new angle."

"Very well," said Melissa, "have Ted Gavin come to her house on Thursday at two." She slammed down the phone, cursing Fatima, Tina Brown, Anna Wintour and every other female editor she could think of.

Seeing that his boss was off the phone, Phillip rose quickly from his desk and strode into her office. "Melissa," he said, "could I talk with you for a moment?"

"What is it?" she asked irritably.

Phillip approached Melissa's desk, his resolve growing with each step. "I understand that Claudio will be going out with Lori Seefer tonight to the premiere of the new Meryl Streep film. And that he's going to be present during her *Personality Magazine* interview."

"That's right. What's it to you?"

"Well I also heard that he's gotten a one-hundred-dollar-a-week raise."

"Overtime is overtime."

"But Claudio has only been here a month. I've been working for you for two years now. Don't you think I should have the opportunity to take Lori out and make that extra money?"

Melissa regarded him coldly. "Phillip, Claudio is going out with Lori for one reason and one reason only: to create the illusion that they are having a romance. He is, in short, a beard. Now to be a beard one must exude a manly, virile, heterosexual quality. Claudio fulfills this one requirement admirably. You, on the other hand, are noticeably lacking in the heterosexual allure department. Now, should we, say, get Mel Gibson as a client and he tells us that he wants the public to perceive him as a homosexual, you would be the perfect man to show up on his arm at a movie premiere. Until then, however, I'm afraid your services as a beard are not required by this office."

Melissa picked up her jade-handled letter opener and began tearing open her mail. Phillip retreated at once, visions of the burning of Atlanta swarming through his brain.

Lori paced nervously in the kitchen, dressed in a black Armani silk gown and a fake fur. It was 6:45 and Claudio was due to pick her up any moment now. She had cleared the kitchen floor of all the broken plates and glasses Maria had decorated it with, but she couldn't shake free from the memory of her departed Mexican lover.

She felt as if she was betraying Maria by going out with a man. A man! She hadn't done that since her high school junior prom and then she'd thrown up for two hours straight after her date dropped her off. Would Claudio have the same effect? Probably not; she'd drunk half a bottle of Kaopectate before slipping into her Armani.

There was a knock at the door. Opening it, she was confronted by the vision of a tall, swarthy man in a black tuxedo holding a single rose.

"This is for you," Claudio said tenderly, handing the flower to Lori. She blushed in response as he offered her his arm. "Now come with me to the movies."

In the limousine Claudio regaled her with tales of his childhood in a small fishing village near São Paolo. His father had been a fisherman, the only profession for males in his family until Claudio, on vacation in Brazil, had been discovered by a scout who urged him to move to Los Angeles to pursue modeling. His mother was a schoolteacher who adored all five of her sons. "From her I learned how to love and protect a woman," he said huskily.

Arriving at the theater he took a firm grasp on her hand as they got out of the car. "Don't worry," he said, smiling. As they faced the mob of photographers clustered in front of the theater, Claudio smoothly put his arm around her waist and drew her close to him. Lori felt like a little girl who had been swept up in the arms of her protective daddy.

The movie, *Foreign Accents*, was the usual upscale Meryl Streep vehicle. She played a teacher of English as a second language who goes schizophrenic and begins assuming the personalities of her students. The role allowed the blond Oscar winner to speak in Latvian, Serbo-Croatian, Hebrew, Armenian and Farsi. Everyone agreed no one could have played it better than Meryl.

After the film the crowd adjourned to the Armand Hammer Museum. While Meryl Streep danced the hora, the Irish jig, the samba and the hokey-pokey, Claudio brought a plate of chocolate-covered strawberries over to Lori.

"That wasn't so bad, was it?" he said, picking up one of the berries.

"I guess I just get nervous in public," blushed Lori.

"Everyone's nervous on a first date," replied Claudio.

"Yeah," laughed Lori, "but this was really a first date for me." Claudio joined her in the laughter, holding out a strawberry. Lori leaned forward and bit into it.

Across the room, Ted Gavin grabbed Fatima Bulox by the arm. "Unhand me," she hissed, "this isn't Islam."

"Look over there," whispered Ted, "Lori Seefer is being fed strawberries by a big hunk who looks like he's on leave from Chippendale's."

Fatima grabbed her pince-nez and peered through it. "He's probably just some overzealous fan."

"I don't know," said Ted. "She's pretty cozy with him for a fan. Look at what they're up to now."

Claudio had slipped his arm around Lori's waist as she fed him a strawberry in return.

"What do you think, Fatima? Has Lori Seefer gone over to men?"

"Don't be ridiculous."

"Stranger things have happened," said Ted.

"Only in the U.S. Congress and my bedroom," snapped Fatima, who nonetheless could not stop staring at the handsome couple across the room.

"This is Michael Musto for *The Gossip Show* on E!, and do I have dish for you. Tongues are wagging over, and a lot of wags like me wish we were tonguing over, the hunky Brazilian stud Lori Seefer was seen with at the recent premiere of Meryl Streep's new film *Foreign Accents* in Hollywood. Lori, who, in the words of Lerner and Loewe's *My Fair Lady*, has always seemed like a 'confirmed old bachelor and likely to remain so,' was this close with her handsome date, feeding him chocolate strawberries and later joining him and Meryl Streep in a French Apache dance. Lori, an Oscar nominee for *Losing Sofia*, really seems to be losing it over the new man—and in her case this is all very new—in her life. On another front, I'm sorry to announce I've learned that another Oscar nominee, Fiona Covington, and her husband, Colin Tromans, have gone the way of Liz and Dick and Ryan and Farrah. The tony British couple discreetly announced their separation yesterday through their lawyer in Santa Monica. No word yet on who gets possession of all their quiet good taste."

19

Karen gazed out the glass doors in the rear wall of her living room at a beautiful sight: Johnny Dante, fresh from a dip in her pool, sunning himself on a chaise longue. His taut, lean body brought to mind such words as sinewy and steely, and his tight bikini briefs barely reined in a curiously copious cock. It lay coiled between his legs, like the asp in a straw basket that delivered the fatal love bite to Queen Cleopatra so many centuries ago in Egypt. Karen wondered idly if she should open Johnny's basket and face down the venomous rattler that lay within.

But she'd had enough sex for today. Colin had phoned her at eight o'clock this morning, pleading for release. Fearing for her role as Lady Macbeth, Karen quickly went over and met him in the lobby of CAA where he was scheduled to meet with a potential set designer for the film. With no time to go anywhere, she gave him a quicky hand job in the elevator of the agency and then headed home. And though it had been brief, Karen knew that Colin had loved every second of her shocking sexual expertise. She figured it was the best Hollywood hand job since Guber and Peters jerked off Sony in the early nineties.

She was just about to join Johnny by the pool when the phone rang. "Hello," she said, picking up the cordless phone while pulling a cigarette out of her Chanel purse.

"Karen, it's Susan."

As in Sakowitz, her publicist. Ugh. "What is it, Susan?"

"I just wanted to let you know that I confirmed your RSVP to the Davises' party tomorrow night." Marvin Davis was the richest man in Los Angeles, twice the size, if not quite twice the wealth, of David Geffen. Having sold Twentieth Century Fox some years ago, he and his wife Barbara now devoted themselves to a series of annual charity galas. The party this week was to benefit a national shelter movement for the homeless.

"That's very nice, Susan," said Karen, softening a bit. "I've always wanted to see their house."

"And it's a chance to help the homeless."

"That too."

"They don't provide limousines, so you'll have to get there on your own. I sent a map over by messenger this morning."

"I didn't get anything."

"Were you home?"

"Actually, I was at CAA for a while this morning."

"But you're with ICM."

"Yes, but there was a little something hanging at CAA so I went over there and handled it."

"I see," said Susan, who was now thoroughly confused.

"Maybe you better send that map over again."

"Sure. Have a nice day."

A nice day? Karen was planning on having a great day. She'd taken care of Colin and now she could lie by the pool with her blue-collar stud. And later, if she felt horny . . . God, it was great to be a movie star.

"Hey, lover," teased Karen as she tossed an ice cube at Johnny, hitting his left nipple.

"Doll, how are ya," he replied, squinting into the sun.

"Fine. And you? Improving your mind?" she asked, glancing down at the Superman comic book that lay at his feet.

"Just waitin' for you," he replied, pulling her toward him and crushing her lips with his. His tongue slid into her mouth like a warm knife through a pound of soft butter. Karen felt his cock throbbing against the side of her leg. It seemed so big today. Had he been taking hormone shots?

She pulled herself away and sat on the chaise opposite him. "We've got the whole day to play," she said.

"So what do you wanna do?"

"Oh, I don't know. Just maybe laze around, order in some lunch, listen to music." Karen was careful to try and keep Johnny hidden on the grounds of her house.

"Sounds cool. Only I was thinking maybe we could go out."

"Where would you like to go?" asked Karen cautiously.

"Oh, I dunno. I was thinking maybe to this place." Johnny reached into the crotch of his swimsuit and pulled out a large folded piece of paper. He smoothed it out and held it in front of Karen's face. It was the map to the Davis house; no wonder his cock had looked so big.

"Where did you get that?" stammered Karen.

"A messenger brought it over while you were gone. I just thought I'd keep it close to my heart," chuckled Johnny, shoving the paper back into his crotch.

"Give me that," she snapped. "That has to do with my career."

"Oh, and here I thought you were all bent out of shape about the homeless," drawled Johnny. "After all, you took me right in."

"Johnny, I can't discuss this with you now."

"What's the matter, doll? How come you haven't invited me to this big fancy shindig? Ashamed to be seen in public with me?"

"That has nothing to do with this."

"Fast food and slow fucks, that's your story."

"I've already committed to go with someone else. It's a business thing. I'm supposed to make a movie with him."

"Who is he?" demanded Johnny.

"Colin Tromans."

"Colin Tromans?" roared Johnny incredulously. "He's a big fag."

"No he's not," shot back Karen. "He's British."

"Same thing."

"Don't be absurd."

"So you're gonna go to this hot party with some limp-dicked Englishman while I sit here and wait for you?"

"Something like that," replied Karen evenly.

"Nothing like that for me," said Johnny, getting up from the chaise. "If I'm good enough to fuck you for four hours straight then you ought to trust me not to pick my nose in public."

"Johnny, please," said Karen. "Sit down. Let's talk."

"Let's not and say we did," retorted Johnny, summoning up a fourth-grade witticism from somewhere deep inside him. "Ask Prince Charles if he'll fuck you when he comes over tomorrow night."

Johnny stalked through the house, grabbed his clothes and jumped into the convertible he had parked in Karen's driveway. He was halfway down the block before she got to the front door.

Damn, thought Karen, slamming the door and leaning against it as Joan Crawford had done in so many movies before her. Why did men seem to only come in two sizes: smart or well-hung? Her meditation on this eternal truth was abruptly cut off by the ringing of her phone.

"Yes," snapped Karen, picking up the phone.

"Is this Karen Kroll?" inquired a genteel voice.

"Yes it is. Now what can I do for you?"

"Well, dear, you could recite the Gettysburg Address for me."

"Who is this?"

"You did it so well for me in your Sophomore Monologues class," said the caller, reverting to her normal voice.

"Ida Gunkndiferson," said Karen weakly. "How are you?"

"Oh I'm fine, dear," replied the old lady. "I've been trying to reach you for weeks."

"I've been very busy."

"I just called to congratulate you on your Oscar nomination. And to tell you what's been happening back here on the home front."

"I'm afraid this isn't the right moment," protested Karen.

"I don't know if you've forgotten it, but your fifteenth class reunion is this spring and I was wondering . . ."

"You know, Ida," said Karen quickly, "I'd love to stay on the line and chat with you, but I'm expecting some people for lunch."

"Oh my, how exciting. Who all is coming?"

Was there no way to get rid of this old bat? "Like I said," continued Karen, "I'd really like to talk with you but . . . oh my gosh, here come Tom Cruise and Nicole Kidman. They just arrived."

"Mercy, Tom Cruise with Nicole Kidman."

"Yes, and I've got to feed them lunch."

"Then I guess the rumor about him isn't true."

"What rumor?"

"That he doesn't like to eat lunch."

"Well he's here now and he's hungry as a bear," replied Karen wearily.

"What are you serving? Pot luck?" pressed Mrs. Gunkndiferson.

"I hate to cut you off, but Tom Hanks just walked in the

door with the biggest submarine sandwich you ever saw in your life. Oh, and here comes Carrie Fisher with a jar of pickles."

"You know I just loved her mother in that *Unsinkable Molly Brown*. She was robbed of the Oscar. You tell little Carrie I said that."

Karen kept going through her Rolodex for Ida, but she wound up missing her own lunch that day.

20

Fifth Avenue rushed by Amber in one big blur, tinted by the window of the limousine she was riding in and sweetened by the potent drug cocktail she was floating on. The Pierre Hotel looked as if it had been dragged across the Atlantic intact from Stonehenge while the Plaza resembled nothing less than the world's largest Pez dispenser. Amber popped another stick of Juicy Fruit into her mouth and offered Billy Walsh one. They had been staying at the Mark on Madison Avenue and 75th for the past three nights, courtesy of MTV, on whose award show they were scheduled to appear tonight.

To do that, however, they first had to get to Radio City Music Hall. Amber had wanted to walk, but when she decided to French-kiss all the store windows on Madison Avenue, Billy saw the logic of a limo. An ambulatory Amber wouldn't have reached the Music Hall before dawn.

They had started smoking grass in the early afternoon, then switched to coke to help them get dressed. Right before they left they did some Ecstasy, washed down by an aperitif of Romilar Extra Strength Cough Syrup. For now, happily buzzed, Amber was content to settle on Juicy Fruit as her drug of choice.

"This city is too fucking clean," groused Billy, staring out the window. The sentiment, which Mayor Rudolph Giuliani might have paid his constituents to echo, came naturally to Billy. A rocker who'd been raised on Kurt Cobain and Eddie Vedder, he could never be confronted by too much filth. Last night after the run-through for the show, he and Amber had overturned all the garbage cans on a five-block stretch of Madison Avenue and then took turns peeing in the gutter. Ah youth!

"We'll have a food fight at the party after the show," promised Amber.

"You're sweet," gurgled Billy, burping softly in her ear.

The limousine lurched to a halt at the stage door of Radio City and they poured out of it. Police barricades held back an army of hungry fans who had come to cheer the rock stars who were in the show.

"Billy, please spit on me!" begged a teenage girl sporting a pierced eyebrow and a tattoo that read, "Humanity Sucks." As he went over to her, Amber caught sight of a young male fan feverishly waving a newspaper at her.

"Amber, please sign this," he pleaded.

Why not, she thought. After all, they were the ones who bought the tickets. Amber glanced at the newspaper as she autographed it. There, on the cover of the *National Enquirer*, was a picture of her mother, Shana, wearing a grease-stained bathrobe and a filthy yellow bandanna. The headline next to it read, HEARTBROKEN, PENNILESS MOM THROWN OUT ON STREET BY DRUG-ADDICTED OSCAR NOMINEE AMBER LYONS.

Her blood froze and her vision blurred simultaneously. That bitch! She'd sold her story to the tabloids! There she was on the cover of the *National Enquirer* making Amber look like a heartless druggy viper. Great PR for the Oscar. God, how she hated her.

"Amber, it's so cool that you threw your mother out," said the young boy.

Right, like you're an Academy voter, thought Amber. What

played in Bensonhurst didn't necessarily play in Beverly Hills. She felt Billy's hand grab her and drag her through the stage door.

"Anything wrong, babe?" he asked. "You look pale."

"It's just something I ate."

"But we haven't eaten all day. We've been doing drugs."

"It's something I ate as a child. I'm reliving it."

"Awesome," murmured Billy.

A production assistant brandishing a clipboard rushed up to them. "Thank God you got here," he exclaimed. "You're on in five minutes."

"I have to go to the ladies' room," said Amber, breaking away.

"Don't you want to meet Dick Clark?" asked the p.a. "You're giving him the award."

"I'll meet him onstage," said Amber. She rushed down the hall and into the backstage ladies' room. A row of porcelain sinks and a full-length wall mirror were in front of her. Examining her face in the mirror (I still look good, she thought, tossing her red hair over her shoulders), Amber reached into the Chanel bag she had bought yesterday at Bendel's and fished out her beloved silver foil packet.

She was interrupted by the sound of retching coming from the last stall. Moving down to it, Amber saw Courtney Love bent over the toilet bowl vomiting into it.

"Drugs?" inquired Amber coolly.

"Nerves," replied Love. "I'm closing the show tonight."

"Good luck," replied Amber. At least she didn't have to worry about that. Returning to the mirror, she unfolded the packet and scooped all the heroin in it onto her fingernail. She brought the nail to her nose and inhaled deeply. The back of her head felt like it had been whacked by a soft, wet pillow. Fantastic, she thought as she threw away the packet, snapped her purse shut and tottered to the doorway.

Billy was waiting for her. "Amber, come on. We're gonna miss our cue." He grabbed her by the arm and hustled her through the crowd to the side of the stage. A pleasant-looking older man was waiting there.

"This is Dick Clark," said Billy.

"Click Dark," woozed Amber, "nice to meet ya."

She tried to shake his hand as she heard Rosie O'Donnell, the show's host, say "And now welcome Billy Walsh, lead singer of Toxic Naomi, and Amber Lyons, Oscar-nominated star of *As if . . . Chillin'*."

Suddenly she felt bright lights hitting her in the face as Billy led her out onto the stage of Radio City. There was a burst of applause followed by silence. Billy grasped the lucite podium and stared out at the TelePrompTer.

"We're here tonight to honor a man who has been instrumental in the history of rock and roll," he said. Then he turned to Amber.

She looked back at him. So, who was this man, she wondered?

There was a pause. Billy smiled nervously and said, "Amber, who is this man?"

That was just what she wanted to know. Another pause. She could hear Rosie O'Donnell muttering softly from the other side of the stage.

"Should I tell you?" Billy asked.

"Nooo," drawled Amber. "Lemme guess." Now she could hear muttering from the first few rows of the audience.

"Here's a hint," said Billy, as he began to sweat. "This man hosted the most popular rock and roll show in the history of television."

Amber furrowed her brow, but her forehead was warm and throbbing, as if someone were beating a heated drum inside it.

She couldn't move yet she felt as if she was swaying wildly on the top of a windswept hill.

"Well, I'm gonna tell you," erupted Billy. "His name is . . ."

"No," whined Amber. "Lemme guess." Another pause, the longest one yet. Then it came to her.

"I know," she said. "It's Click Dark."

Pockets of nervous laughter sprang up in the audience which then fell back into an immediate silence. Just as suddenly, the theme song from *American Bandstand* issued from the orchestra pit as Dick Clark strode out onto the stage. He joined Billy at the podium, putting his arm around Amber.

"I love the way you kids put on an old man like me," he said, flashing the warm, sincere smile that had convinced four decades of parents that their children would not be lost to sex, drugs and rock and roll. "You have a wonderful sense of humor, young lady," he continued. "Hang on to that."

Amber desperately wanted to hang on to something, but the thought of moving her arm was too exhausting to contemplate. Instead she stood still as Dick Clark said, "You know, when we started *Bandstand* in Philadelphia in the fifties . . ." His voice droned on, but Amber couldn't make out the words he was saying. She was too busy trying to understand what was going on inside her body. The pounding in her head had subsided, only to be replaced by a whirling sensation in the pit of her stomach that felt like the last spin cycle of a rickety old clothes dryer. Her mouth was dry and her hands felt clammy.

And it was into those hands that Billy placed the Lifetime Achievement Award that Amber was to hand to Dick Clark. Rather than anchoring her, the large metal object tilted her forward; she was swaying toward Dick Clark like a listing tree in a strong breeze.

"Whoa there, young lady," television's most famous disk jockey said, as he extended his hands to accept the award.

It was at that moment that Amber felt the bile rising from the depths of her stomach. She opened her mouth to warn Dick Clark, but a stream of vomit spewed out instead, hitting him right in the face and dribbling down to cover the award he had just accepted.

The audience erupted into pandemonium as Rosie O'Donnell screamed "Cut to commercial!" Dick Clark was speechless, for possibly the first time in his life, while Amber mustered up the presence of mind to cover her mouth with both hands.

Feeling like the little Dutch girl who tried to save her city by sticking her finger in the dike, Amber caught sight of the mobile cameraman circling the podium. As if on cue she dropped her hands, hiccuped and sprayed him with vomit. It hit the lens of his camera, creating a visual that *Time* magazine would later name one of the ten most interesting Television Events of the year.

Her work done, Amber promptly collapsed on the stage of Radio City Music Hall.

"AS IF ... HURLIN'. This is Kurt Loder with MTV News, and that's what most people were saying at our annual awards show last night where actress Amber Lyons may have hurled away her chances at the Oscar by hurling chunks at beloved rock icon Dick Clark. Lyons was taken to St. Luke's Hospital where she is being held for observation. In other news, Courtney Love managed to upstage Lyons's vomit fest with a stunning rendition of 'God Bless America' that closed the show. Most observers agreed that Love's version of the classic song even overshadowed Natalie Cole's at last week's Presidential gala for the Vietnam Vets where Cole was a last-minute replacement for shoplifting superstar Connie Travatano."

21

The huge white tent the Davises had erected in their yard for the homeless benefit rose fifty feet in the air at its apex. Heaters boomed warm air into it so that the scantily clad movie stars, executives and lawyers who came to the party could mingle in relative comfort. But the heat caused the top panels of the tent to balloon upward, and the outside of the dome had a huge pink dot painted in the center of it. From the air, it looked as if a giant breast had landed in the backyard of Marvin and Barbara Davis.

Sergio Falucci, however, was beyond worrying what the tent looked like from the many traffic helicopters that buzzed over it on their way to the 405 freeway. As director of operations for Ravenous Meals, Beverly Hills' most prestigious catering firm, he had a staff of two hundred cooks, waiters, ushers and valet parkers to command. It was now 6:45, fifteen minutes before the arrival of the first guests, and Sergio was hovering somewhere between apoplexy and dementia.

"Lena," he barked into the headset that gave him the appearance of having not one, but two, moustaches, "Mrs. Davis wants to know where the soft-shell crabs are."

"You can tell her they're off the coast of Maryland, hibernating," responded Lena Platz, the fish chef, over her headset. "That's what they do in the winter."

"But she wants to see them," demanded Sergio. "Here. Tonight."

"I can bring her a picture of one, if that would help," replied Lena. "But I can't serve her one until April. The shells of those little babies are as hard as Charlie Sheen's cock right now."

Sergio muttered in disgust and walked through the tent into the Davis mansion. Arrangements of fresh flowers lined the hallways and eucalyptus logs blazed in the baronial master fireplace in the living room. The three hundred guests were to be served cocktails and hors d'oeuvres on the first floor of the house and then proceed into the tent for dinner and entertainment. Trays of caviar, fresh salmon and cold asparagus wrapped in prosciutto were waiting to be passed by the catering staff. Bottles of chardonnay, cabernet sauvignon and Cristal champagne stood ready on the bar tables that had been imported for the evening. And a three-man Dixieland jazz band was perched on the front steps of the mansion, waiting to serenade the guests as they walked through the portals.

It was going to be a great party, thought Sergio, if only Mrs. Davis could forget about the fucking soft-shell crabs.

Connie shifted uneasily in the backseat of the limousine and held on to Morty's hand for comfort. After her calamitous shopping expedition at Barneys she had considered canceling, but not to show up at the Davis party, after stiffing the President of the United States, would have had her running sixth in the five-woman race for the Best Actress Oscar. Better to go and hold her head up high, she told herself. Maybe she'd get points for courage. It had worked for Hugh Grant; maybe it would work for her. So she had decided to attend, fortifying herself in the bath with two extra-dry vodka martinis.

The silence in the car was broken by Morty cutting a fart. "Egg salad for lunch," he grimaced. That was Morty for you, thought Connie: eats like a delicatessen, sounds like a munitions factory. Still, she was grateful to have him by her side for her first public appearance since the arrest. And the Davises, out of consideration for their famous guests, had banned all media from their property, other than a photographer and a society writer from the *Los Angeles Times*. There'd be no pictures of a shamefaced Connie getting out of the limo on *Hard Copy* tomorrow night.

While Morty stared out the window, Connie reached into her purse, the Chanel she'd bought years ago, and fumbled for her flask. As she did, her hand brushed over the envelope she'd received in this afternoon's mail and hastily stuffed into the purse. Opening it, she read the short, typed note inside:

> Dear Bitch,
> Why don't you stop stealing handbags and start singing songs again? Or have you ruined your voice after too many blow jobs?

Jesus Christ! Some angry, unhinged fan. But how had he gotten her address? She paid over a thousand a year to a security firm to keep things like that and her phone number private and unlisted. This was just what she needed to get up for this goddamned homeless party. Bringing the flask to her lips, Connie took a long swig of vodka as the limousine swept through the gates of the Davis mansion and up the driveway.

Walking into the foyer, past the Dixieland trio, Connie spotted Kurt Russell and Goldie Hawn holding hands.

"Kurt, Goldie," boomed Morty.

Kurt Russell grabbed his hand. "Morty, Connie, good to see you," he said.

"Congratulations, Connie," beamed Goldie. "Hope you win."

"Thanks," gulped Connie. "I just hope I don't lose to Amber Lyons."

"Hey," joshed Kurt, "she's young enough to be the daughter of any of us."

"If she were my daughter," giggled Goldie, "I'd throw her in jail." There was a slight pause and Kurt Russell shifted his feet. Why not ask me how the prison food was, thought Connie bitterly.

"So," smiled Kurt, "got your dress picked out?"

"I haven't got a clue," muttered Connie, wishing she could reach into her purse and suck on the vodka for reassurance.

"Why not run into a store and just grab something off the rack?" suggested Goldie.

I already did that at Barneys, thought Connie. She couldn't help noticing that the eternally youthful blond star was clutching her purse protectively. Don't worry, Goldie, she thought, I won't steal it.

"What's everybody drinking?" asked Morty, punctuating his inquiry with yet another fart. Morty and his damn farts, seethed Connie. If they installed a Bic lighter at the seat of his pants he'd have the eternal flame lapping at his asshole.

"Nothing for me," said Goldie.

"Me neither," added Kurt.

"Stoli on the rocks," said Connie, "make it a double." She turned to Kurt and Goldie, shrugging, and said, "I'm nervous."

"Don't be," smiled Kurt, "you look great." Morty waddled off, leaving the three of them.

"Well," said Kurt, "we should probably head into the living room and say hello to the Davises."

Wouldn't want to hang around me, thought Connie. You might wind up in a police lineup.

"We've already been here an hour and we haven't met our hosts," explained Goldie.

"So it's a good party?" asked Connie.

"It's a lot of fun," said Kurt.

"Everybody's here," said Goldie. "And there's tons of food, great music and just a nice relaxed feeling. It's like Burt Reynolds's New Year's Eve party back in eighty-seven. Remember that?"

"How could I forget it," snapped Connie. "The ball dropped and then his ass fell."

Kurt and Goldie quickly retreated into the living room, shocked at Connie's viciousness.

"Hand me some ice cubes," said Karen, pointing to the silver bucket on the far side of the limousine's backseat bar.

"Are you feverish?" asked Colin.

"Not a bit," she replied, slipping her thumbs under the straps of her gold lamé Vera Wang cocktail dress and pulling the front of it down to expose her breasts.

"What's come over you?" sputtered Colin as he held the bucket in front of her.

"Just an old trick I learned in my soft-core days," said Karen. She reached into the bucket, scooped up two handfuls of ice and pressed them to her breasts. Colin stared at her in utter amazement.

"Makes your nipples hard as thumbtacks," Karen said, throwing the ice back into the bucket and pulling the top of her dress back on. "Now, doesn't that look nice?"

Iced nipples, thought Colin incredulously. I'm going out in public for the first time since my separation from Fiona with a woman who has iced nipples!

"See how good they look," purred Karen, pushing her chest against the fabric of the dress. Colin had to concede that her nipples now stood out like a pair of twin signposts. But signposts to what, he wondered fearfully; this way lies madness?

"Why do you keep drinking that stuff?" asked Morty timidly.

"Because if I didn't, I might sober up and then I'd have to smell your farts," said Connie, polishing off her third double Stoli on the rocks and placing the now-empty cocktail glass on the head of a life-size Renaissance Italian cherub that Barbara Davis was especially fond of.

"God help me," muttered Morty as he picked up the glass and brought it back to the bar. Connie instantly regretted her remark, but it was too late now. And anyway, she'd been insulting people all evening. After Kurt Russell and Goldie Hawn fled from her she had run into Angie Dickinson. "Why don't you do something about that hair, Pepper?" Connie hissed and Angie headed right back to where she came from. When Diane Keaton, dressed in a 1920s English butler's uniform, approached her and asked her if she had seen Steve Martin, Connie laughed and said, "Don't get excited, honey. *The First Wives' Club* was a fluke!"

She was, of course, petrified that everyone was talking about her recent arrest. And that awful note she'd gotten in the mail had only further unhinged her. It was as if all the guests at the party were laughing at her and plotting against her. It would never occur to Connie Travatano that her colleagues might be genuinely concerned over her and her welfare.

"Let's go into the tent," said Morty, in the hope that the predinner entertainment would sober her up. He put his arm through hers and began to steer her through the living room. Halfway across the huge Oriental rug they ran into Colin and Karen.

"Well, it's a night for the nominees," said Morty.

"Hello, Connie," said Karen. "Do you know Colin Tromans?"

"No," said Connie cautiously. "Nice to meet you."

"I'm a big fan of your records," said Colin, trying to smooth things over. "I loved *Where Am I Now That I Need Me?* when I was a little boy."

"Really," replied Connie. "I recorded it when I was a middle-aged woman." Wasn't he supposed to be married to Fiona Covington? What was he doing with this overpriced tramp?

"That's terribly droll of you," said Karen with a mock laugh.

Connie hated Karen's condescending manner. "Where's your wife?" she said, turning to Colin.

"She's at home," snapped Karen, "listening to one of your old records. A seventy-eight, I believe."

"Karen," said Connie, inspecting her rival's dress, "your nipples look as big as olives. What did you do, have them stuffed?"

"Love your purse, Connie," said Karen. "Where did you steal it from?"

"Your face belongs on an arsenic bottle," hissed Connie.

"Let's see what's for dinner," said Morty. He grabbed Connie's elbow and pushed her forward, through the living room French doors and toward the huge tent that lay outside.

"That pizza-tossing bitch," huffed Karen as Colin moved her to the bar. "I hope the Davises aren't using their own silver. She'll swipe that too."

"I'm sure she didn't mean it," mumbled Colin. As tawdry as the scene had been, Colin was secretly thrilled by it. Two glamorous women snarling at each other and almost getting into a catfight. It was too Aaron Spelling for words. Colin felt the vague stirrings of an erection at the mere thought of it.

Those stirrings instantly subsided into a nuclear winter when Colin reached the bar: Fiona and Lionel were standing there sipping chardonnay. Colin's face went white, but, alas, not white enough to blend into the wall he was standing next to. Fiona spotted him at once.

"Colin," she stammered in confusion.

"Fiona," he managed, "I didn't know you'd be here."

"Clearly not," she replied. "This was Lionel's idea." And a bloody bad one it was, she thought.

"Is it possible for us to act terribly Noel Coward about all this?" asked Lionel hopefully.

"I don't know," said Fiona coolly. "I've never been a middle-aged British homosexual."

"Have you met Karen Kroll?" said Colin, his face flushing fuchsia.

"No," said Fiona, "but clearly you have."

"I've admired your work," said Karen.

"So much so that you seem to have taken some of it home with you," noted Fiona tartly.

"Can't we behave like three mature adults?" asked Colin.

"Why, when it's so much more fun to behave like badly brought up wee ones," replied Fiona, her lower lip quivering ever so slightly. Her sangfroid was beginning to slip into senti-mentality as she gazed at the man she loved on the arm of a woman who routinely displayed her breasts like a pair of marked-down melons at the Covent Garden marketplace.

"Fiona," pleaded Colin. "Don't embarrass us all. Please don't cry."

"Why should I cry," she gulped, as the first tears anointed her hitherto dry cheeks. "Just because my husband has shown up at a party with the tart of the century."

"Now wait a minute, sister," barked Karen.

"Let me handle this," interrupted Colin. "Fiona, Karen and I are merely a recent friendship."

"Are you planning to vote for her for Best Actress, Collie?" asked Fiona, dabbing at her eyes with a cocktail napkin.

"You're mussing yourself," said Colin, genuinely concerned.

"Maybe you should cast your new friend as Lady Macbeth," sobbed Fiona. "I daresay you'd save on costumes."

"He's already done that, honey," purred Karen.

"Oh Collie, you rotter!" wailed Fiona as she threw down her wineglass and fled to the ladies' room.

Karen's victory over Fiona was watched carefully from the other side of the room by Jeffrey Klein. A man capable, only with the greatest difficulty, of deciding whether he wanted chicken salad or tuna fish for lunch, Jeffrey was nonetheless the head of production for Marathon Studios. His unlikely ascension to this hallowed position had occurred when a Japanese business consortium bought the studio in the early nineties. Politically well-connected, Jeffrey managed to land the job to the astonishment, and envy, of most of Hollywood. An inveterate backslapper and ass-kisser ("Try doing both of those at the same time," cracked one of his many enemies), it was said of Jeffrey that he never met a movie he didn't like. He proved that to be true when he assumed the reins of power at Marathon, green-lighting such unlikely projects as *Dracula Sings!* (a horror movie musical with Neil Diamond and Debbie Allen that returned $3 million on a $47 million budget), *Wampum Woman* (Demi Moore as a squaw who becomes an inside trader on Wall Street; $5 million on a $52 million budget) and *Mickey Mouse Is Dead!* (an action film starring Tom Arnold as a divorced father trying to stop a terrorist plot to overtake Disneyland; judged unreleasable and sold to cable for $2 million, despite its $60 million budget).

Jeffrey's reverse Midas touch—he had also made *Idiot Snot*, the only unprofitable Jim Carrey movie—had somehow escaped the notice of his Japanese bosses, but not that of Hollywood's creative community. Most of the agents and stars were loath to make deals with him, convinced that it could end their careers. This only increased his frenzied deal-making, which is why he had been observing Karen, waiting for the right moment. Convinced that this was it, he handed his half-empty champagne glass to a homeless person and approached her.

"Karen Kroll," he beamed.

"Jeffrey Klein," she smiled, "I don't believe we've ever met."

"I just wanted to tell you how underrated *Casino* was. You were great in it."

"Thank you," said Karen, "that was Sharon Stone."

"Just testing you," laughed Jeffrey. This was known as "the Jeffrey Klein save," a maneuver he used thirty or forty times a day to cover his errors. Just yesterday he had congratulated Jeff Bridges on "eclipsing the career of your father, Beau."

"Guess why I want to talk with you," said Jeffrey.

"To tell me how much you loved my work in *Basic Instinct*," teased Karen.

"You're too much," grinned Jeffrey.

"By the way," said Karen, "this is Colin Tromans."

"I've always been a big Shakespeare fan," said Jeffrey, shaking Colin's hand. "Ever since *West Side Story*."

"That's nice," replied Colin, quite distracted. He kept wondering if he should have followed Fiona to the ladies' room and tried to comfort her.

"And I'm Lionel Latham," said Fiona's agent, who wouldn't have followed his dying mother to the ladies' room if there was a studio head in the vicinity.

"I've been thinking that Marathon Pictures and Karen Kroll should be talking," said Jeffrey.

"And what do you think we should be talking about?" asked Karen, fixing him with a killer stare from her cobalt baby blues.

"Oh, a multiple-picture deal, to follow up your success in *Sacrilege*," said Jeffrey, trying to sound casual.

"But I have so many projects on the table right now," parried Karen.

"At Marathon we believe in rewarding talent," Jeffrey reminded her.

"How big a reward are we talking about?" asked Karen, smiling provocatively.

"How does ten million a picture sound to you?"

Karen tried to mask her shock. Jeffrey Klein had just offered her twice her current asking price. But then, he was famous for overpaying talent. Just last year he had offered Barbra Streisand half a million dollars if she would come to the Marathon lot and sing "Happy Birthday" to him in his office on the day he turned fifty. To her eternal credit, Streisand turned down Jeffrey's offer, although she did send him a Barbra coffee mug from her national concert tour.

"I think Marathon Pictures and I can have quite a nice conversation for ten million dollars a picture," said Karen, a big grin spreading over her face.

Fiona's sobs echoed through the ladies' room, muffling the sounds of the Dixieland jazz trio that the Davises had thoughtfully arranged to be piped into all their bathrooms. "It may help the constipated," said Marvin Davis, who was a great believer in music therapy.

Wiping her eyes, Fiona stared into the vanity mirror and steadied herself for another assault of tears. Just as they arrived an attractive young waitress, one of the many who proffered hors d'oeuvres and champagne to the invited guests, entered the room.

"Forgive me," said Fiona, choking back a sob. "I can't seem to stop crying."

The young woman smiled at her sympathetically while Fiona tried in vain to stop the tide of tears with a bedraggled tissue.

"I've been crying for two weeks now," she whimpered, feeling oddly calmed by the woman's steady gaze. "Ever since my husband told me he was leaving me, it's been one long stream of tears. I've cried in front of him, in front of my agent, in front of Robert De Niro and now here at this splendid party. Sob, sob, sob; it's all I seem to do.

"And the worst part of it is," moaned Fiona, wiping her runny nose, "I hate this sort of blatant sentimentality. I've always been so British, so stiff upper lip, if you know what I mean."

The woman's smile grew warmer and broader; Fiona sensed that she did know what she meant.

"Here I am, nominated for an Academy Award, living in Hollywood, I should be the happiest girl in the world. And yet I'm engulfed in this torrent of tears, a veritable Niagara coursing down my cheeks, staining my bosom and leaving a large puddle at my feet. Oh," wailed Fiona, "will there never be an end to this?"

The smiling woman reached into her purse and extended a fresh tissue to Fiona. "No more tears," she said warmly. "Enough is enough."

"Enough is enough," murmured Fiona. "Where have I heard that before? Is it from . . ."

"Donna Summer and Barbra Streisand," said the woman. "It was a disco song in the seventies."

"Well, yes," said Fiona, "it didn't sound like Coleridge, come to think of it. I suppose there's wisdom to be found everywhere, even in the bygone doggerel of disco. I mean, 'young man there's a place you can stay' and all that."

"You talk too much and you cry too much," said the woman.

Fiona emitted a peal of laughter. "How right you are. My Lord, how long it's been since I've laughed."

"I know what it is to pine for your true love," said the woman, "but I never let it stop me from laughing."

"How terribly sensible of you," said Fiona, dabbing at her eyes and throwing the tissue away. "How I wish I knew you, and your marvelous philosophy, better."

"Would you like to have coffee sometime?" asked the woman.

"That would be lovely," smiled Fiona. "How do I get in touch with you?"

"My name is Maria Caldone," said the woman as she handed Fiona a card. "You can reach me at this number."

"**H**urry up," commanded Sergio Falucci. "Mrs. Davis is waiting."

"I don't like this one bit," said Lena Platz as she arranged several pieces of fish around an iced silver bowl of cocktail sauce.

"I employ you to chop the heads off fish," seethed Sergio. "Not to give me your opinion. Now hurry up!" Distraught over the lack of soft-shell crabs, Sergio had sent an assistant to a local fish market. He had returned with a half pound of imitation crabmeat which Lena was now feverishly arranging into an impromptu crab cocktail.

"This isn't even shellfish," complained Lena. "It's pollock that's been dyed to look like crab. This stuff bears the same relation to real crab that Newt Gingrich does to a human being. It looks phony and tastes like shit."

"Back to your mackerel!" ordered Sergio, whisking the silver bowl away from Lena's fish-encrusted fingers. It wasn't enough that he was having trouble meeting a simple request from the wealthiest woman in Beverly Hills; he also had to put up with the political diatribes of a head fish chef.

Bolting from the kitchen, Sergio made his way through the crowded living room. He wanted to place the crab cocktail at Mrs. Davis's place setting before she was seated. And he would have made it too, had he not been distracted by the fracas that erupted at the bar.

It was Karen Kroll screeching, "What the hell are you doing here?" that stopped him in his tracks. Karen had been talking and laughing with Jeffrey Klein, Colin Tromans and Lionel Latham when a tall, muscular man in Levi's and a leather jacket approached her. Sergio had no idea who he was.

But Karen did: it was Johnny Dante.

"What the hell are you doing here?" she repeated.

"Just thought I'd check out how the better half lives," sneered Johnny.

"How did you get in here?" she demanded angrily.

"The valet parker is a friend of mine."

It figures, thought Karen, her face reddening at the tangible reminder of her relentless libido in the midst of her attempt to seduce Jeffrey Klein into a sweetheart deal.

"Might I inquire what this is about?" asked Colin timidly.

"Cool your jets, Shakespeare," spat Johnny.

"He's a fan," mumbled Karen, not even believing the lie as she spoke it. "He's been following me for weeks."

"We must call security," said Colin.

"A fan!" howled Johnny. "That's not what you call me when you're sitting on my cock for four and five hours at a time."

Jeffrey Klein's ears perked up instantly. He adored cheap gossip. Lionel was not uninterested either.

"Now see here," protested Colin.

"When I'm fucking you," continued Johnny, "I think what you like to call me is Big Daddy. Ain't that right, doll?"

"If I had a gun," said Karen, her face blazing with shame.

"If you had a gun you still couldn't get off the way you do with this," said Johnny, grabbing his crotch.

"I must ask you to leave," said Colin, summoning up all his courage, despite a growing awareness that he was probably hearing the truth about Karen.

"Get fucked," sneered Johnny, grabbing a cold, prosciutto-wrapped asparagus stalk and shoving it up Colin's left nostril. He then picked him up and hurled him onto a loveseat where Alec Baldwin and Kim Basinger were sitting.

Karen gasped.

Lionel groaned.

Alec and Kim left.

"Oh God, let's get out of here!" implored Karen, rushing over to Colin.

"What a disaster," muttered Colin, taking her hand and heading to the front door.

People were shocked at the incident, but a loud bell reminded them that it was time to be seated for the entertainment and dinner in the tent. Gossiping amongst themselves, everyone began to leave the living room.

Everyone but eternal naïf Jeffrey Klein. His eyes aglow at the spectacle he had just witnessed, Jeffrey sidled up to a still-pissed Johnny Dante.

"Hey," said Jeffrey, "have you ever thought of making action movies?"

Sergio put the crab cocktail in front of Mrs. Davis just as she and her husband were being seated at table #1, at the foot of the stage that had been erected on the far side of the tent.

"A crab cocktail, Mrs. Davis," smiled Sergio. "I personally tested the soft-shells and found them not up to my standards. I hope this will be an adequate substitute."

"How sweet of you," smiled Mrs. Davis. "But you needn't have gone to all this trouble."

"It was my pleasure," said Sergio, bowing and retreating into the crowd. It never failed to amaze him how gracious a billion dollars could make a person.

Billy Crystal was onstage, concluding his opening remarks. Having joked about each of the major studios, he was now ready to bring on the main act. "Ladies and gentlemen," he said, "please welcome Liza Minnelli."

"Jesus," muttered Connie, "do we have to sit through *Cabaret* one more time just to get to the roast beef?"

"Connie, please," pleaded Morty. They were seated two tables away from the Davises, and he was terrified that she would make a scene. She had already scared off Geena Davis by fixing her with a stare and asking, "When the hell are you going to learn how to act?" Whoopi Goldberg had proven to be a tougher customer. Asked the same question, Whoopi shot back, "Soon as you learn how to hold up a store, Bonnie Parker." She then sat directly opposite Connie and stared her down.

That pushed Connie onto her sixth vodka, but who was counting? (Morty was.) She gazed at Liza on stage, feeling a mixture of resentment and envy. There she was singing Sondheim's "Children Will Listen," and Connie could only think that it could have been her. But her voice gave out because she blew a Mexican pool boy, and then she got caught shoplifting a purse in Beverly Hills. So there was Liza up onstage and here she was, drunk in the audience. Connie licked the rim of her glass, wishing she had another vodka.

Liza finished the number and the crowd applauded heartily. Some of them even yelled "Bravo!" Enough, thought Connie, get her off. But Liza wasn't finished yet. The orchestra began a familiar refrain—dum, dum, da da dum/ dum, dum, da da dum—and Connie shuddered. She wasn't really going to sing *New York, New York*, was she? But she was, and what's more, people seemed to like it. "Go girl," murmured Whoopi, tapping her fingers on the table.

Who could ever want to hear her sing this thing again, thought Connie bitterly. Kurt Russell and Goldie Hawn apparently, since Connie now noticed that they were humming and nodding their heads in time with the music. Christ! Didn't anyone have any standards left? Liza was standing center stage, her legs apart, seeming to inhale the audience's enthusiasm. "My little town blues," she sang.

Oh no, thought Connie, here comes that fucking arm. And sure enough, Liza began to whirl her right arm around in a dizzying circle as she pushed the song toward its climax. Round and round her arm spun. Maybe this time she'll take off, hoped Connie, and we won't have to hear the end of this goddamned song.

Instead Liza shot her arm straight up in the air as she bellowed "I'll make a brand new start of it, in old New York," and the audience went wild. Kurt, Goldie and Whoopi all stood up and started to cheer. So did several hundred others. Mrs. Davis threw kisses.

Connie was so mad she could spit. So Liza could sing. Big deal! So could she. And better than Liza. She'd show them, the ungrateful Hollywood bastards! She'd show them once and for all. Throwing caution, as well as her napkin, to the winds, Connie stood up and strode toward the stage. Morty tried to grab her, but he was too late. Liza was just coming down the steps as Connie charged up them.

"Connie!" exclaimed Liza.

"Out of my way, Sally fucking Bowles," Connie slurred as she grabbed the microphone out of Liza's hands.

Staggering onto the stage, Connie turned to the orchestra leader and mumbled, "Start the intro to 'Cabaret.' " Not wanting to create a scene, the man nodded to his pianist and the music swelled as the audience stared at Connie in hushed amazement. She began to sing.

> *I once shared songs and laughs with my friend Liza,*
> *Who wanted all the fans to idolize her,*
> *She wasn't what you'd call a major player,*
> *In fact she paid the chorus boys to lay her.*

There were gasps in the audience.

Connie, oblivious to the havoc she was creating, sang on:

> *The day she sang the audience came to boo her,*
> *They said she stank like freshly shat manure,*
> *But when I saw her singing like her Mom . . .*

As Connie hit the word *Mom* she staggered forward and caught her heel in the cord of the microphone. Tumbling forward, she fell off the stage. And right into Mrs. Davis's crab cocktail.

22

"**W**ho was that bully?" demanded Colin, pulling bits of asparagus from his nose as the limousine sped east on Sunset.

"Nobody," sighed Karen, "nobody at all."

"Big Daddy, I think he said you called him?"

"If you don't trust me after all this time."

"You've never called me Big Daddy," whined Colin.

Junior would be more like it, thought Karen. "What we have is special," she purred.

"You've been bonking him on the side, haven't you?" challenged Colin.

"It's an old thing," protested Karen. "It's been over for ages now."

"You've been bonking him when I've been away," grumbled Colin. "Well I won't have it. I won't be a stand-in for your *Fatal Attraction* boy toy."

"You could never be a stand-in," murmured Karen, trying to draw his lips to hers.

"I should say not," stated Colin, moving to the other side of the car. "But you, I venture, could be. Perhaps I should revisit the idea of Fiona as Lady Macbeth, with you as a fallback should she turn me down."

"Yes, but then who would you have to turn you on?" asked Karen. As she did, she crossed and uncrossed her legs. Karen knew that the mere sound of her nylon stockings meshing together could rouse Colin to a priapic frenzy.

He stared out the window, trying to ignore her entreaties. But when her hand slid into his crotch, his resolve weakened and his libido sparked. "Not here," he said weakly, "not in the backseat."

"Where do you want to do it, in the trunk?" She smirked, unzipping his pants.

"But the driver," protested Colin.

"He can't see a thing through the tinted window," said Karen, hiking her dress up around her waist and straddling Colin.

"This isn't right," he moaned feebly. "Not after you've betrayed me." Colin sat back in the seat, trying to frustrate Karen's attempt at insertion. But just then the limousine went over a speed bump at Sunset and Doheny, and Colin entered her with a swift thump.

Their bodies moved together in the animalistic frenzy that Colin had grown addicted to. Two more speed bumps and he had climaxed.

Perhaps that's why he didn't notice the red and blue lights of the police car in the back window.

Fiona drew the covers of her comforter to her chin, taking one last sip of hot cocoa and opening the dog-eared copy of *Silas Marner*. Perhaps the humble folk of George Eliot could dispel the anguish that tonight's party had caused, populated, as it was, by creatures from the land of Harold Robbins and Jackie Collins. Fiona desperately needed to feel one thing: cozy.

The phone rang abruptly, causing her to spill the cocoa and drop her book. "Bloody hell," she cursed as she picked up the receiver. It was Lionel.

"Turn on the telly at once," he ordered.

"American television is the last thing I wish to experience at this moment," she said.

"Channel Four, and do it now," said Lionel.

Fiona picked up her remote and switched on the TV. Kelley Lange, the blond newscaster who so reminded her of Petula Clark, was speaking.

". . . were arrested tonight on Sunset Boulevard on a charge of lewd behavior," said Kelley Lange.

Mug shots of Colin and Karen Kroll filled the screen. Fiona stopped mopping up the spilled cocoa and paid keen attention.

"This is the second time in a week that an actress nominated for the Academy Award has been arrested by the Beverly Hills Police," continued Lange.

A policeman identified as Thomas Ponzini came on the screen. "Yeah," he said, "last week it was Connie Travatano for shoplifting, tonight it was Karen Kroll for hanky-panky. This place is becoming *Hollywood Squares*."

"Lionel," said Fiona, "has Collie been arrested?"

"And so has Karen Kroll," beamed the British agent. "They were caught in flagrante in the back of their limo at a stoplight."

"How frightful," exclaimed Fiona.

"How delightful," crowed Lionel.

"Lionel, don't be cruel," scolded Fiona. "Collie needs us now."

"Colin needs a good lawyer," responded Lionel. "You need to simply be quiet and rise above it all on a ballast of good taste. The scenario we've envisioned has come to pass: you're now the scorned wife and Colin is the public cad."

It was true, pondered Fiona, Lionel's dastardly plot had come to pass. Her heart was broken, but her star was rising in the East. Well, she thought, at least there's one thing left for me to do.

"Lionel," said Fiona firmly, "I want you to fire that squalid little flatfoot, Ralph Spivak. The last thing I want to do is help to support such a terrible person."

"But I've promised him an advance of five thousand dollars," he sputtered.

"Send him my best wishes instead," said Fiona coolly as she hung up. Poor Collie, his passions had got the best of him. Now he was in trouble with the authorities, and she could lead a peaceful, civilized existence, doing the things she liked to do. Like having coffee with that young woman Maria who'd been so lovely to her this evening in the ladies' room. Pulling the covers to her chin once again, Fiona finally began to feel cozy for the first time in weeks.

Connie tried to bring her eyes into focus, but all she could conjure up was a beige blur. Her memory was as shaky as her vision, and she could only recall tiny flashes of what had happened to her in the past twenty-four hours.

There had been some sort of a party, with lots of people and lots of vodka. She remembered insulting the former and drinking the latter. And Liza had been there, only her arm had turned into a propeller and then she had turned into an airplane . . . no, that couldn't be right. Connie still couldn't see clearly and her memory was shot, but there was one thing she was certain of: her hair smelled like imitation crabmeat.

Slowly the beige blur smoothed itself out into a wall. She was lying in a bed, staring at a beige wall. But how could that be? None of the walls in her house were beige.

Then an attractive, middle-aged woman with light brunette hair appeared at her side. Connie had no idea who she was.

"Hello, Connie," said the woman gently. "I'm Betty Ford."

23

Melissa knocked briskly on Lori's front door. Claudio was at her side, dressed in a pair of overalls that offered a full view of his hairy, well-pumped chest.

"Remember," said Melissa, handing him a rake and a straw hat, "you're to say that talking to her plants made all the difference."

Lori opened the door and Melissa breezed in. "Here we are, darling," she said, "the farmer in the dell and Little Nell." Melissa waved a copy of *US* magazine, open to its celebrity photo section. "Just look at this marvelous picture of you two lovebirds."

Lori studied the photograph of her and Claudio from the premiere of *Foreign Accents*. His arm was around her and she was gazing adoringly at him. The caption read, "Oscar nominee Lori Seefer brushes up on her Brazilian with date Claudio Farenconi at the premiere of Meryl Streep's multilingual *Foreign Accents*."

"It also went out on the AP wire," said Melissa, snatching the magazine back as she dropped a pair of soiled sweat socks and some Nike running shorts on Lori's coffee table.

"What are you doing?" asked Lori.

"Just 'hetting' the place up a bit, dear," said Melissa. "Have you hidden all those dyke detective novels down in the cellar with your old Nancy Drews?"

"I don't read detective novels," protested Lori. "And why does Claudio look like Johnny Appleseed?"

"I want him gardening in your backyard during the interview, so Ted Gavin can see him while you talk. He'll be a silent presence. Silent but virile."

"Hello, Lori," said Claudio, blushing at the outfit that Melissa had forced him to wear.

"Nice to see you again," she responded with a shy smile.

"There's no time to lose," reminded Melissa, moving into the bathroom, taking a toothbrush, a razor and a can of Cruex Jock Itch Powder out of her handbag and arranging them around the sink.

"Melissa, this is really too much," said Lori. "You don't have to make my place look like the Y."

"When you're out to gild a lily," said Melissa, tossing a pair of Calvin Klein bikini briefs onto the showerhead, "you can never apply too much bronze. We must fabricate, fabricate, fabricate!"

Lori stared at her in wonder. When it came to lying, Melissa made Pinocchio look like he'd just had a nose job.

"When did you get interested in gardening?" asked Ted Gavin. In the past hour he and Lori had covered her career, her teen stardom and her hopes for the Oscar. It was now time, apparently, to move on to gardening, a topic that Melissa had been hinting at so blatantly that Ted had begun to wonder if she had picked up the Burpee Seed Catalogue as a new client.

"Gardening," replied Lori, "oh, Claudio is the one who really got me into that." Melissa had told her to say it and so she said it.

"So he's the one who does most of the work, the watering and the weeding?"

"Yes." Actually it was Maria who had cultivated the garden in the backyard. Lori couldn't help feeling like a traitor as she spewed out her carefully rehearsed story.

"Are there any plants he specializes in?" inquired Ted.

"Actually," piped up Melissa, "Claudio tends to Lori's parsley." Lori shuddered at the heavy-handed double entendre, but there was no stopping her determined publicist. When Melissa was pushing an angle she was about as subtle as a two-dollar whore on payday.

"Do you think I could get a gardening tip or two from Claudio?" asked Ted.

"Of course," gushed Melissa. "Claudio, put down your Miracle-Gro and come join us." She beckoned.

Not bad, if it's true, thought Ted as he watched the swarthy Brazilian stride from the garden into the living room. If Lori Seefer had gone straight, at least she'd picked the right man to do it with. Patti-Sue, the checkout girl at the Piggly-Wiggly in Austin, Texas, who Ted always thought of as his archetypal reader, would certainly be impressed by Lori's new love interest.

"Ted Gavin, from *Personality*," he said, extending his hand.

"Nice to meet you," said Claudio, shaking Ted's hand and seating himself next to Lori on the sofa.

"So," continued Ted, "how would you two characterize your relationship?"

"It's a woman and her gardener," said Melissa. "It's all been terribly *Lady Chatterley's Lover*."

"If you don't mind, Melissa," said Ted, "I'd like to have it in Lori and Claudio's own words."

"Well," said Lori hesitantly, "Claudio is a new person in my life."

A new *kind* of person, at least, thought Ted, as he scribbled down her words.

"He's brought new experiences, new feelings into my life."

I hope you didn't faint at the sight of it, he thought.

"It's all very new and exciting for me. We're just at the beginning," concluded Lori.

"That's great," said Ted. Actually it wasn't so great. What it was was starlet boilerplate #101 for a new relationship. Ted had heard the same stream of gush everywhere, from the set of *Friends* to Linda Evangelista's dressing room. But what the hell? Patti-Sue would eat it up.

Ted leaned forward to pick up his tape recorder from the coffee table. Reaching into the sunlight, his blue blazer fell open. A sharp reflection, from somewhere on his chest, struck Claudio in the eyes.

"Thanks a lot, Melissa," said Ted, gathering the rest of his things.

"The photographer is coming over on Monday?" she inquired.

"Yes, but Fatima will give you a call before then." Ted was at the door, just about to leave, when Claudio spoke up.

"Excuse me, Mr. Gavin," he said.

"Yes," replied Ted, turning to face him.

"I think you've picked up something of Lori's by mistake."

"What do you mean?" replied Ted, feigning mystification.

"That gold pen in your breast pocket. It was on the coffee table." It was the reflection that had caused Claudio to notice it.

"Oh my God," said Ted, blushing, "you're right. You know, I get so used to picking up pens in my profession, I do it automatically."

"Maybe you should keep it," offered Melissa. "As a memento of a lovely interview."

"I wouldn't dream of it," said Ted smoothly, taking the pen out of his pocket and handing it to Lori. "With my apologies."

"Oh, forget it," she replied. "I probably would have never missed it."

"Nonsense," replied Ted. "And besides, I don't want you to think I'm some sort of kleptomaniac, going around swiping things from people's houses!"

God, that was close, thought Ted, as he lit up a joint and headed to Fiona's house in Santa Monica. He'd never been caught stealing before, and the experience had given him a queasy, electric thrill. Rather like masturbating with a live wire. Screw it, he figured, there'd be something good to pocket over at Fiona Covington's.

"Admiring the unbound Auden sonnets, are we," said Fiona, emerging from the kitchen with a fresh pot of tea.

Ted jumped in response, since he had been only seconds away from stowing the manuscript in his briefcase. "I just love his work," Ted said, putting the sonnets back on the bookshelf.

"Ah yes," murmured Fiona, as she handed Ted his tea. " 'We must love one another or die.' One lump or two? Or Equal?"

"Equal," he responded, impressed by Fiona's ability to glide from great twentieth-century poetry to artificial sweeteners without batting an eyelash. "Speaking of love," Ted continued as he stirred no less than three packs of Equal into his tea, "I'm afraid I have to ask you the status of your relationship with Colin."

"Ah yes," sighed Fiona.

"I mean, what with the arrest for lewd conduct with Karen Kroll and all that," said Ted, looking for a juicy quote that would satisfy Fatima's literary bloodlust for petite disappointments.

Fiona put down her teacup and stared Ted straight in the

eye. "I can only quote Auden," she said. " 'Let no man be my judge in the brothel of ideas.' "

"Yes, I see," said Ted, writing it all down while wondering what the hell it meant.

Actually, it meant nothing. Fiona had made it up on the spot. Over the past few weeks she had discovered that the best way to silence nosy American journalists was to throw a phony, yet tony, quote at them. They wrote it down and moved swiftly on to the next topic, not wanting to reveal what they feared was their ignorance. It worked every time.

"Shall we move on to the Oscar, then," said Ted.

"Onward," smiled Fiona, pleased that Ted had proven to be no brighter than the rest of his colleagues.

"Do you have any special thoughts?"

"Only one," offered Fiona, demurely lowering her eyes. "In the past you Americans have been bloody generous with your Oscars, giving them to Glenda Jackson, Julie Christie and Emma Thompson. I can only hope that you will consider taking this bundle from Britain to your bosom as well." God that was saccharine, she thought. It could use a little of that Equal he had dumped so promiscuously into his tea.

"Do you think that the voting will be affected by Colin's scandal?" asked Ted, still digging for dirt.

" 'In the jungle there is rain, on the moon it never snows,' to quote Auden once again," responded Fiona gamely.

This time Ted was so befuddled he had trouble getting the quote down. Sensing his discomfort, Fiona leapt up.

"I know what we need," she said. "Shortbread." She bustled off to the kitchen again as Ted wrote down the last of her gibberish. Putting down his pad, he glanced stealthily around the living room. Something personal, he wanted something that would make him feel close to her. His eyes fell on a half-folded note sitting on the desk. Moving quickly, Ted went over and picked it up. "Dearest Fi," the note read, "How wonderful that you should receive a nomination for the Academy Award. I'm ever so envious of your honor, and yet oh so determined that you should win it. As the only nominee to carry the colors of our beloved Union Jack, rest assured that you have my vote. Sincerely, Emma Thomp . . ."

"Snooping in the mails, now, are we?" said Fiona with mock dismay as she carried a plate of shortbread into the room.

"Oh," gasped Ted. "I was just trying to get a little background for the piece."

"I daresay you were," said Fiona, smiling pertly and taking the note from his hand. "If a missive from my fellow thespian Emma Thompson so intrigues you, I must surely keep my love letters under lock and key."

"Well, you know," said Ted, desperately trying to recover, "it's like Auden said."

"What was that?" inquired Fiona.

"What was what?" said Ted weakly.

"What Auden said?" she persisted.

"Well," stammered Ted, "I think it was, 'We must lock up our letters, to keep them from our betters.' "

"Did Auden really say that?" said Fiona, wondering if Ted had caught on to her game.

"Didn't he?" replied Ted warily.

"Actually," said Fiona, "I think it was T. S. Eliot."

"Yes, yes," mumbled Ted. "It was Eliot."

He's as dumb as he looks, thought Fiona triumphantly.

Christ almighty, cursed Ted, how was he ever going to steal something from this poetry-spouting bitch?

24

The sunlight that filtered into the breakfast room of the Betty Ford Clinic was neither yellow nor golden, but, rather, a pale jaundice, as if a thoughtful color consultant had dimmed its vibrant hue in view of the facility's exclusive clientele. It carefully illuminated the individual breakfast trays of grapefruit, soft-boiled eggs and tea that had been set out for the clinic's patients.

Connie would rather have had a boilermaker and black coffee, but there was no chance of that. Breakfast at seven, chores at eight, group therapy at nine, lunch, then more group therapy: the routine at the clinic was as unchanging as one of Demi Moore's two facial expressions. I haven't had soft-boiled eggs since parochial school, thought Connie grimly.

"Miss Travatano?"

Connie turned to see who was calling her. It was Grace, the West Indian attendant who had told her yesterday that she had always thought that Bette Midler was overrated. Connie liked Grace.

"Yes, Grace."

"Mail call," smiled the hefty black woman, handing her four envelopes.

Who knew she was here? Connie's mind set off on a paranoid journey worthy of Nixon during the last days of Watergate. After coming to, she learned that she had been checked into the clinic by Morty and her assistant Erika. Both had been sworn to secrecy. But of course, she had made a drunken spectacle of herself in front of half of Hollywood at the Davises' party. It was inevitable that word of her whereabouts would circulate.

Connie opened the first letter, recognizing the handwriting instantly.

Dear Connie,
My thoughts are with you at what must be a very difficult time in your life. Please know that I've been there, and that it does get better. If you ever want to talk, sistah to sistah, please pick up the phone. I know you're going to put this behind you; you're too wonderful a person not to.
All my love,
Liza
P.S. I voted for you for the Oscar!

Tears welled up in Connie's eyes for the first time since she had seen *Terms of Endearment.* How could Liza be so decent and sweet when Connie had cruelly mocked her in front of hundreds of their contemporaries? Was she just naturally a good person, free from the envy and vanity that had driven Connie around the bend, over the edge and into the abyss? Connie's cheeks flushed vermilion with shame.

She didn't recognize the script of the second letter-writer.

Dear Connie,
Remember that love is the answer. We're all just

marionettes, weaving and bobbing through the dance of life. You can make it if you'll just reach out and . . .
Touching you, touching me,
Diana
P.S. Get out of the Park, girl, it's starting to rain!

The third letter was short and to the point.

Dear Connie,
Have you ever considered directing?
Barbra

Connie almost gagged on her soft-boiled egg, contemplating how pathetic she must seem to her rivals in divadom. Fearing the worst, she opened the final letter.

Oh Great Washed-Up One,
Hope you're having fun cleaning toilets at Betty Ford. I've heard Tidy-Bowl works best. Don't worry about working when you get out; Mickey Rooney can always use another has-been for his next tour of *Sugar Babies*.

Her hand trembled as she read the letter a second time. How was this possible? Someone seemed to know everything that was happening to her, and then writing her these awful letters. It was the same envelope, the same typewriter. She was being stalked!

Pushing aside her breakfast, Connie stumbled toward the doorway. Grace was waiting there to meet her.

"Miss Travatano," she said.

"Not now," protested Connie, pushing her away.

"But you have a visitor."

"Nobody's supposed to know I'm here," wailed Connie.

"He's waiting in the lounge," said Grace, unperturbed. "And he's very handsome."

His blond hair was somewhat disheveled, and his skimpy T-shirt offered a better view of his torso and biceps than his previous outfit. Still there was no mistaking him: it was Eric Collins, the Beverly Hills police officer who had arrested Connie little more than a week ago.

"What are you doing here?" demanded Connie.

"I wanted to see if you were all right," said Eric, rising to meet her.

"How did you know I was here?"

"It was in *USA Today*. On the front page."

Good Christ! Why not just hang a bell around my neck and make me walk the streets shouting "Unclean! Unclean!" thought Connie.

"My sister and I are in Palm Springs visiting my mom, so I thought I'd stop by," Eric continued. "I've been worried that my arresting you may have helped lead to this."

"Thanks a lot, Father Flanagan," spat Connie.

"Recovery is a powerful process," said Eric, ignoring Connie's anger. "My dad went through it in the late eighties and it made all the difference in our family."

Connie was unnerved by his sincerity, but her worst impulses still reigned. "Where's Dad now? Back on the sauce in some Van Nuys gin mill?"

"No," said Eric quietly. "He was gunned down in a drive-by shooting while helping an old crippled woman across the street."

"Yeah, well, I'm sorry about that," mumbled Connie. "But it's not doing much for me seeing you here."

"Then I won't bother you anymore," said Eric. "But I can give you the name of my mother's priest if you're ever interested in some spiritual counseling."

"Thanks," snapped Connie, "but I don't think there are any young boys around here for him to molest."

"Actually Father Karras prefers lepers. He's worked with them in a colony in Haiti for a decade now. He's just in the desert on sabbatical." Eric smiled at her peacefully.

Goddamn it, this kid made the driven snow seem like slush. Had he been taking lessons from Liza?

"Anyway," continued Eric, "I have to get back to this orphanage where my sister and I do volunteer work. It's called Kids for Christ. You can call me there if you need me."

"Thanks," said Connie in a low voice.

"And remember the old saying, 'You're only greater than your greatest problem.'"

"Who said that?" demanded Connie.

"W. H. Auden," said Eric. "I just read it in an interview with Fiona Covington."

Returning to her room, Connie was filled with shame over her behavior with Eric. Maybe he had been sincere in coming to see her. But years of being used by people in the entertainment industry had left her suspicious of everyone from David Geffen to her garbage man. There was always an angle.

Still, he had looked awfully cute in his white chinos and gray T-shirt. She wondered exactly how old he was. Thirty-three? Thirty-five?

It was while she was running these actuary tables in her mind that the door opened. A pale young redhead entered the room.

"Hi," said the new arrival. "I'm Amber Lyons. Your new roommate."

Ted sat in his office surrounded by a mountain of memorabilia. *Personality Magazine* would never be mistaken for *The New Yorker*, but it prided itself on the thoroughness of its research staff. For the article on the nominees for the Best Actress Oscar Ted had been supplied with everything from Fiona's first review as an intern at the National Theatre ("oddly appealing, despite a nattering speech pattern; she suggests Sandy Dennis after a brisk tromp on the moors") to a teenage fanzine profile of Lori while she was on *Magnum, P.I.* ("this blissful babe is positively panting over all the Hawaiian hunks"). Right now he was feverishly paging through Karen Kroll's file, trying in vain to construct a chronology of the blond sex goddess's life.

His search was interrupted by the ferocious click of Fatima Bulox's tiny high heels as they strode toward his office. What did the Ayatolahess want now?

"Drop everything," seethed Fatima as she reached his doorway.

"I'm not holding everything," smiled Ted, grasping for the kind of limp witticism that Steve Martin usually managed to wring a laugh out of.

"Save your comedy for the unemployment line," snapped the steely editor. "I've just gotten a call from Amber Lyons's agent. She's checked into Betty Ford and she's willing to talk to us about her recovery. I want you in the desert by sundown."

"But I've been researching Karen Kroll," complained Ted.

"Drop that blond slut like hot cow dung," commanded

Fatima. "Not only is Amber Lyons willing to talk; it turns out that Connie Travatano is her roommate. You can interview her as well."

"But she turned our request down flat," said Ted.

"That may be harder to do when she realizes that her roommate is talking to you, willing, with only a little provocation I'm sure, to dish the dirt on the broken wings of our little Sicilian songbird. Get to Connie while you're there. Make her talk to us."

"And just how am I supposed to do that?" sputtered Ted.

"Tell her if she doesn't give us an interview, we'll make her the most hated woman in American life since Ethel Rosenberg." Fatima turned on the proverbial dime and goose-stepped back to her office.

The desert by sunset! But *Friends* was on tonight. Oh hell, sighed Ted, there was no use battling Fatima when her scimitar was drawn. He might as well pack up and hit the road right away. At least he could mellow out during the drive there by smoking the hash he had bought this morning. Ted reached into the pocket of his blue blazer and pulled out a briarwood pipe with the words "From Fiona, all my love," engraved on its stem. It would be perfect to smoke the hash in. Lucky for him he'd stolen it from her bedside table yesterday.

═══

"I adore the ravioli with fava beans and raw twigs," says Sharon Stone of chef Pierre Mauvais's signature dish at his new Beverly Hills bistro La Nature (that's nature in English). Combining the natural foods trend with classic French cooking, chef Mauvais has come up with a menu that both startles and delights: pebble soup, composed of saffron, chicken broth and sand ($9); Loire Valley foie gras sautéed and served with mung bean potstickers ($16.50); mud risotto (hasn't it always tasted like that?) ($19); and sauteed halibut garnished with an earthworm coulis. Feasting on a dessert of crabgrass sorbet and kiwi crisp, Sharon noted, "It's either Fiona Covington or Lori Seefer for this year's Oscar. They're the only ones who haven't been thrown in jail or rehab."

—George Christy
"The Great Life"
The Hollywood Reporter
March 10

25

A warm breeze wafted through Fiona's freshly washed hair as she sauntered down the street. She had used an herbal rinse twice this morning and now her entire head smelled like an English garden in full bloom. Oh how she missed London!

However it was not the King's Road, but trendy Montana Avenue in Santa Monica that Fiona was laying leather to this morning. Store windows filled with overpriced Italian sweaters, most of them made by illegal Chilean laborers, swam by her as she noticed the many toddlers being pushed in their expensive strollers by their devoted Mexican nannies. Despite being the progeny of Jewish sitcom writers and mini-skirted development executives with voluminous hair weaves, most of these kids would learn Spanish before they mastered English.

The thought of young couples building a life together suddenly filled Fiona with the same ineffable sadness she felt every time she watched *Brief Encounter*. Were she and Colin truly finished forever? Were they, like Trevor Howard and Celia Johnson in Sir David Lean's sentimental masterpiece, destined to depart the train station of life, never to see each other again?

Feeling her resolve beginning to slip, Fiona increased the pace of her march down Montana Avenue. Push on, she thought, I've simply got to push on. To new experiences, new adventures. Her mind snapped back to the English girls' boarding school she had attended and the hymn she and her classmates had sung after every Sunday service. Softly she began to sing "Onward Christian Soldiers" to herself. It was the first time it had been heard on Montana Avenue in decades.

Fiona entered "Mocha Choca Latta, Ya Ya," a hip, interracial coffeehouse on the corner of Montana and 9th Street. Passing by the bulletin board filled with flyers for poetry readings, performance art and reflexology courses, she peered into the invitingly dark room filled with out-of-work actors and models.

"Over here," waved Maria, who was sitting at a corner table and nursing a cup of tea.

"I'm so glad you accepted my invitation," said Fiona, seating herself at the table. "You gave me such a good laugh at the party the other night, and I'm determined that we shall repeat that lovely event."

Maria smiled faintly at the verbose greeting. It was Fiona's tenderness, not her laughter, that had kindled the fires of her radical Mexican heart.

A handsome young waiter, who not two hours earlier had given a terrible reading for the role of an ambulance driver on *Baywatch*, approached the two women. "Morning," he said to Fiona. "Can I get you something?"

"Ah," murmured Fiona, "the moment of decision. One ponders it so."

"We've got a special," droned the waiter. "A double decaf, iced, nonfat latte with a shot of Italian raspberry syrup. It's seven-fifty."

Fiona thought for a second. "Would a simple cup of coffee be out of the question?" she inquired gently.

"You're the customer," he said, sauntering back to the counter.

"You Americans with your elaborate coffees," said Fiona to

Maria. "It's like Mexican food. The same three ingredients served forty different ways."

"I was so happy you called me last night," said Maria, whose mind was on passion, not caffeine.

"As I said," responded Fiona, "you gave me my first spot of laughter in too long a time."

"Has it been that bad?"

"It's quite dreadful to be publicly cuckolded. Especially by such a brassy tart as Karen Kroll."

"You must be in such pain," empathized Maria.

"I daresay life is a good bit rougher than they told us it would be as schoolgirls at Hollingsford-on-Mews." Fiona thought fondly of her school days, merrily making mud pies and reciting Beatrix Potter to her classmates. It had all been so Masterpiece Theatre.

"Are you still crying all the time?" inquired Maria, inhaling the floral scents emanating from Fiona's auburn hair.

"Got that under control," grinned Fiona. "I turned to writing poetry as an outlet for my grief."

"I just rely on tequila," shrugged Maria.

"In fact," said Fiona, digging into her Chanel purse, "I think I have one of my poems with me."

"I'd love to hear it," said Maria.

"And you shall," smiled Fiona, unfolding a piece of yellow paper. Slipping on her wire-rimmed glasses, she began to read from it.

> *Whilst I wandered*
> *weakly wilting,*
> *when my will*
> *was wickedly wounded*

While the willow
wantonly wondered . . .

"I haven't got a clue what you're talking about," interrupted Maria.

"Haven't you, though?" said Fiona. "It's quite simple, really. You see I'm depicting myself as utterly lost, wandering like a . . ."

Maria put her hand tenderly across Fiona's lips. "Don't say a word," she murmured softly.

Fiona withdrew in puzzlement. If she couldn't talk what could she do?

"Just let me look into your eyes," said Maria softly.

"But whatever for?" inquired Fiona.

"You are someone I'm very attracted to," replied Maria.

The waiter arrived with her coffee, providing Fiona with a moment to gather her wits. This young woman was clearly expecting more than a cursory morning chat. Fiona thought of the girls' field hockey team at the Hollingsford-on-Mews School for Young Ladies and the rumors that had circulated about it.

"I fear you are here under a misapprehension," began Fiona gingerly.

"I'm here because I wanted to see you," replied Maria.

"But I thought you told me you had known the pain of losing a true love yourself. I thought that was part of what we shared."

"We do," said Maria. "I was Lori Seefer's lover up until two weeks ago."

"Lori Seefer," said Fiona in shock. "Are you planning to sleep with all the nominees for the Best Actress Oscar?"

"Only you," answered Maria with a smile.

Fiona stared at her for a moment, and then broke into laughter. "Ah, what tangled webs we mortals weave."

"Please," protested Maria, "no more poetry. English lit is my worst subject."

"Don't misunderstand me," said Fiona consolingly. "I've nothing against your sexual preference. I learned of it fully in my Women's Studies Group at Oxford. Virginia Woolf, Vita Sackville-West, those long Sunday afternoon picnics on the lawn at Bloomsbury."

"I didn't say anything about Bloomingdale's," said Maria.

"Bloomsbury," repeated Fiona.

"You've never made love to another woman?"

"I've never robbed a bank, either," replied Fiona. "I shall go to my grave curious about both experiences."

"You're a tender woman," said Maria gravely. "And you've been hurt badly by your husband."

"You're right about that," said Fiona quietly. She cursed herself as she thought of how desperately she'd pursued Colin, only to be thrown over for a blond harlot.

"You need someone to hold you, to take care of you," whispered Maria huskily.

"Perhaps," murmured Fiona, "but it shan't be of my own sex." Her right eye began to blink as a tear rolled out of it.

Maria took her hand. "You're crying again."

"I've got something caught in my eye," said Fiona as she brushed at it.

"Here, let me," said Maria. She wrapped a napkin around the tip of her finger and gently probed at Maria's eye until the particle was removed. Somewhere in the back of her mind Fiona began to hear a schoolgirl choir sing "Onward Christian Soldiers." Her resolve began to wilt like a sailor's hard-on when confronted by an overly friendly chaplain.

"That was sweet of you," breathed Fiona.

"This is sweeter," said Maria, leaning over and kissing her on the lips.

Fiona withdrew in shock, worried what the coffeehouse's clientele might think. But on this lazy weekday morning in Santa Monica the customers of Mocha Choca Latta, Ya Ya had better things to do than to spy on an innocent lesbian flirtation. Maria leaned over and kissed Fiona again.

"How do you feel?" she asked her.

"Cozy," replied Fiona, her cheeks blushing redder than Prince Charles's.

They walked hand-in-hand on the beach, the wind at their backs, the tide nipping at their feet. Fiona gazed at the seagulls that circled and flew above them.

"Do you think they can love, Maria?" she asked.

"God wants everyone to be loved," she replied.

"Ah," murmured Fiona, who hadn't read Kahlil Gibran or *Jonathan Livingston Seagull* while at Oxford and was therefore unaccountably impressed with such gush. Or maybe it was Maria and the effect she was having on her. Certainly after a year of being virtually ignored by Colin, Fiona felt flattered and touched to be the object of such boundless affection.

As for the possibility of making love with Maria, she remained uncertain. Fiona had never really thought much of intimacy with her own sex. She had rented *The Children's Hour* once from Blockbuster Video, but had fallen asleep before the end of it.

One thing she was certain of, though: sex between women couldn't be as humiliating as her last romp in the hay with Colin. And after all, hadn't scholars recently theorized that Jane

Austen might have been a lesbian? What was good enough for the classics was good enough for her.

Which is why she was so touched when Maria leaned over and kissed her. "You see that gull up there," Maria said, pointing to one particularly persistent bird that had been swooping around them for the past five minutes. "That bird is our love."

"Oh, how sweet," sighed Fiona. "The seagull of happiness." With such a bird in the air, not to mention such sentiments, it was inevitable that Fiona and Maria would wind up back at her house. Fiona offered her tea, but Maria refused. It was honey pot nectar she yearned to feast upon.

Maria pushed Fiona down on the sofa, pressing her lips and body upon her. She writhed in passionate abandon as Fiona shifted uncomfortably.

"I'm getting wet," moaned Fiona.

"That's good, baby," whispered Maria huskily.

Maria gently pulled down Fiona's panties and began to tongue her. Like freshly microwaved popcorn in a warm kitchen, Fiona's love juices filled the air with an oozing, palpable lubricity.

"It's never been like this before," gurgled Fiona.

"Oh baby, I want you so bad," breathed Maria, delving deeper, ever deeper.

Fiona heaved and thrashed, her body pulsing with a passion that was wholly new, yet oddly familiar. This love that had dared not speak its name was now crying it from the highest hilltop. Desire permeated her every fiber.

As Maria continued licking and kissing her, Fiona found herself clinging to a small branch on the precipice of abandon. Slipping down it, she gave herself over to the first orgasm she had experienced in more than a year. As she did, she burst into song. The words echoed through the canyons of the Santa Monica mountain range:

The hills are alive,
with the sound of music!

Some hours later, the very same seagull that hovered over Fiona and Maria lost its way and circled warily over Bronson Canyon. It sighted a small Spanish cottage and darted toward it. Lori looked up, mystified, wondering what a seagull was doing so near her house.

The bird shat on the terrace and flew back to Santa Monica.

We recently had the chance to chat on the phone with Oscar nominee Karen Kroll and found the blond sexpot to be as opinionated, and funny, as ever.

Asked if she thought her recent arrest for lewd conduct in a limousine with director/actor Colin Tromans would hurt her chances for an Oscar, Karen simply brushed the incident off as "a routine traffic violation."

Karen said the Beverly Hills police were "perfect gentlemen, although they did confiscate my panties as evidence."

When I asked Karen what effect she thought the incident would have on Colin's shaky marriage to fellow nominee Fiona Covington, she discreetly replied that she "didn't want to come between the two British stars."

Well all right then, but it seems to me that Karen did a pretty good job of that when she staged her little backseat lovefest.

—Liz Smith

Syndicated columnist

March 16

26

Jeffrey Klein sat at his table in the Marathon Studio commissary, working diligently on the *Los Angeles Times* daily crossword puzzle. The clue for five down read "a jerk." It was a five-letter word beginning with "i." Jeffrey thought of imbecile, but that was eight letters. Any idiot knew that.

Putting down his pencil, he sipped on his passion-fruit iced tea and pondered the problem that lay ahead of him. Having offered Karen Kroll a multiple-picture contract at ten million dollars a film, he now had to decide whether or not to proceed with it in the face of her public sex scandal. Jeffrey hated big decisions, since he knew that someday he might be held accountable for them. He had even turned to a Ouija board when it came to green-lighting *Wampum Woman*, the Demi-Moore-as-a-squaw-on-Wall-Street vehicle. The board said yes, Jeffrey said yes, and nine months later Janet Maslin in the *New York Times* said, "*Wampum Woman* is the biggest setback to Native Americans since the slaughter of the Sioux nation."

And now this! A star he had promised millions of dollars to caught screwing in the backseat of a limo with a still-married director. And he needed stars. After all the flops he had produced at Marathon, the big names had become wary of signing with him. Just last week at a party he had overheard Jack

Nicholson say, "There are only two things in this town I won't do: heroin and a picture for Jeffrey Klein."

He shook free of his mental anguish and rose as Karen sashayed across the commissary toward his table. She was wearing a white jersey mini that left nothing to the imagination, but she knew she didn't have to worry. Jeffrey had no imagination.

"Jeffrey dearest," she squealed, giving him a big hug and sliding into the banquette next to him.

"Thanks for coming to see me at the studio," he said.

"I just love big executive lunches," declared Karen, laying her Chanel purse on the table. "Let's order martinis and steaks and drink the afternoon away."

"Actually I ordered the Julia Roberts special while I was waiting," said Jeffrey. "It's a soybean loaf with mushroom sauce. And I already have my iced tea."

"So," teased Karen, "this is going to be a sober, healthy occasion?"

"I thought we could talk about our deal," said Jeffrey calmly. Karen decided to settle for a chicken salad and a Perrier. Lunch wasn't going to be as much fun as she'd thought.

"You're not having second thoughts, are you?" she asked warily.

"Not at all," protested Jeffrey, who lived by the Hollywood executive credo of never saying no until the other party was either dead or working in television. "I just think we should examine our timetable. I don't want either of us to be the victim of a first impulse."

"First impulses, huh," she murmured.

"They can be deadly," said Jeffrey.

Karen saw the waiter approaching out of the corner of her eye.

Unbuttoning the top button of her dress, she thrust her breasts against the fabric, wishing she'd had time to ice her nipples.

"Watch this for a first impulse," she said to Jeffrey as she turned to the waiter. "Hi," she smiled.

"Hello, Miss Kroll," said the tall blond young man. He was handsome, twenty-four and, thanks be to God, thought Karen, looked to be straight.

"So what have you got that's special?" she asked, letting her voice drop when it reached the word *special*.

"Well, today we have the Julia Roberts soy loaf."

"Hmm," mulled Karen, "that's not the kind of loaf I usually eat."

The waiter blushed. "Would you like to see a menu?" he stammered.

"Is that all you're willing to show me?" teased Karen.

"Is there something you like?"

"I think you know what I like if you've been reading the papers. But this afternoon I guess I'll have to settle for some chicken salad and a Perrier." Looking down, Karen noticed that the boy's crotch was swollen. Bull's-eye!

"Very good," he said, retreating hastily to the kitchen.

"He was sporting a woody, Jeffrey," Karen said triumphantly.

"You're quite an actress," he smirked.

"Just remember what Bob Evans always says, 'Hard dicks buy tickets.' "

Had Bob Evans really said that? Jeffrey couldn't be sure; having once mistaken him for George Hamilton, he had always been too embarrassed to strike up a conversation with the legendary mogul. But he saw Karen's point.

"So you don't think the scandal has hurt you?" he inquired.

"On the contrary," said Karen, rebuttoning her dress. "I think it's helped. It's pushed me out to the edge. Audiences are intrigued."

"Okay then, let's talk business," said Jeffrey, who loved accentuating the positive. "Any ideas for your first picture?"

"Why not *Macbeth*?" responded Karen.

"But you're supposed to be doing that with Richard Gere and Colin, at TriStar."

"Yeah, but my agent tells me Mel Gibson is interested in it. And he'd like to direct it too." Karen had been waiting to drop this little bombshell since the day after her arrest.

"Mel starring and directing," gushed Jeffrey. "It'll be *Braveheart* all over again."

"You got it," said Karen with a big grin.

"There's just one thing."

"What's that?"

"What about the rights?"

"The rights?" said Karen in amazement.

"Yeah," continued Jeffrey. "TriStar must own the rights to the script. How do we get them?"

"Jeffrey," said Karen patiently. "*Macbeth* is a four-hundred-year-old play. There are no rights. It's in the public domain."

"Cool," said Jeffrey.

Richard Mulvehill poured himself another Fresca and looked at the can. Contains water, corn syrup, fructose, artificial flavoring, saccharine, sodium and reconstituted fruit juice. Richard had been on the wagon for three weeks now and his stomach was killing him.

Well, it wasn't as bad as this week's cover story. Heartbroken, Penniless Mom Thrown Out on Street by Oscar Nominee

Amber Lyons. Richard had headed up the Los Angeles bureau of the *National Enquirer* for the past five years and was long past being titillated by a domestic problem. What he yearned for was a good, juicy sex scandal. The Karen Kroll–Colin Tromans lewd behavior arrest was perfect, but the daily papers had covered it to death. He would still do something in next week's issue, but, with all the coverage it had gotten, he wasn't sure the story was strong enough for the cover. That was the problem with the mainstream press today: they were replacing the tabloids.

Which is why Richard broke out into a big grin when Ralph Spivak entered his office. Almost as sleazy as Anthony Pellicano, Ralph had delivered the goods on a number of celebrities over the years.

"What have you got for me, Ralph?"

Ralph flipped up his eye patch—possessed of twenty-twenty vision, he wore it only for effect—and tossed an envelope of photographs on Richard's desk. "I think you're going to be very happy with these," he said.

Richard ripped open the package and began flicking through the photographs. Two women were holding hands and kissing on a beach.

"Who are the broads?"

"The redhead's Fiona Covington. The brunette's named Maria Caldone."

"Is Covington a dyke?"

"What do you think?"

"I think it's a possible cover. What do you want for them?"

"Twenty thousand."

"Let me call Florida. How'd you get them? Someone pay you to follow her?"

"No," said Ralph, drawing the toothpick from Tony's Steak Hut out of his gums. "Someone didn't pay me and I decided to get even."

"**F**asten your seat belts," hissed Bette Davis, "it's going to be a bumpy night."

Phillip Castleman hit the rewind button on his remote and watched her say the line again. What style she had! What venom! Phillip rented *All About Eve* at least five times a year from Video West in West Hollywood, never ceasing to be amazed by Davis's performance. If only he could be like her!

But of course he couldn't. That kind of high-handed behavior was completely out of Phillip's range. He was closer to Celeste Holm, the knowing wife who tactfully pulls up the collar of her cloth coat while everyone else is happily drowning in a blizzard of ambition and barbed repartee. It was the awful Melissa, his boss, who was Bette Davis.

Phillip sighed and hit the stop button. Somehow *All About Eve* just wasn't doing it for him tonight. He pulled the cassette out of his VCR and reached for the other tape he had rented this evening after leaving the CPR offices. Here it was, *Butthole Banquet*. It seemed like a logical replacement for *All About Eve*: dumber dialogue, actually no dialogue, but better bodies.

He hit play and opened his robe in anticipation of the pleasures to come. But just as he was becoming aroused, he saw something that instantly wilted his newly minted enthusiasm. He leaned forward and stared at the screen, fascinated by what he saw.

27

Doctor Angus McFardle stared out the window of his office at the Betty Ford Clinic as he finished his first cigarette of the day. Yearning for a final puff, he raised the smoking butt to his face. Alas, he stuck it in his left nostril instead of his mouth.

The sad truth was that, despite all his degrees and years of practice, Angus suffered from a debilitating spastic twitch on the left side of his body. When it came on, his left leg, arm and one side of his face jerked up and down in a frenzied, chaotic dance: he resembled nothing less than a marionette during a 7.1 earthquake. Over the years the good psychotherapist had managed to largely tame his twitch through modern medicine, namely Valium, and a knowledge of what brought it on, stress and anxiety. Unfortunately the latter two promised to be in great abundance today.

Angus had warned the administrators that it was a mistake to put Connie Travatano and Amber Lyons together. After a brief flare-up over who would use the bathroom first, Amber moved out to a private room. She had retreated into silence, saying nothing during the group therapy sessions. Connie found herself a new roommate in Magda Burke, a fading starlet whose sole claim to fame, other than an addiction to Percodan, was a Häagen-Dazs and sex orgy with Elvis Presley right before he died. An unknown was fine with Connie, who just yesterday had broken down and admitted that she hated herself for the nasty way she spoke to people, in particular the young policeman who had arrested her at Barneys.

But if people were to heal, they had to learn to deal with all the attendant pressures of their daily lives. Half-measures were not the chosen path at Betty Ford. With the Oscars only two and a half weeks away, Angus felt it was time Connie and Amber confronted the issue that had both joined them and been responsible for their being here. But it wasn't going to be easy, he thought, as his twitch returned full force.

Stubbing his cigarette out in his ear, Angus stood up and headed toward the group therapy room.

"**W**hy do we always have to listen to what Connie says?" whined Gil, a stand-up comic who had done enough speed over the past three years to keep the entire population of the United States awake well into the millennium. Right now he was eating a cherry cheese danish, his third of the morning. Since coming to the clinic and kicking amphetamines, Gil had put on forty pounds.

"Just because she's a star doesn't mean that everything that happens to her is important," he said, licking the sugary pastry crumbs from his lips.

"You can't hate Connie for being a star," chided Magda. "It's like Elvis told me when we were together, 'You've got to eat what they put in front of you.' "

"That's why that putz is dead," said Sophie. "He never stopped eating. I heard he thought mayonnaise was a vegetable."

A grandmother of four, Sophie had realized that her penchant for afternoon martinis had gotten out of hand when she greeted the cable man one day in the nude.

"God, how I wish I'd fucked him before he discovered Ring-Dings," sighed Magda.

"Amber, what do you think?" asked Angus. He'd taken two Valium before the session and was feeling much better. But Amber was slouched in a corner, picking at her aquamarine nail polish.

"Amber," he repeated, "how do you feel about Gil's question?"

"Umm, I really wasn't listening," she replied, not looking up.

"Well then, why don't you stop playing with your nails and join the group," said Angus. "Gil thinks that Connie gets special treatment because she's a star. And Magda thinks that's okay. What do you think?"

"I don't really think a whole lot of Connie," Amber said.

"And why is that?"

"Because she used up all my papaya conditioning shampoo in the shower."

"I replaced it and you know it," insisted Connie, stung to the quick.

"Yeah, with a cheap bottle of Head and Shoulders." Amber flung her hair behind her shoulders.

"Let's not quarrel over little things," interrupted Angus, feeling the slightest tremble in his left hand. "Connie, Amber, you two have never really gotten along, have you?"

"We're different generations," shrugged Amber.

"Yes," nodded Angus. "But you do have one thing in common." There was silence. "Isn't that right, Connie?"

"What?" she replied, befuddled. "We both wash our hair twice a day?"

"You've both been nominated for the Best Actress Oscar," said Angus.

"I always dreamed of being nominated for an Oscar," sobbed Magda, whose most recent role had been as a dead body on a two-hour *Matlock*.

"I always dreamed of shtupping Clark Gable," shrugged Sophie. "Deal with it."

"Connie," asked Angus softly, "do you feel a kinship with Amber?"

Connie took a deep breath and stared up at the ceiling. This was not a time to be bitter, she told herself. Being bitter had gotten her here in the first place. "May the best woman win," she said through clenched teeth.

"She'll probably win, anyhow," pouted Amber. "She's got everybody's sympathy because she was drunk in public."

"What about you?" said Connie. "You vomited in front of the entire world."

"Big deal. They think I'm a rebel."

"Well, you are."

"Yeah. And you're old."

"Old enough to rip your eyes out, Bo Peep."

"Try it, Granny."

"Ladies, ladies!" exclaimed Angus, whose left shoulder was now whacking the side of his head. "This is not why we're here."

"It's druggies like you that are ruining the business," blazed Connie.

"When was the last time you played the Music Hall?" taunted Amber.

"They drummed you right out of Broadway," spat Connie. "So you came crawling back to Hollywood. Well Hollywood doesn't go for booze and dope."

"Stop it, stop!" begged Angus. But he was in no condition to make the two women do that. His left arm was flapping to and fro wildly, as if it were caught in a Mixmaster. He tried to hold it down, but to no avail. It flew up, hitting Sophie in the jaw and sending the upper plate of her false teeth flying across the room.

"You've been sending me these, haven't you," said Connie, pulling a crumpled piece of paper out of her pocket and waving it at Amber. It was a third hate note, which she had just received this morning.

"You're nuts," said Amber, grabbing the note from Connie.

"Give me that," shrieked Connie.

But Amber darted to the other side of the room, thrusting a chair in Connie's way. Unfortunately it fell directly in Angus's path. He tripped over it and spun over to the far side of the room, crashing into the venetian blinds. Magda rushed over to help him. Gil calmly started in on another danish.

"Dear Susan Hayward," read Amber from the note. "Why don't you cry tomorrow and keep drinking today? You'll be dead from booze before I get a chance to put a bullet through your skull anyway."

"That's evidence!" howled Connie, vaulting over the chair as Amber scrambled away from her.

"Evidence that you've lost it," said Amber, coolly whipping out her lighter and setting fire to the note.

Connie jumped on Amber and they fell to the floor, clawing and hissing at each other like two cats battling over a plate of Fancy Feast. Angus was hopelessly entangled in the venetian blinds, the flailing of his left hand causing them to rise and fall with an ear-shattering bang. Sophie was on all fours, searching for her lost upper plate. And Gil was calmly finishing off his fourth cherry cheese danish.

That's when the attendants arrived.

I've really lost it this time, thought Connie, her head pressed against the pillow to absorb the bitter tears that coursed down her cheek. How could I let that little pothead get under my skin? Why couldn't I realize she's no threat to me and just walk away?

And yet, hadn't it always been thus? Back as far as Newark, Connie had always gone on the defensive when she felt threatened. It had started with her mother Rose and the arguments they had had over Connie's going into show business. Connie always won those fights, but, deep down, she never got over the fear that someday it would be Rose's turn.

The fights had continued with Morty, with her assistant Erika and, worst of all, with Jimmy Perls, her arranger who had become her husband in the late seventies. Studio technicians still talked about the five-hour running battle they had over Connie's conviction that "Send in the Clowns" should be done to a bossa nova beat.

"Why do I always have to fight for my vision," she complained bitterly.

"Maybe because you're not secure enough in it to accept other people's input," shot back Jimmy.

Connie had always insisted "it's my way or the highway," so it should have come as no surprise when, in the midst of a bitter argument on the way to their beach house in 1985, Jimmy pulled the car over to the side of the road and got out. Despite her pleas, he kept on walking down Pacific Coast Highway until he reached a motel. He checked in and had his clothes delivered the next morning. Five days later he was working for Tina Turner.

The breakup of her seven-year marriage only confirmed Connie's worst fears. There was no man, no person, who could ever fully understand her drive for perfection. She would have to fight for it for the rest of her life.

And this is where her fighting had led to: a tear-stained pillow at a glitzy celebrity rehab center.

Drying her eyes, Connie grabbed some change off the nightstand and headed to the pay phone. Maybe there was one more chance.

Dialing 411, she waited impatiently for the operator.

"This is Terry, what city?" said a bored voice.

"Palm Springs," replied Connie. "I'd like the number for an orphanage called Kids for Christ."

She had tried booze; she had tried rehab. She might as well try religion.

"Let's face it," said Amber, drawing a last drag on her Marlboro Light, "I've blown the Oscar out my ass."

"Do you really think so?" asked Ted Gavin. They were sitting in the solarium of the clinic where they'd been talking for the past hour.

"After what I did on the MTV Awards? And that stuff with my mother?" Amber stubbed out her cigarette and made the kind of face Shirley Temple had fifty years ago when confronted by a plate of spinach. "RuPaul's got a better shot at Best Actress this year than I do."

"Don't be so sure," said Ted. "I sense a lot of sympathy out there for you."

"You do?" said Amber.

"Oh yes. The letters we got on the photo spread we ran of you at the Music Hall? More than half of them took your side."

"Who's writing these letters?" asked Amber, mildly intrigued.

"Patti-Sue," answered Ted.

"Who the hell is Patti-Sue?"

Ted briefly explained his theory of Patti-Sue, the Texas checkout clerk who was the archetypal *Personality* reader. By the end of it, Amber was giggling helplessly.

"Well," she drawled, "I might be a big deal at the ole Piggly-Wiggly, but I don't think the Academy voters shop there. They're never going to think of me the way Patti-Sue does."

"They might, if you'd just open up and tell me your story," said Ted, going for the jugular.

"It's such a long story," sighed Amber. "And besides, why do it to win the Academy Award? I don't even have anybody to go with. Billy won't talk to me since I puked on him on television."

"I'd go with you," murmured Ted, who had noticed the supple curve of Amber's breasts beneath her tight-fitting overalls.

Amber sighed again and stared at the floor. When she looked up, Ted noticed that there were tears in her eyes. "I had a very difficult childhood," she said softly.

28

Colin grimaced as he lowered himself onto the stool of the coffee shop in the Shangri-La Motel. It had been over a week since he had been arrested for lewd conduct and he had spent the intervening days dead drunk. He had gone into seclusion after leaving the police station, trying only to contact Karen and TriStar by phone. Neither of the calls had been returned, so he repaired to the mini-fridge in his room, draining the miniature bottles of vodka, scotch, bourbon and Grand Marnier. He then ordered a pint of Smirnoff vodka from room service. A bottle of that and a plate of watery scrambled eggs had been his diet for the past eight days. Fearful for his career, bereft and horny over the presumed loss of Karen, he had been giving a fair approximation of Nicolas Cage's performance in *Leaving Las Vegas*. At his lowest point he had attempted masturbating to Martha Stewart while she refinished a pair of shutters on her cable show.

He had thought of calling Fiona, but held off doing so, secretly hoping she might have pity on him and call herself. But why should she after that ugly scene at the Davises' party? Another bridge burned.

Peering into the mirror this morning with bloodshot eyes, Colin had been shocked by his appearance. He hadn't bathed in three days and the film that had begun to form on his body resembled nothing less than soap scum. His scraggly beard only furthered the impression that he was not Richard Burton or Peter O'Toole gone on a glorious bender, but a pathetic skid row bum who held the door open for customers at the 7-Eleven in hopes of a tip. He promptly emptied the vodka bottle down the toilet, showered, shaved and dressed for breakfast. Mercifully he hid his eyes behind a pair of Italian sunglasses.

Sipping on his coffee, he opened the trades. This is what you're supposed to do when you're waiting for the phone to ring out here, he told himself. His bloodshot eyes fell upon the headline of a front-page story in the *Hollywood Reporter*:

MEL GIBSON TO STAR IN AND DIRECT *MACBETH*

FOR MARATHON PICTURES IN MAY

OSCAR NOMINEE KAREN KROLL TO BE HIS LADY

Colin's hand shook so badly that hot coffee splattered all over the newspaper. Good Christ! That bitch had gone behind his back and signed for a rival production of the very film he was supposed to be making! He dropped the coffee cup, cracking it in half.

"Had a little accident?" said the attractive young waitress behind the counter.

"Just something I read in the paper," stammered Colin. "It upset me."

"You're acting like it was your obituary," she joked, picking up the broken china and mopping up the coffee.

"Not quite," said Colin. "I'm not dead yet. Just mortally wounded."

"You want to read something wild," continued the waitress, "you ought to read this." She waved a copy of the *National*

Enquirer that she had been carrying under her arm. "Stuff you wouldn't believe."

Colin caught sight of a headline that read, OSCAR NOMINEE FIONA COVINGTON IN LESBIAN LOVE NEST. He gasped and grabbed the paper from the young woman.

"Big story about that English actress, Fiona Covington, making love on the beach with another woman," said the waitress. "Right here in Santa Monica."

"You don't say," mumbled Colin as his eyeballs were seared by picture after picture of Fiona hugging and kissing Maria Caldone.

"Seems like her husband split so she decided to switch teams," giggled the waitress. Colin's hand shook wildly as he tried to flip the pages of the tabloid. He needed a drink so badly right now he would have gladly tried to suck vodka from a potato.

The waitress leaned over and assumed a confidential tone. "And another thing. The husband's supposed to be staying here. Only room service tells me he just sits in his room and drinks vodka all day. Guess he's pissed that someone else is sampling the home cooking."

Colin rose on legs as wobbly as the reputation of the Royal Family. "Thanks for the gossip," he said as he staggered to the door. If he hurried he could be drunk again by noon.

Lori stared at the copy of the *National Enquirer* that sat on her coffee table. She had dropped a twelve-dollar bottle of imported olive oil when she saw the tabloid in the supermarket. Since then, she had looked at it more than forty times, first in shock, then in anger, finally in resignation. Maria was having an affair with Fiona Covington. Incredible! It was to spite her; it had to be. Maria was so passionate, so primitive. She probably thought that if she went with another nominee, Lori would come running back to her. Didn't she know that would happen anyway? If only she could wait until the goddamned Oscars were over with.

Lori picked up the remote and flicked on the television, desperate for something to divert her. Terri Murphy's vacuous face filled the screen. Ugh! *Hard Copy*. The worst.

"Some shocking developments," hyperventilated the blond anchor, "about the escort of a superstar."

Lori sat up in shock as a picture of her and Claudio at the premiere of *Foreign Accents* came on the screen.

"It was just a few weeks ago that all Hollywood was wondering about the identity of the hunky Brazilian who accompanied Oscar nominee Lori Seefer to the Westwood premiere of *Foreign Accents*," continued Murphy breathlessly. "He goes by the name of Claudio Farenconi, but *Hard Copy* has learned that's not his only name. Claudio, it seems, has another life. One night he's on the arm of a star. Next night he's on all fours."

The image on the television screen suddenly became grainy and flesh-colored. The camera pulled back to reveal Claudio's face as he moaned and threw his head back in abandon. Pulling back further, it became painfully clear, despite digitalized computer graphics to mask the objectionable parts, that Claudio was on his hands and knees, completely nude, with another man, also nude, right behind him. Claudio was getting buttfucked on national television!

Lori shrieked in terror as Terri Murphy chattered on. "In this scene from a popular gay porno video entitled *Butthole Banquet*, Claudio assumes a few positions we doubt he's ever struck for Lori Seefer. And, for his silver screen debut, Claudio has taken a new name. Viewers of *Butthole Banquet* may recognize Claudio by his nom de porn, Brad Bottoms."

"No! No! No!" screamed Lori. But Terri Murphy kept right on going. "We asked Claudio what it's like going out with a movie star," she said.

A close-up of Claudio's face filled the screen as he moaned feverishly, "It's hard. Oh God, it's so hard."

"And what would he do if Lori won the Oscar this year?"

"I want to sit on it all night long," groaned Claudio, beads of sweat rolling down his face.

"And finally," chirped the blond scandal hound, "what would he say if Lori asked him to marry her?"

"Mount me like a dog and don't stop until I collapse," panted Claudio in the throes of passion.

"This isn't happening!" wailed Lori. "This isn't happening!" But it was, and Terri Murphy seemed all the better for it. With a smile that oozed insincerity, she leaned forward and looked directly into the camera.

"Lori, if you're watching, you might want to check out *Butthole Banquet* for yourself. It's available, in a plain brown wrapper, from All-Male Fetish and Kink Video for only forty-nine-ninety-five. We can guarantee you'll like Claudio's work. Why, right on the box, no less an authority than *Gay Male Video News* says, "Brad Bottoms gives an unforgettable performance as the Holland Tunnel.""

"It's all a ghastly mistake," said Melissa, frantically juggling the receiver from ear to ear. "I'll have it under control by tomorrow morning."

"A mistake?!" howled Lori at the other end of the line.

"You've been sending me out in public with a gay porno star. I'm ruined! I'm a laughingstock!"

"People survive scandals all the time," insisted Melissa. "Look at Rob Lowe and Hugh Grant."

"They weren't dating the star of *Butthole Banquet*," shot back Lori.

"You're a victim," said Melissa. "You've been cruelly deceived in your first major love affair, and the public will rally to your side."

"Oh yeah?" replied Lori. "What public? The public that's waiting for the comeback of the Village People?"

"The victim angle will work, Lori. You have your interview with Barbara Walters in five days and you can put it out then. It's the perfect opportunity for you to break into tears. The Jewish mother in Barbara will drive every heterosexual in America faklemt."

"And what about Claudio?" said Lori angrily. "Did he get a raise for this?"

"I dismissed him not more than an hour ago. His desk is being cleaned out as we speak."

"Why are you cleaning out his desk?"

"Unfortunately he left a number of oversized dildos in his wake."

"Jesus Christ, Melissa," whined Lori. "Is this how you prove I'm straight? By setting me up with the biggest fag since Liberace?"

"Don't worry, pet, don't worry," soothed Melissa. "We can use spin control to make this work for you. Just remember, you're a victim, you've been wounded. Please, believe me."

Despite her closed door, Melissa's voice carried to the outside hallway. It sounded frantic and fearful and, to Phillip Castleman, utterly delicious. Lori was raking Melissa over the coals and Phillip was getting to listen to her flesh melt. Right now he felt like Scarlett O'Hara and Bette Davis with a dash of Sharon Stone thrown in for good measure. He popped one of Polly's Pralines into his mouth, savoring the taste of the brown sugar as it melted on his tongue, and walked into his boss's office.

"Melissa?" he inquired.

"What is it?" she huffed in exasperation.

"There was a phone call while you were on the line."

"Who was it?"

"Mel Gibson's agent. He said Mel decided to pass on your offer of representation. Even at the reduced rate."

"Out! Now!"

The green room for *The Tonight Show with Jay Leno* was surprisingly small. Just five under-upholstered chairs, two tables and a large television on which the show was broadcast during its taping. When big stars arrived with their entourages the door was left open and the various agents, managers and make-up people spilled out into the hallway.

I've been in lavvies bigger than this, thought Fiona to herself as she looked around.

She'd rarely been in a jam as tight as this, however. Having agreed to appear on the show weeks earlier, as a boost for her chances of winning the Oscar, Fiona's first impulse was to cancel her appearance once the *Enquirer* story broke. Lionel was certainly in favor of it.

"Back out immediately," he counseled. "Tell them you've come down with something. Then we'll put out a statement to refute the story in that unspeakable rag."

But Maria had an entirely different take on the situation.

"Why would you deny something that is true?" she asked. "Our love is a fact, not a scandal. Stand up for who you are."

Fiona was no gay liberationist—she was, in fact, not entirely certain how gay she really was—but the directness and simplicity of Maria's approach appealed to her. She'd played the game Lionel's way for weeks now and wound up going directly to jail time after time. Maybe there was something, peace of mind, perhaps, to be gained from simple honesty.

It was easy to think that way cuddling naked in front of the fireplace while watching a Martina Navratilova tennis instruction tape, as Fiona and Maria had done last night. It was harder to hang on to while you sat in a deserted green room waiting to face an audience of millions of gossip-hungry viewers. Maria had wanted to come with her, but Fiona felt it would only create more scandal and begged her to remain at her parents' home where she was now living. With Lionel, she was more succinct.

"Your instincts are such that, had you been a young boy at the time, you would have doubtless canceled your swimming lesson to book passage on the *Titanic*. I shall fight this battle alone."

Fiona stared at the television in the green room. Jay Leno was talking to a twelve-year-old boy from Fresno who had taught his dog to sing "Dixie" by belching. The vagaries of American chat TV never failed to amaze Fiona.

"Miss Covington?" It was a page.

"Yes," replied Fiona.

"Would you come with me? You're on next."

Fiona popped a Tic-Tac for courage. Following the young man, she left the room, stepping over the maze of cables and through the army of crew members who nightly delivered Jay

Leno into the homes of American viewers. Soon I shall pulse through these cables and enter those humble lives, thought Fiona. Let my journey be a peaceful one.

Standing behind the curtains, Fiona heard Jay Leno say, "Please welcome a nominee for the Best Actress Oscar, Miss Fiona Covington." The curtains parted and Fiona stepped through them to the accompaniment of the band's intro music. She thought she heard a vague rumbling in the audience as the applause died down and she seated herself next to Jay Leno.

"Nice to have you on the show," he said with a huge grin.

"Nice of you to ask me," replied Fiona, who was amazed at the size of the comic's chin in real life. Lantern-jawed was inadequate, only bucket-jawed could truly describe him, she decided.

"Now tell me about this Oscar thing," continued Leno. "I mean, are you excited? Do you think you'll win? Do you have your dress picked out? Are your folks coming over for the show?"

"Yes, no, maybe and I forget the question," quipped Fiona. There was a burst of laughter from the audience as well as Jay Leno. Fiona began to feel more comfortable.

"So now, tell me," smiled Leno, "how are you finding America?"

"With a compass and a guide book, the same way Columbus did," joked Fiona.

"Okay," said the host, picking up a pencil and making a mark on a pad of paper. "That's one for you." Fiona had the odd sensation of being in a tennis match, constantly required to lob the ball back over the net. She thought of Wimbledon and the many gloriously sunny spring and summer days she'd spent there watching tournament matches. Sitting here bantering with Jay Leno she could almost feel the clay courts beneath her feet. Better that, she decided, than feet of clay or, worse yet, a roman à clef. She shuddered at the thought.

"You like it here?" Leno asked of her.

"Well of course. It's a land of new experiences."

"Ah ha," he grinned, "new experiences. What could that mean?" A knowing groan came forth from the audience. Fiona blushed as the comic grinned amiably.

She picked up the pencil and made a mark on the pad. "Now we're even," she smiled.

"What do you mean?" asked Leno, feigning innocence.

"You know perfectly well what I mean," replied Fiona in a voice that verged on prim. "I'm sure you read the tabloids at the market like everyone else in America."

A hush fell over the audience. Jay Leno suddenly looked a good deal more serious. "I just wondered what you meant by new experiences," he explained. "It wasn't meant to be personal."

"But alas, it always is personal, isn't it?" said Fiona with the mock earnestness that had endeared her to Anglophiles across America. "I've had a new experience in my personal life, and now suddenly the entire country is peering into my bedroom window." There was a scattering of applause in the audience.

"Let's talk about your movie," said Leno.

"Let's not," said Fiona, feeling that the ball was in her court. "Everyone seems to want to know of my new experience, so let's have at it."

"Well, um, without getting too nosy," stammered Leno, "I mean, what we've been reading, is this a new experience for you?"

"Absolutely."

"And you're blaming it on America?" A laugh erupted from the audience.

"Not blaming," smiled Fiona. "I simply mean that a new environment can lead to new experiences."

"So you feel being here has given you a certain, um, freedom?"

"Most assuredly," said Fiona, seeing an opportunity to slam one over the net and right down the center of the court. "I figured that if you Americans could put a woman on the Supreme Court, you could surely put one on me."

A huge whoop went up from the audience, while Jay Leno broke into laughter. Fiona was feeling on top of her game.

"So you're really enjoying this, huh?" chuckled Leno. "I mean it's a big change and all."

"I didn't say I've changed," said Fiona modestly. "I said I've had a new experience. One swallow doesn't make a spring."

"You swallowed?" replied Leno in mock amazement. Another whoop from the audience. Clearly he had returned her volley.

"Now you're getting quite personal," observed Fiona tartly.

"Well, look," shrugged the host, "let me ask the question everybody wants to ask you. Are you a lesbian?"

"Are you my only alternative?" replied Fiona. There were cheers, mixed with howls of laughter, from the audience.

Game, set, match.

Lori felt numb as she watched the *Tonight Show*. She hadn't gotten this much bad news from television since the day they read the verdict at the Simpson trial. First her attempt at appearing straight had been revealed as a pathetic masquerade with a sleazy porno star. And now this! Fiona Covington was coming out on national television and people were cheering her! The very thing she had been petrified of, and this English-woman was becoming a heroine for it.

Lori reached for the remote control and switched channels. She was desperate for something, anything, even an infomercial, to distract her. David Letterman's face filled the screen. "I think it's great what you've done," he said. "People are really proud of you."

"Thanks, Dave," said Ellen DeGeneres as the cameraman panned over to her. "I was just trying to be myself."

Lori hit the off button instantly.

29

"**T**his is the trashiest thing I've read in ages," said Fatima Bulox, waving the first draft of Ted's interview with Amber Lyons. "I simply adore it."

"Thank you, Fatima," replied Ted. He had been certain there was some crisis when Fatima summoned him to her office. What a pleasure to be wrong for once.

"It's so juicy," gushed the Middle Eastern editor. "Born out of wedlock in a trailer park, a lush for a mother, molested by her stepfathers. She gets an abortion at sixteen, then leaves a job at The Gap to come to Hollywood. It's really got that white trash thing. It reminds me of those fabulous songs Cher used to sing in the seventies. You know, 'Gypsies, Tramps and Thieves,' 'You Better Sit Down Kids,' celebrations of the banality of the American dream. Ah, how we boogied in the shadow of the mosque to those tunes."

"I don't know that it's that profound," blushed Ted.

"And the things you got her to say," continued Fatima. " 'I blew the Oscar out my ass,' 'I started smoking pot to relieve my hemorrhoids.' Who says they don't write great dialogue anymore? I'm telling you, Ted, New York is going to turn this into a cover. Just on this kid alone."

"What about the other actresses?"

"Their stories are out there already."

"Even Fiona Covington's lesbianism?"

"Screw that stale bowl of English porridge. She saves her best stuff for Jay Leno. No, this is what our readers want. She sins and then she asks for forgiveness. Works every time. There's just one thing more we need."

"What's that?"

"I want some more stuff on her estrangement from her mother. Does she see them reuniting in the future? Can they be friends? All that Meg Ryan/Demi Moore, famous daughter on the outs with mom crap. Think you can get it for me?"

"I know I can," said Ted, smiling confidently. "Amber's out of rehab and I happen to be meeting her for lunch today."

"And is this business?" asked Fatima, eyeing him shrewdly.

"Over the course of doing this piece, we've become quite close. Amber has even asked me to accompany her to the Oscars," said Ted proudly.

"Are you fucking for a story?" blazed Fatima, secretly jealous that Ted had gotten such an invitation while she was condemned to a Beverly Hills Oscar party complete with clam dip and Doritos.

"No," said Ted, rising from his chair and heading to the door. "I'm fucking for pleasure. The story is just business."

Actually Ted wasn't fucking Amber, not yet anyway. But that would come in time—hopefully before he did—and what had happened so far had, he was convinced, radically altered the trajectory of his once not-so-glorious life. Amber had talked to him for four hours at Betty Ford, pouring out the details of her squalid upbringing. She left out nothing: her teenage pregnancy, her drug-taking, even the fact that she used to slip shards of jagged glass into the sweaters she folded at The Gap. At one point, moved as deeply as he'd been when Ali MacGraw died in

Love Story, Ted reached out and cradled Amber in his arms. She wept into his chest, her tears flowing through his Brooks Brothers shirt and soaking the chest hair beneath it. Unbuttoning the shirt to dry his pectorals with a floral potholder, Ted looked over to Amber and realized he was falling in love with her.

This infatuation with an interview subject had happened many times before, with Heather Locklear, Courtney Cox and Rachel Ward, to name just three. The difference this time was that Amber seemed to have a similar interest in Ted. Driving back to Los Angeles, they had fallen into a shared silence, her head on his shoulder. She invited him into her condominium and they talked late into the night over a bottle of chardonnay that Shana had inadvertently left behind. There was no sex, but before he left Amber showed Ted how to make S'Mores. He dipped his tongue in Bosco, she dipped hers in Marshmallow Fluff and then they French-kissed until the two flavors combined in their mouths.

Small wonder then that Ted was humming the ultraromantic "Lara's Theme" from *Dr. Zhivago* as he sped down Sunset Boulevard to Chin Chin, the open-air Chinese restaurant where he was to meet Amber. He had always dreamed of being in love with a movie star, becoming a player, and now it seemed to be within his reach. Amber had asked to see his script, *Heavy Artillery*, and, along with a dozen condoms, Ted had thrown a copy of it on his dashboard. If they were to have an affair, and she were to star in his script . . .

I'll be the most powerful writer in Hollywood, thought Ted, blissfully unaware that such a title would place him two or three notches below David Geffen's dry cleaner in the hierarchy of Hollywood's power elite.

Ted turned into the parking lot of Chin Chin and gave the

keys to his car over to the valet parker. Located in a densely populated area of the Sunset Strip, the restaurant was a trendy spot favored by young agents, development people and hookers who had gone freelance now that Heidi Fleiss was out of business. They all chatted incessantly on portable phones during lunch, a phenomenon that made a meal at Chin Chin seem like being at a company picnic for telephone operators.

"Ted," cried Amber as she spotted him making his way through the thicket of tables that dotted the sidewalk.

"Sorry I'm late," he said as he reached her table.

"It's good to see you again," she smiled, the sun playing against her red hair. Then she leaned over and kissed him.

Oh my God, thought Ted, I'm being kissed in public by a movie star. He looked around to see if anybody had noticed. A young female agent, with her de rigueur crimped hair and Armani suit, was looking up from her Italian *Vogue* with an expression on her face that lay somewhere between mild curiosity and smelling cauliflower. It wasn't much, but it was enough for Ted. Eat your heart out, bitch, he thought joyously.

"Did you have a good morning?" asked Amber.

"Yeah," smiled Ted, "actually it was pretty good. How about you?"

"Oh," sighed Amber, "I lost a role at Disney. I was going to be one of the voices in an animated version of *To Kill a Mockingbird*. My agent said they don't want to touch me after what happened at the MTV Awards. But you know something? That's to be expected. All part of my growth curve. Anyway, it probably wasn't much of a part."

"Which one was it?" he inquired.

"I think the Tippi Hedren role," she murmured, flinging her hair over her shoulders.

Rather than correcting her obvious error, Ted moved on to

something much closer to his heart. "I brought my script," he said, passing it over the table to her.

"Oh great," she said, flipping through it. "Does it have a good role for me?"

"Well actually, it was written for John Candy. But I can fix that in the rewrite."

"Natch," replied Amber. "Anyway, he and I are basically the same type. You know, born in the same century and all that." Amber giggled and Ted joined in.

"Listen," he protested, "it's an action comedy. A perfect change of pace for you."

"You're right about that. Ever since *As if . . . Chillin'*, all I seem to get are these heavy, heavy dramatic roles. Like I'm, ugh, Meryl Streep or something. This could be just the thing for me."

"I think you'll like it," said Ted confidently.

"You know I have my own production company," boasted Amber.

"I know," replied Ted. "Lyons' Den."

"And we're bankrolled by Marathon Pictures. I could buy this for a couple hundred thousand out of my housekeeping fund and they'd have to pick up the tab for it."

"How did you get a deal at Marathon?" asked Ted, his head swimming at the big money that seemed to be just within his grasp.

"I ran into Jeffrey Klein at the Farmer's Market the day after *As if . . . Chillin'* opened," Amber said. "He signed me up at the beef jerky counter."

"Hey listen," jumped in Ted, "I just have to ask you a few more questions for my story. And by the way, my editor thinks it may be a cover."

"Cool," said Amber. "What do you want to ask me?"

"It's about your mother."

"Oh Ted," she groaned, "it's so hard for me to go there. I shared all that with you at the clinic."

"It's just a few things," he reassured her. "I have to turn the piece in tonight."

"Oh all right, fire away."

"All I need to know," said Ted, "is whether or not you see yourself and your mother reuniting in the future. Or is this split for good?"

"How can I say?" mused Amber. "I'm not even sure where she is right now."

"Have you thought of looking for her?" asked Ted gently.

"I suppose that's a pretty good idea. Maybe when the Oscars are . . ."

There was a sudden screech of brakes and a scream from the street. "Oh my God," cried Amber, springing to her feet.

A young woman had been sideswiped by a Jeep that was now barreling down Sunset, away from the site of the accident. "Help me! Help me!" cried the woman.

Amber rushed over to her and sat her gently down on the curbside. Pushing her head between her legs, she protectively ran her hands up and down the woman's body, looking for injuries.

"It's gonna be all right," she said, grabbing a portable phone from one of the hookers and punching in 911. "Get an ambulance to Chin Chin on Sunset at once," she barked.

"Hey," protested the hooker, "I was on a business call."

Amber threw the phone back at her and returned to the distressed young woman. "We'll have you at the hospital in no time," she told her.

"Is she okay?" asked Ted, coming over to the curb.

"Seems it," replied Amber. "But I want to go to the hospital with her to be sure."

"That's so nice of you," said Ted. "There's just one thing. I have to get back to the office, and I need to finish asking you about your mother."

"Ted," said Amber solemnly, "at a time like this?"

Shamefaced, Ted returned to the table as Amber helped the woman into the ambulance that had just arrived.

"I've brought you a Bloody," said Lars as he handed Karen a tumbler filled with tomato juice and vodka.

"Thanks, doll," she replied, taking a sip and putting the drink next to her portable phone on the poolside table. "I'm still waiting for that little bitch I pay three thousand a month to for publicity to call me back."

Karen had been feeling oddly restless and empty for the past week or so. She was finished with Colin, and Johnny hadn't tried to reach her. Without a man in her life to distract her, she had begun to dwell on her chances of winning the Oscar. The ebb and flow of public opinion—as ceaseless as the tides, as mysterious as the popularity of Mariah Carey—was of great concern to her. In George Axelrod's cult classic, *Lord Love a Duck*, the heroine, Tuesday Weld, kept saying "Everybody has got to love me." Karen knew the feeling.

The phone rang and she snatched it up eagerly.

"Hi Karen," said Susan Sakowitz, feigning brightness.

"What have you got to tell me?"

"Well, the *Today Show* will take you next Tuesday if you'll fly to New York. Katie Couric will do the interview."

"I can't be interviewed by Katie Couric," bristled Karen. "With those fucking Peter Pan collars and that smile she'll make me look like a slut."

"She's the one who wants to do it," replied Susan, who couldn't help thinking that even if she were stark naked in a room with twenty sailors and a tequila bottle Katie Couric could make Karen look like a slut.

"I don't come off well with women. What about Jay Leno?"

"He's booked until after the balloting for the Awards is over."

"I saw Fiona Covington on there the other night," said Karen testily.

"She came out as a lesbian," reminded Susan.

"So what?" snapped Karen. "I'll come out as a Republican. In Hollywood that's worse."

"Leno's booked," repeated Susan. "I can see about Letterman if you'll go to New York."

"What about Ted Koppel?"

"That's politics."

"And what do you think the Oscars are about? Art?" demanded Karen.

"Let me see if Leno has a cancellation," said Susan, eager to get off the line.

"I'm free Thursday."

"He's got Madonna booked that night."

"Tell him she's busy taking an acting lesson." Karen clicked off the phone, softly muttering "Shit."

"You really want that Oscar, don't you?" said Lars.

"Just watch me," replied Karen evenly. "Now be a pet and put some more vodka in this."

Lars headed to the kitchen while Karen stared sullenly at the jacaranda trees that bordered her property. Her moodiness over the Oscar race was threatening to ruin what had started out as a perfectly lovely day with Lars. She had invited him over for brunch and gossip, a ritual they'd indulged in since their days on the set of *Jacuzzi Madness*. She always told Lars that, like the song said, they were sisters who were "doing it for themselves." But his amusing patter about who was sleeping with who and which one had just checked into rehab couldn't divert Karen from the emptiness she felt closing in on her. It was an emotion she'd known for years, one she held at bay with sex and ambition. But now the Oscar had brought her face-to-face with it. The truth was, Karen didn't just expect the Oscar to change her life; she wanted it to fill it, make it whole.

Had Karen been literate she would have recognized herself as the heroine of a Joan Didion novel: vain, shallow, unfulfilled and heading toward disaster. Alas, she hadn't picked up a book since finishing *The Sensuous Woman* by "J" in junior high, and so had to settle for comparing herself to the leading lady in a Joan Collins miniseries.

The phone rang and Karen picked it up. "Hello?"

"Karen, dear, it's me."

"Ida, I don't have time for you now," snapped Karen.

"I just wanted to tell you about the fifteenth-year class re-union. It would mean so much to the faculty and alumni of Semi-nole State if you would come down here and make a speech."

"I can't," begged Karen. "I'm too busy."

"It's the least you can do," chided Mrs. Gunkndiferson, "after all I've done for you."

"What you did for me is in the past," retorted Karen. "Now stop calling me!" She slammed the phone down on the table.

Lighting a cigarette, then stubbing it out just as quickly, Karen began to sob. The sobs came in large, wailing gulps, tears running down her cheeks until she felt the sudden chill of an ice-cold Bloody Mary pressed against her backbone.

"Come, come, darling," said Lars, putting his arm around her, "this will never do."

"Oh Lars," she moaned, "sometimes I think it's all too much. I'd just like to quit and move to a private island."

"You're tense," he said softly. "Anyone would be."

"It's more than that," said Karen, drying her eyes with a cocktail napkin. "I feel so empty inside."

"Oh, darling," laughed Lars, "we all feel that. Vivien Leigh syndrome."

"But I've always felt it," insisted Karen.

"Always?"

"Well, ever since sophomore year at Seminole State. That's when I decided to become an actress."

"And you think running away would solve your problems?" asked Lars.

"It seems like I have to fight for everything," moaned Karen, "my career, my roles, the Oscar. I want everything so badly, but nothing comes easy. Sometimes I do think I'd be happier if I just gave up."

"That's not you, darling," said Lars. "You couldn't just walk away from all this. What would happen to all your drive? You're the Energizer Bunny of movie stars."

"I wish," whimpered Karen. "The truth is I get so tired of the struggle. I really do think of just walking away from it." A fresh batch of tears began to roll down her cheeks, plunking into her Bloody Mary and rendering it undrinkable.

"Listen to me," said Lars, who was now growing concerned. "Life is full of choices. We can be happy, or we can be sad. We can work hard and play when the day is over, or we can sit on the sidelines and watch life pass us by. And, most important of all, we can either be Mary Richards, or we can be Rhoda Morgenstern."

"What are you trying to tell me, Lars?" asked Karen, whose sorrow had now been replaced by befuddlement.

"I'm telling you that you're not Rhoda Morgenstern and you never will be," said Lars, seizing Karen by her shoulders. "Now get out in the middle of the street, do a turn and throw your fucking hat in the air!"

30

The sunlight streamed through the stained-glass windows of the First Lutheran Church of Christ in Palm Springs, highlighting the lilies of the valley that stood in vases on the altar of the white clapboard building. A children's choir sang "Amazing Grace" as the minister dismissed his humble congregation. They rose in pairs and made their way down the aisle and out into the desert heat of Palm Springs.

Jesus Christ, thought Connie, I haven't even been in a church since Steve McQueen's funeral.

Released from Betty Ford yesterday, Connie was walking out with Eric Collins at her side. The other churchgoers had been discreet during the service, but now it was over and all bets were off. A large woman in her fifties, clad in a yellow muumuu and smelling distinctly of chocolate chip cookies and Elizabeth Taylor's White Diamonds, approached Connie and Eric.

"Miss Travatano?"

"Yes," replied Connie, forcing a smile.

"I just want you to know you're my favorite star," enthused the woman. "I've loved you ever since I saw you in *Where Am I Now That I Need Me?* I think you should have gotten the Oscar for it."

"That's very kind of you."

"I hope you win this year," the woman continued. "For *Garlic and Emeralds*."

"Thanks," said Connie. "By the way, it's called *Tomatoes and Diamonds*."

"We're having a bake sale behind the rectory," said the woman. "Would you like to come by? Marge Lufenstaffer has made her famous Hawaiian coconut and grape jelly fudge balls."

"Thanks," grimaced Connie, "but I actually prefer Baked Alaska."

"Well all right then," trilled the woman. "May the Lord bless you on Oscar night." She sauntered away happily, leaving Connie and Eric to themselves.

"I hope that wasn't too hard on you," said Eric, leading her to his car.

"I'm never at my best with my public," shrugged Connie. "I'm always afraid they want a piece of me."

"Maybe they just want to enjoy you," offered Eric, opening the passenger-side front door of his five-year-old Honda Civic. Connie slid in and he closed the door. She couldn't help thinking that, despite all evidence to the contrary, Eric was just like her fans. He too wanted something from her, something she was too defensive or possessive to give up. These thoughts evaporated as she gazed out the front window and noticed the taut symmetry of his Irish ass as he rounded the car.

"Where are we going?" she asked as he got into the driver's seat.

"Home for Sunday dinner," he grinned.

"What's on the menu?"

"Pot roast, duchess potatoes and a broccoli soufflé. And save room for dessert. Mom makes a mean Baked Alaska."

"**S**usan Hayward was a real sweetheart," said Mary Collins, her heart-shaped face framed by a pageboy of silver-white hair. While her children, Eric and Laura, cleared the table, Mary, a former stuntwoman, and Connie had been trading war stories about lives lived on a movie set.

"I did stunts for Susie in a picture called *White Witch Doctor* for Zanuck back in fifty-three," recalled Mary. "Bob Mitchum was her costar, and, as usual, all the ladies on the crew had their eye on him. But he really wanted Susie. She was happily married; couldn't have cared less. But I was still single then and crazy for Mitch. Susie knew it and decided to help me out.

"One night we all went down to the hotel bar for drinks. We were on location, with Carlsbad doubling for Kenya, if you can imagine that. Mitch was doing boilermakers like they were going out of style and coming on to Susie between rounds. She tells him to go up to his room and wait for her. Then she grabs me and says, 'Hey, Mary, go take my place with the great white hunter. He's so drunk he'll never know the difference with the lights off.' So I did, and the next morning Mitch is playing cock of the walk on the set, sure he's had his way with his leading lady. To the day he died I'll bet he thought he put her away."

"Mother!" cried Laura from the kitchen.

"My kids hate to think their old mom once had a life," laughed Mary.

"So how was Robert Mitchum?" asked Connie, joining in the laughter.

"Drunk, he was better than most men are sober," replied Mary, sipping on her coffee. "Of course that was before I met Paul and had the kids. Movies were just something I did when I was a wild young kid."

Connie couldn't help envying Mary's common sense and down-home wisdom. Maybe she'd been wrong about the little people all these years.

"Hey, Mom," said Eric, "I want to steal Connie for a walk around the neighborhood."

"You just want me to finish the dishes for you," grinned Mary. "Now get out of here, both of you."

They walked down the sunbaked street in front of Mary's house, quietly enjoying each other's company. But Connie, as usual, couldn't give up her hectoring ways.

"Why did you arrest me at Barneys?" she said suddenly.

"Because you stole something," Eric replied.

"So what?" Connie sniped back. "I've got enough money to buy everything in that store."

"Then go ahead and buy it. But don't steal it. That's a crime, and I make my living by trying to prevent crime."

He was so fucking virtuous! How could someone grow up in Los Angeles and remain so square?

"So how come you're not married?" she probed.

"Just haven't found the right woman yet," he replied evenly.

"I don't know what's holding you back. You're a nice-looking man."

"Well thanks," he grinned.

"Are you sure you're not gay?" She hated herself the second she said it.

"No I'm not," replied Eric. "But my sister Laura is. I'll set you up if you're interested."

Well I earned that one, she thought to herself grimly. She could either try to make amends or head back to Betty Ford and watch *60 Minutes* with Magda and Sophie.

"Listen," sighed Connie, "I know I'm on edge. I can't help

myself. The past few weeks have been hell for me. I've been drinking, making a fool of myself in public. I've even been getting notes from a stalker."

"That's serious," said Eric.

"Tell me about it. Whoever it is must be following me around. They seem to know everything I do."

"Where are these notes?"

"Right here," said Connie, reaching into her Chanel purse and handing them to Eric.

"Why don't I take them to headquarters when I go back to LA tomorrow," he said. "We've got a special unit assigned to stalkers." He put the letters in his shirt pocket. "Any idea who it could be?"

Connie shook her head. "Morty, my manager, and Erika, my assistant, are the only two people who know my life that well. She's my dearest friend and he's too busy farting to write a grocery list, much less a death threat."

"Let's see what I can do," offered Eric.

"Thank you," replied Connie, humbled at last.

Later they went down to the rec room of the tiny desert house with Mary and Laura and played Parcheesi. Connie squealed with delight as she rolled doubles and got to roll again. The image of Marie Antoinette playing at being a shepherdess on the lawn of Versailles flashed through her mind, but she dismissed it. Especially after she won the game.

"Connie, there's one favor I'd like to ask of you," said Mary as she folded up the Parcheesi board.

"Ask away," replied Connie, still glowing from her victory.

"Do you think you could sing a few bars of 'Where Am I Now That I Need Me?' It's always been my favorite song of yours."

That song again. It was like Sinatra with "My Way." The cornier they were, the more they wanted you to sing them.

"We can just go over to the piano in the corner," said Mary. "I don't even need the sheet music. Know the damn thing by heart."

Connie glanced over at Eric, who offered her a noncommittal look. She was on her own with this one. Oh, why the hell not? She liked Mary, even if she hated the song.

"Sure, Mary," she said. "Let's all stand around the piano and sing it." Like the Lennon Sisters, she almost added, but for once she caught herself in time.

Mary sat down at the keyboard while Connie, Eric and Laura gathered round. She played the opening bars as Connie began to sing:

> *In love it seems*
> *It's all unspoken,*
> *You whisper words,*
> *Your heart is broken*
> *And yet they say*
> *It's just that way*
> *From Mandalay to old Hoboken.*

Now Eric and Laura began to sing with her.

> *Tell me, where am I now that I need me?*
> *Why does your heart always bleed me?*
> *When will your love come and feed me?*
> *Tell me, where am I now that I need me?*

I've got to be out of my mind, thought Connie joyously. I'm staging a comeback in a rec room in Palm Springs.

31

Lori stood behind a large elm tree, gazing at the ramshackle house that lay beyond it. There was a strong wind tonight, and she shivered as it blew through the thin T-shirt she had thrown on in haste. Raising the tequila bottle to her lips, she took one final swig and threw it in the gutter.

A broken liquor bottle wouldn't cause a stir in Maria's old neighborhood, but the sight of a movie star trying to spy on her former lover surely would. Lori had been drinking behind the tree for over an hour; now that night had fallen, she knew what she must do.

She had been heartsick over Maria for two days now. The media coverage of her and Fiona had been relentless, each story driving yet another arrow into Lori's heart, which had begun to resemble a pincushion. Why had she listened to Melissa and cast off her lover to pretend she was straight? For the Oscar? What good was that without love? A bedroom with only one person in it, reflected Lori, was the loneliest place in the world.

And so she had grabbed her Chanel purse and a bottle of Cuervo Gold and headed to the home of Maria's parents in the rundown Echo Park area. The tequila had emboldened her, given her the courage she needed to apologize to Maria. And it had made her horny, letting her mind drift back to the fiery lovemaking they had shared. Now, after drinking behind the tree for an hour, her passion for Maria thundered through her like an electrical storm on a sultry summer evening.

Wobbling ever so slightly, Lori tiptoed over to the side of the house, sidling up to the window of Maria's bathroom. She quickly raised it and slipped into the room. Moving stealthily into the darkened bedroom, she saw the outline of a voluptuous figure lying in the bed.

"Maria, it's me," she said quickly. "Don't scream or be upset, please. I had to talk to you, and I knew you'd hang up if I phoned. Oh God, if you knew how I've missed you. These past few days have been the worst of my life. But they taught me something: I love you. I love you and I want to be with you again. Oh please, my darling, remember how hot it was?"

Moving to the edge of the bed, Lori kept talking, fearful that Maria would cut her off. "Remember the love we made? How we feasted on each other's flesh like wild beasts? Oh my love, please don't refuse me. I come to you a starving woman stumbling out of the desert of desire."

With that Lori pulled away the bedsheet and buried her head in her lover's honey pot. She licked and burrowed deep into the channel of lust, hungry for the nectar that lay therein.

A hand reached out and turned on the bedside lamp. Lori looked up to discover that her face was buried in Fiona Covington's crotch.

"I'm sorry to inform you that you're mowing the wrong lawn," Fiona said tartly.

Lori gasped and reared back. Just then Maria entered the room completely nude, her breasts covered with bean dip.

"What is this?" stammered Lori.

"We were about to have a Mexican dinner," replied Fiona,

gathering the sheets around her, "until you came in and started munching on the appetizers."

"Maria, I came to see you," said Lori urgently.

"Our love is a dead chihuahua," sneered Maria.

"How could you let another woman touch you?" begged Lori.

"How could you let a man touch you?" Maria shot back. "And how did you get into my house?"

"Like the Beatles," observed Fiona, "it seems she came in through the bathroom window."

"No one can ever love you the way I did," said Lori.

"You didn't love me," replied Maria. "You loved your career. So now you've got your career, and I've got a new lover."

"I don't care about my career," pleaded Lori. "I want you."

"But you can't have me, baby," said Maria softly. "Fiona's got me. We're going to have dinner and then she's going to read to me from Chauncey."

"Chaucer," volunteered Fiona.

"Please, Maria," said Lori, beginning to tremble.

"No, it's too late."

Lori burst into tears and fled the room. Maria struggled for a second, wondering if she had been too harsh. But when she heard the front door slam she turned back to Fiona.

"I daresay this is all becoming just a bit over-the-top for me," murmured Fiona.

"Amber, it's Ted."

"Oh hi."

"I called to see how you were doing."

"Fine. I just went with the girl to Cedars-Sinai to make sure she was all right. And she is."

"That's great. I'm sorry I couldn't come with you."

"Well, you said you had your story to finish."

"Yeah, duty calls. Anyway, I want you to know that I rewrote the piece and put in how you helped that girl today."

"Oh, Ted, please. That's embarrassing."

"No, I think it was very nice of you. And she's okay, huh?"

"Well, yes. Except for her insurance."

"What's the problem?"

"She didn't have any."

"Bummer."

"So I just told Cedars to send me the bill."

"Get out. Hey, I'm going to add that to the story."

"No, you can't. Please, it's like I'm bragging or something."

"Amber, don't you understand that right now the public thinks of you as some cheap little vixen? My piece can help change all that. It can even help you get the Oscar."

"I just don't want to come off as some little kiss-ass. That's not me at all."

"Don't worry. I know the real you, Amber. And I've gotten her down on paper."

"You're so sweet. I wonder what I did to get to meet you?"

There was a short buzz on the line.

"Was that you?"

"Yes, let me see who it is." Amber clicked the line. "Hello?"

"It's Tatianna."

"Oh, hey, hold on." Amber clicked the line again. "Ted?"

"Yeah?"

"I have a friend on the line. Can I call you back?"

"Sure. I'm at the office."

"Give me five minutes." Amber clicked the line again. "I'm back."

"So how'd it go?"

"Fabulous."

"I've been dying to talk to you. But I drove all the way out to Malibu to make sure no cops were following me."

"You're safe. Don't worry."

"So he bought it?"

"Hook, line and sinker. He's even putting the whole thing in the story, just like I told you he would."

"And Brianna?"

"Oh she's fine, just a bruise on the knee. I had the ambulance drop us off at Drai's. We had a couple of martinis, did some blow and then I took her home. She's soaking in a Vitabath and doing her nails as we speak."

"So the story's going to make you out to be a big hero?"

"The way he's talking, I'm Florence fucking Nightingale. And it's a cover."

"Cool."

"I can't thank you enough. I really think this story may help me cop the Oscar."

"Remember, if you win I get to use it as a dildo for a night."

"Deal. Listen, I gotta go. Putz-face is waiting for me to call him back."

"Why bother?"

"I gotta be cool till the story breaks. Besides, he thinks I want to star in a script he wrote."

"A script?"

"About a guy who goes to a fat farm. He wrote it for John Candy, so of course he thinks I'm dying to do it."

"As if."

"You should hear the dialogue. It could bring back silent movies."

"Wanna go to the Sky Bar tonight?"

"Sure. Pick me up?"

"At eleven."

"Great. Now let me go and kiss off Ernest Hemingway."

"Bye."

"Bye."

Amber clicked off the line. She heard a double click in response.

Which was not surprising since Ted, through the kind of accident the phone companies like to think can never happen, had been connected to the call for its duration.

My life is over, he thought calmly as he put down the phone. Ended by a druggie slut actress who uses phrases like "hook, line and sinker." The very kind of phrases I'll be using for the rest of my life as a writer of celebrity profiles for *Personality*. Unless, of course, I end my life. And why not? After all, my life is over.

He thought briefly of phoning the New York office and telling them he had some changes for the article on Amber and the other nominees that he had e-mailed less than an hour ago. But what would he tell them? That he had discovered Amber Lyons was a lying little witch when she duped him into thinking she was in love with him and wanted to buy his script? Not likely.

The phone rang. Ted looked at it grimly, each shrill ring piercing what precious little there was left of his soul, like Barbara Stanwyck in *Sorry, Wrong Number*. The rings continued, far past the point they should have. Does that bitch think I'm going to answer, thought Ted. Still they continued, ring, ring, ring. In a fury, he picked up a pile of books and papers on his desk and flung them at the phone. It crashed to the floor along with the other articles. The receiver fell free, and from it Ted heard Amber's sullen voice.

"Ted, Ted," she said, "are you there?"

Ted rushed over to the receiver and began to stomp on it, splintering the plastic that encased it into thick, jagged shards. Amber's voice disappeared under the repeated stomps of his Doc Martens.

The other phone on his desk began to ring. Damn that bitch! He'd show her. Ted grabbed the receiver.

"Go to hell!" he screamed.

"What?" said a frightened voice.

"Go to hell and suck the devil's cock!"

"Is Ted Gavin there?"

Ted's stomach lurched wildly. Clearly it wasn't Amber on the other end of the line.

"Who is this?" he asked weakly.

"Do I have the wrong number? I was trying to reach Ted Gavin."

"This is Ted Gavin," he sighed. "Who is this?"

"This is Ida Gunkndiferson, Karen Kroll's college drama teacher. You spoke to me last week about the article you're writing on Karen and the other Oscar nominees? Remember?"

"Oh gosh, Mrs. Gunkndiferson," fumbled Ted. "Sure I remember you. You caught me right in the middle of rehearsals for a play I'm doing. *The Devil's Disciple* by George Bernard Shaw." Ted winced at the feebleness of his excuse.

"You must be doing a version of it that I'm unfamiliar with," said Mrs. Gunkndiferson. "But no matter."

"What can I do for you?" asked Ted, relieved that the old lady was willing to let his bad manners pass.

"Well, Ted," began Mrs. Gunkndiferson, "I have something to tell you about Karen that might be of use to you in that article you're writing."

32

Ted careened up Laurel Canyon, his car hugging the winding canyon road as if it had been attached to the side of it with Velcro. He had driven this whiplash trail hundreds of times before, but never with such impatience and anxiety. His destiny, he felt, was lying at the top of it, on a deserted stretch of Mulholland Drive.

The roller coaster of life never ceased to amaze him. Just an hour ago he had been listening to Amber and Tatianna, convinced that all hope of a viable career in film was gone. Now he was racing to meet Karen Kroll, a blond sex goddess who could grant his every wish. He felt like a condemned man whose electric chair had morphed into a poolside chaise longue, complete with a sun umbrella and a tall, cool drink with a parasol floating in it.

He swerved onto Mulholland, heading past the mansions where Jack Nicholson and Warren Beatty and Annette Bening lived. Soon he might well be a neighbor, stopping over to borrow a cup of flour or compare a crabgrass remedy. Hey Jack, how are they hangin'? He shivered in an ecstasy of anticipation.

He braked quickly as he approached the lonely outlook, spotting Karen's silver Mercedes. She was leaning against it, wearing a tight black mini-dress and a pair of Ray-Bans. You had to hand it to her, she always knew how to dress.

"This is such a strange place to meet," said Ted, jumping out of his car and approaching her.

"Raise your hands," she ordered as she approached him.

He did so and Karen frisked him, checking his pockets and up and down his trouser legs.

"What is this," joked Ted, "*Mod Squad*?"

"You think I'm going to take a chance that you've got a tape recorder hidden somewhere?" she shot back.

"I told you over the phone," said Ted, dropping his arms, "this is just between you and me."

Karen retreated back to the side of her Mercedes. "Okay, what's the deal?"

"I don't want you to think of this as blackmail," he began gingerly. "I think we should think of it as an exchange. I've got something you want, and you've got something I want. We'll work out a trade."

"How much do you want?"

"I don't want money."

"You want to fuck me?" she asked incredulously.

"Yes," said Ted, "what man doesn't? But that has nothing to do with the deal."

"Then what is it?"

"I have a screenplay, an action comedy entitled *Heavy Artillery*. With a little rewriting, you'd be perfect for it. So I want you to option it, for half a million dollars."

"Where do you think I can get that kind of money?" she said.

"I read you've got a production deal with Jeffrey Klein over at Marathon. Have him option it for you."

Perhaps there was some method in his madness, she speculated. After all, last year there had been a rumor that Jeffrey, in a state of high confusion, had optioned his housekeeper's shopping list for three hundred thousand dollars, bringing it to the studio and insisting that they try to sign Paula Abdul as Salsa and Jim Belushi as Liquid-Plumr.

"And what do I get in return?" asked Karen coolly.

"My silence," responded Ted with a smile.

"Your silence?!" she sneered. "For how long? You can bleed me for the rest of your life with this."

"And what if I can?" shrugged Ted. "Isn't it worth it to make me writer/producer on a couple of your movies? Or would you rather have the world know that the glamorous Karen Kroll had an illegitimate child when she was a sophomore in college? A child she gave to her drama teacher, Mrs. Ida Gunkndiferson, to raise as her own. Which was especially appropriate considering that Mr. Gunkndiferson was the father."

Karen stepped forward and raised her hand. She slapped Ted hard across the face. Then she did it again. He felt, deliciously, as if he were in *Chinatown* and had to restrain himself from muttering, "my sister, my daughter, my sister, my daughter."

"How did you find out?" hissed Karen.

"Mrs. Gunkndiferson called and told me. She's very upset that you're not planning to attend the fifteenth-year class reunion," replied Ted.

That old bitch, seethed Karen. Would she never be free of her?

"You shouldn't try to turn your back on the past," continued Ted. "Personally, I never miss a class reunion."

"Lots of people have illegitimate children," countered Karen calmly.

"Yes," replied Ted, "but not all of them desert them. Mrs.

Gunkndiferson told me you never even sent little Kevin any Christmas presents."

"You can't prove that!" said Karen as she paced the ground angrily.

"No, but I can prove that you didn't even show up at the funeral six years ago when Mr. Gunkndiferson and Kevin died in a car crash. Now that's what we at *Personality* call a cover story." Ted leaned back on his car and grinned.

"I was on location," protested Karen.

"In Miami with Jean-Claude Van Damme," replied Ted. "I checked. You were just a few hours away."

"I had a big scene that day," insisted Karen.

"What did you have to say to Jean-Claude?" asked Ted. "Pass the ammo?"

She paused and looked at him. "Is it a good screenplay?"

"Do you care?"

"What assurance have I got that you won't print this?"

"My word," said Ted crisply. He had her and he knew it.

"Do I have to make this movie," she asked, "or is it enough that I buy the screenplay?"

"Why not make it," grinned Ted. "Who knows? Maybe you'll get another nomination."

Karen sighed deeply and stared at the darkening sky. It would be night soon. "All right," she said, "you've got a deal."

"Congratulations," replied Ted, "I'll make you come off beautifully in the article. And I'll tell Mrs. Gunkndiferson that *Personality* doesn't print unsubstantiated rumors."

Karen turned away, walking back to her car in disgust. Ted looked out over Mulholland Drive, down into the San Fernando Valley that lay thousands of feet beneath it. The lights in the homes and businesses in Studio City and Burbank were just beginning to be turned on. They formed an elaborate, electronic grid, twinkling as they stretched to the mountains beyond, a perfect setting for the world's largest toy train set. How wonderful it's going to be, thought Ted, to be staring down at this every night for the rest of my life.

It was at that moment that Karen rushed up behind him and pushed him off the side of the cliff.

33

The score from *West Side Story* came booming out of Lori's CD player. But it had been programmed in a most unusual manner. There was no "Somewhere," no "Tonight." Not even an "Officer Krupke." Instead, the digitalized disc kept repeating only one song: "Maria." Lori had been listening to it, and doing straight shots of Cuervo Gold tequila, for two days now.

Her eyes were bloodshot and her tongue was thick and fuzzy with alcohol, but she didn't care. The confrontation at Maria's house had left her devastated. Having finally admitted to herself that nothing, not even the Oscar, was more important than Maria's love, she had been shut out by another woman. Unlike the tragic Diana Barrymore, who suffered from too much, too soon, Lori was suffering from a case of too little, too late. Brushing back her tears, she rose shakily from the sofa to search out the tequila bottle for one more hit.

Heading into her kitchen, Lori saw something that made her gasp. A busty, middle-aged woman, in heavy makeup and a flashy Pucci print dress from the sixties, was sitting on one of the stools at her breakfast bar. The woman had teased black hair the color of tar, blood-red lipstick, a wrist full of clanking silver bracelets and huge jade earrings in the shape of pagodas. Lori thought she had two tiny tarantulas on her face until she realized that the woman was wearing the biggest fake eyelashes she had ever seen. She was also sipping vodka on the rocks from an enormous tumbler and sucking greedily on a Kent.

"Hiya, kid," said the woman in a baritone so deep it suggested Lauren Bacall imitating a truck driver.

"Who are you? What are you doing in my house?" stammered Lori in half-drunken shock.

"I'm Jacqueline Susann," said the woman, stubbing out her Kent.

"You're who?" said Lori in disbelief.

"Jackie Susann," repeated the woman. "You know, the doll who wrote *Valley of the Dolls*."

"But you're dead," gasped Lori.

"Doesn't stop me from getting around," said Jackie, lighting up another Kent with a gold Cartier lighter.

"I don't understand this," said Lori, groping for some sort of rational explanation.

"I'm just on a little field trip," smiled Jackie.

"From where?"

"Hell," said Jackie.

"Hell?" echoed Lori, who was now growing somewhat scared. "You live in Hell?"

"Well, actually it's Celebrity Hell," offered Jackie. "It's where all the naughty stars and media types go when we die. It's got condos, a pool, a Jacuzzi. Actually, it's just like Hollywood, only no one can get any work. That's why it's Hell."

"And all the bad stars go there?" asked Lori, not quite believing she was having a conversation with a woman who was technically a ghost.

"Oh yeah. Dean Martin checked in last year and he's been having a blast. He and Lana Turner are fucking like a couple of seventeen-year-olds," said Jackie, grinning lewdly.

"And this is where you live?"

"They've put me up in the Bad Women Writers Cottage. I share a bedroom with Grace Metalious. We're waiting for Julia Phillips and Danielle Steele to join us. Actually," said Jackie, stubbing out her second cigarette, "I don't mind Hell that much. But you can't get decent Chinese down there. Say, how about ordering out for some lobster cantonese and shrimp toast?"

Lori held on to the kitchen counter for balance. She was either dreaming or hallucinating; this could not actually be happening. And yet the woman got up, poured herself another vodka and raised the glass in Lori's direction.

"Bottoms up, kid," said Jackie, taking a healthy slug of her drink and settling back down on the stool. "Why don't you pour yourself one. Looks like you need it."

"Oh, Miss Susann," sobbed Lori, giving up all hope of understanding the situation. "I'm so confused."

"Join the club, doll. Join the club."

"I never thought it would be like this," sniffled Lori, pouring herself another shot. "I always thought I'd become a successful actress and win an Academy Award and everything would be all right."

"You have to climb to the top of Mount Everest to reach the Valley of the Dolls," commiserated Jackie, quoting the first line of the poem that opened her classic novel. "And when you get there, the loneliness is devastating." She grabbed her lighter and lit up a third cigarette. With her thick, black eyelashes, her dangling jade earrings and smoke coming out of both nostrils, Jacqueline Susann looked like a fire-breathing dragon on the front door of a Chinese restaurant.

"I miss my girlfriend so much," confessed Lori.

"Lesbo stuff, huh?" replied Jackie. "Know all about it. I even tried muff diving Ethel Merman back in the sixties, but the bitch blew me off to make *It's a Mad, Mad, Mad, Mad World.* Could have used some dykes in that one."

"I thought success would make me happy," said Lori, taking another gulp of tequila.

"So did Neely."

"Neely?"

"Neely O'Hara, one of my dolls in *Valley*," said Jackie. "Neely was a kid star, great voice, hit it big in the movies, then started marrying fags and hit the bottle."

"That sounds just like Judy Garland," said Lori.

"Listen, kid," hissed Jackie, "I write fiction. If my stuff feels familiar, it's because it's so true to life."

"Why is it always such a struggle?"

" 'Cause that's the way the big kahuna rigged it," replied Jackie, jerking her thumb upward. "Face it, show business is tough on women. Look at me. I practically invented the shlock blockbuster novel. Then I kick, and who comes along to steal my thunder? Men! Sidney Sheldon, Tom Clancy, Robert James Waller. Fags, all of 'em."

"But what should I do?" asked Lori. "I don't want to leave the business. It's my whole life."

"That's what Neely said. It practically killed her."

"Oh this is such a mess," cried Lori, starting to weep again.

"Hey, hold on, kid," said Jackie, putting her arm around Lori. "I've got something for you. Why don't you try some of these?"

Lori looked at Jacqueline Susann's outstretched palm. In it was a small cluster of capsules, carefully color-coordinated as if they were on a book jacket. There were pink pills, black pills, red pills.

"What are they?" asked Lori.

"Dolls," said Jackie, taking a last, long drag on her Kent. "Take ya where ya wanna go. Up, down, sideways out your wazzo."

"But aren't they addictive?"

"Bullshit," sneered Jackie. "I've been taking them for years. Never missed a night." She poured the pretty pills into Lori's hand. "Wash these babies down with a shot of hooch. It'll all seem like a bad memory by morning."

"Thank you," replied Lori, staring at the pills. Would they really help?

"Now I gotta go," said Jackie, sliding off the stool and palming her lighter. "I got an appointment with my proctologist back in Hell. My hemorrhoids are killing me." She walked to the front door and then turned to Lori.

"Oh, and kid?" she said. "If you see Jackie Collins tell her for me that I'm not worried. I've got wigs older than that broad."

Jacqueline Susann slammed the door behind her, leaving Lori alone in the kitchen, pills in one hand, a tequila bottle in the other. She wondered if she should really take the dolls. What if there were side effects? And yet, she was so tired of crying and drinking over Maria. A little rest couldn't hurt.

Suddenly a spasm of energy surged through her. She shoved the pills in her mouth, raising the bottle to her lips. "I'm Neely O'Hara!" she gargled as the liquor washed down her throat. "I'm Neely O'Hara and don't you ever fucking forget it!"

━━━

TED GAVIN, 34, a writer for *Personality Magazine*, was discovered yesterday by members of the LAPD in a gully in the Hollywood Hills, where he is presumed to have fallen to his death. Gavin was working on a cover story on the nominees for the Best Actress Oscar when he died. Authorities are conducting an investigation of the incident. A celebrity journalist, Gavin is perhaps best remembered for the articles " 'I Don't Give a Damn Whether They Like Me or Not': The *New* Sally Field" and "Charlie Sheen's Search for Inner Peace." Survived by his parents.   —*Hollywood Reporter*
March 23

34

Fiona put down her fountain pen and read the letter she had just written. It had taken her all morning, pen in one hand, crumpet in the other, to craft it. Now she had to decide if she had the courage to mail it. Her eyes surveyed the pages.

My Dearest Maria,

After the turbulent melodrama of our last tryst, with Lori appearing at the most inopportune of moments, I felt it might be of great benefit to both of us for me to take pen to paper and set down my feelings for you under the influence of reasoned contemplation, rather than the potent combination of unbridled passion and 100-proof tequila that has hitherto served as our mutual aphrodisiac.

You entered my life at a time of great confusion, offering solace and companionship, to say nothing of a style of lovemaking that was hitherto foreign to the shores of my libido. I have cherished the times we've shared, the long walks, the intimate dinners, the interesting new uses we've discovered for garden vegetables. Our love has burned brightly. And yet I am not sure whether it is an eternal flame, or merely a Bic pocket lighter. Thus I should like to suggest that we take a brief holiday from each other's company.

Before you contemplate homicide, please let me offer an explanation.

When Collie and I first met, we embarked on a blazing affair that rocked the National Theatre to its foundation. Young, filled with ambition and drawn passionately to each other, we carried on with an erotic abandon that was considered quite scandalous. Necking in the balcony was not unknown to us. And yet, after two months together, Collie suggested that we stop seeing each other to discover if we were in the grip of infatuation or had truly made a match.

It was at that moment that my love for Collie flowered.

In this time of confusion, I feel such a respite would clarify things for both of us. Are you truly through with Lori? Is Collie but a bittersweet memory to me? Perhaps some time alone would help us find the answers to these vexing inquiries. Let us take a one-month sabbatical to work on ourselves, if I may lapse into the parlance so beloved by you Americans.

Be well. I shall speak with you after the Oscars.

Fondest Regards,

Fiona

Done, thought Fiona as she munched on some stray crumpet crumbs, and done well. She affixed a stamp, slipped on a butterscotch cardigan sweater and headed to the front door. After mailing the letter at the post office, she'd treat herself to a second cup of Earl Grey at the local tea shoppe.

Thus it was with great confusion that she opened the door

to find herself confronted by two detectives from the Santa Monica division of the Los Angeles Police Department.

"Miss Fiona Covington?" asked the older of the two, whose thick neck and beefy hands suggested an aging sumo wrestler.

"Yes," replied Fiona. "Is something wrong, gentlemen?"

"I'm Harris Ysplanski, LAPD," he said, holding up his badge. "We'd like to ask you a few questions about the death of *Personality Magazine* writer Ted Gavin."

Colin fought his way through the thicket of newscasters and cameramen that clogged the steps of the Santa Monica precinct. Damn vermin, he thought to himself, at least in London we have the Royal Family to distract these electronic vultures.

The call from Fiona had come while he was masturbating to a Kathy Ireland exercise video.

"Collie dearest," she said, her voice trembling.

"Fiona, what a surprise," he replied, reluctantly letting his swollen member slip out of his hand.

"Collie, I'm in desperate straits. I need your help."

"Whatever has happened, Fiona?"

"The police are accusing me of the murder of a writer from *Personality Magazine*," sobbed Fiona.

"Murder?" gasped Colin in shock. "Fiona, have you gone mad?"

"If only it were that simple," she wailed. "If only it were some tatty Agatha Christie one picks up on a rainy weekend in a cottage in Brighton."

"But what do you want me to do?" asked Colin, wistfully gazing at the space between Kathy Ireland's thighs as she performed a series of squats.

"Collie," replied a mortified Fiona, "there may be a question of making bail."

In the end, there was no bail, the district attorney's office having decided to hold off on filing formal charges. But there was a police inquiry that, upon reflection, Fiona decided was more brutal than an audition for Oliver Stone.

The small airless room where Detective Ysplanski led Fiona resembled an actor's worst nightmare of a green room, a cheerless cell in which one might prepare for a one-woman show entitled *The Wit and Wisdom of David Mamet's Women.* In the corner of the left wall, someone had carved the words, "Manson was here."

Fiona sat on a hard, wooden chair, facing Ysplanski and three other detectives from the homicide division. Added together, the four men's annual intake of red meat totaled over seven hundred pounds.

"When did you first meet Ted Gavin?" asked Detective Ysplanski as he stared into Fiona's frightened brown eyes.

"Not more than a week ago," she gulped. "He came to my house to interview me for a story he was writing for the magazine."

"At what point did you become intimate with him?"

"Intimate?" cried Fiona. "I met the poor man once in my entire lifetime."

Ysplanski and his fellow detectives gazed at Fiona coolly, their faces betraying no emotion whatsoever. She felt like Sharon Stone in *Basic Instinct,* confronted by Michael Douglas and a squad room full of policemen. And indeed, perhaps only Stone's antics could have melted these four stony detectives. Alas, Fiona had never smoked and always wore panties.

"What did this interview with Mr. Gavin consist of?" continued Ysplanski.

"Only the usual," responded Fiona. "A pot of tea and a spot of Auden."

Detective Ysplanski shifted uncomfortably in his chair. "How long have you been taking the drug Auden?" he inquired.

"Auden is the greatest poet of the twentieth century," protested Fiona.

"Call the lab," said an unimpressed Ysplanski to the detective at his side. "Ask them if they know of any crack or crystal meth derivatives called Auden. Tell them it's known as the poetry drug." The detective left the room as Fiona's expression turned from one of terror to disbelief.

"Now see here, detective," she began, her voice cracking slightly. "I've a right to know why I'm being interrogated in the death of a man I hardly knew."

"You hardly knew Ted Gavin?" asked Ysplanski.

"I'm on better terms with the man who installed my cable," insisted Fiona.

"Then perhaps you can tell me why we found this in Ted Gavin's jacket pocket when we discovered his corpse." Detective Ysplanski reached into a manila envelope and withdrew a briarwood pipe with the words "From Fiona, all my love" engraved on its stem.

Later, when Fiona rushed into Colin's arms in the waiting room, she told him of the pipe, his pipe, which had mysteriously appeared in Ted Gavin's jacket pocket.

"What utter tosh," exclaimed Colin. "You gave that to me just a few weeks ago."

"I told them that," murmured Fiona through her tears, "but they regarded it as a mere lie, an utter canard."

"I'll back you up," said Colin. "In court if necessary."

"Oh will you, Collie? Will you?"

"Get set for the greatest cross-examination since *Witness for the Prosecution.*"

"Oh Collie," gasped Fiona, sinking into his shoulder, "what a comfort you are."

"Has it been hard, darling?" he asked, slipping his arm around her.

"Remember that awful student production of *The Wild Duck* we saw at Oxford?" replied Fiona.

"That bad?" smiled Colin.

"Worse," sighed Fiona. "At least that was in Swedish."

Amber took her seat and looked around the dining room of Morton's. It had been Ted's favorite restaurant, and Fatima had insisted it be used for his memorial service, even if they could only get it from three to five in the afternoon. She had been surprised when Fatima called to invite her to the memorial; evidently Ted had imagined their relationship to be much more than Amber had ever intended.

"He worshiped you," said Fatima over the phone. "He saw you as the one shining light among the whores and thieves nominated for this year's Best Actress Award."

"That's really nice," mumbled Amber.

"It's all in his final article," continued Fatima. "An article I have personally rewritten as a tribute to Ted. I've dropped the other nominees and concentrated on you and Ted, your relationship. It's called 'The Journalist and the Hellcat.' A real grabber, eh? We tell the story of how Ted's love redeemed you from a hell of drugs and parental abuse. It's got real guts." Fatima pronounced the word guts as "goots," making it rhyme with roots.

"I can't wait to see it," said Amber warily.

"It'll be out Monday, right before the voting closes. You come off very well in it."

"Wow," said Amber, suddenly seeing a very bright silver lining.

So she had borrowed a black dress, hat and gloves from Brianna and sworn off all drugs, except for Thai stick, for twenty-four hours. There had been two photographers in front of the restaurant; both had taken her picture. What the hell, she thought as they clicked away, after all the stories about her mother and the MTV fiasco a little good publicity couldn't hurt.

There were only about fifty people in the room, most of them fellow *Personality* writers and editors. After listening to a tape of "Stairway to Heaven," Ted's favorite song, Fatima rose and walked slowly to the front of the room. She seemed somber and more composed than usual.

"The goats of Mecca are still today," she began. "The shepherds have quietly laid their staffs in the ditch on the side of the road."

Amber raised the large handkerchief she had borrowed from Brianna to her cheek. Her eyes fluttered several times, and then large tears began to pour from them. Fatima nodded sadly in her direction.

Amber was surprised, but then she knew very little about cooking. The raw onion she had placed in the handkerchief was working like crazy.

"This is Dan Rather with *The Evening News*. Our top story tonight is about the upcoming Academy Awards and the rumors of scandal, suicide and murder swirling around two of the nominees for the Best Actress Award.

"At Cedars-Sinai Hospital in Los Angeles, it was confirmed this afternoon that Lori Seefer, the blond actress nominated for her role in *Losing Sofia*, has been in the hospital under observation for the past two days. Rumors persist that Miss Seefer attempted to take her own life in a fit of despondency over a failed love affair. However, in a statement released a few hours ago, the actress's publicist, Melissa Crawley, termed the story 'specious,' adding that Miss Seefer was 'suffering from food poisoning brought on by eating a poorly microwaved pizza.'

"And at the Santa Monica precinct of the Los Angeles Police Department, Fiona Covington, a British actress nominated for her work in the film *Mary*, was released today after questioning in the ongoing inquiry into the mysterious death of *Personality Magazine* writer Ted Gavin. Early, unconfirmed reports suggest that a keepsake from the actress was found on Gavin's corpse.

"Asked if she felt she could find justice in the Los Angeles court system, or if the investigation would harm her chances of winning the Academy Award, Miss Covington replied, 'Kevin Costner and Mel Gibson both have Oscars as best director; Martin Scorsese and Stanley Kubrick have none. Where is the justice in that?' "

35

Karen hurled the *Personality Magazine* across her living room in disgust. She'd almost rear-ended the BMW in front of her when she spotted it at the newsstand on Franklin Avenue. There, sitting in the midst of a sea of *Time* and *Newsweek,* was the new issue of *Personality* with Amber Lyons's angelic face on the cover.

And the article! Karen had flinched when she came across passages such as the one that read, "Deeply troubled, deeply talented, the twenty-something actress felt she had finally found an unconditional love with the man whose weapons were not drugs or abuse, but words. How quickly it all slipped away." Was this supposed to be about a young tramp who drugged her way into movies, or Joan of Arc? She could hardly tell the difference.

The outpouring of sympathy in the press for Amber had left Karen befuddled. She'd been certain the young actress was out of the Oscar race when she tossed her cookies on the stage of the Music Hall. Now she was being made out to be some sort of martyr just because Ted Gavin (who knew they'd been seeing each other?) was dead.

Karen took solace in a CBS News poll that named her and Connie as three-to-one favorites to win Best Actress. She could only hope that Connie's public disgrace as a shoplifting alcoholic would make her own arrest for lewd conduct seem insignificant.

But now there was Amber Lyons to worry about, and Karen didn't know how to strike back at a sob story on the cover of *Personality*. If only Ted Gavin hadn't died.

But then, of course, he had to.

She hadn't spent fifteen years building a career, moving from a community college drama program to soft-core pornos and on to major motion pictures, only to see it destroyed by a creepy magazine writer. Karen had never had a single guilty moment over leaving her child with the woman whose husband she had seduced. It was what she had to do to get where she wanted to be.

In the years between Bascom and Hollywood she had had only one goal: movie stardom and the fame and riches that went with it. Marriage, family, inner peace: those were for the girl next door. Karen wanted only to live on a hill, surrounded by nothing more intimate than a large metal fence that could keep all intruders at bay.

Mrs. Gunkndiferson could never understand that. Which is why she made a better mother for Karen's son that Karen ever could have. At least that's how she had rationalized it over the years.

And now that she had called Mrs. Gunkndiferson and promised to address the class reunion at Seminole State, she figured that her secret was still safe. At least until after the Oscars.

You do what you have to do, she thought to herself grimly. It was something she'd realized to be true from the age of nine when she first saw *The Bad Seed* on television. It still bothered her that little Rhoda Penmark had to pay for her murderous crimes. That kid had deserved that penmanship medal!

Karen had slept dreamlessly ever since her meeting with Ted on Mulholland Drive; no hint of guilt invading her conscious or her subconscious. Which didn't surprise her. You do what you have to do. That poor sap from *Personality* had merely offered her the opportunity to prove it.

She was troubled by one thing, however. It would devastate her if her killing Ted Gavin clinched the Oscar for Amber Lyons.

The call had come early this morning.

"Connie?"

"Yes?"

"It's Eric. How are you?"

"I'm fine. How are you?"

"The same. Connie, I'd like to see you for lunch this afternoon. Are you free?"

"And easy," joked Connie.

"I'll stop by at noon then?"

"I'll be ready, Eric."

Putting the phone back down, Connie felt her heart beating wildly, like a bongo drum played by an epileptic. All week long she had been waiting, hoping that Eric would call. And now he had! She hadn't felt this way since she'd watched Sandra Dee succumb to Troy Donahue in *A Summer Place* at the Loew's Metropole in Newark. Had it really been over thirty-five long years ago?

Well fuck Sandra Dee, she thought. This may well be my last shot at landing a decent man, and I'm going to live it out. Relaxing in a bubble bath, Connie found herself dreaming of a life with Eric. She'd pack him a lunch every day before he left for the Beverly Hills Police Station; dinner would be waiting when he came home. There would be quiet fireside chats in the evening, and church services every Sunday. She couldn't wait to go to the Policeman's Ball and dance a lusty polka with her beloved. And oh those pot luck suppers! Perhaps Rose's recipe for lasagna would come in handy after all.

Drifting into her living room, dressed in an ivory silk caftan, Connie sank down into the pillows of her black velvet sofa. Leaning her head back, she began to hum "Where Am I Now That I Need Me?" By now, it was her favorite song of all time.

The maid led Eric into the room and then retreated. He stood in the archway, sunlight forming a halo around his blond hair. Oh my adored one, thought Connie.

"It's so nice to see you again," she said, managing not to drool. "It's almost been a week since Palm Springs."

"Glad to be back home?" he asked, joining her on the sofa.

"You bet," said Connie brightly. "I haven't touched a drop." Indeed, upon returning to her estate, she had turned it upside down, rooting bottles out of closets, tree planters and any other location she could recall. She gave them all to Helga, her masseuse. "They're for Bjork and his book on Ingmar Bergman," she said. "All writers drink."

"I'm glad you're doing so well," replied Eric evenly.

"What would you like for lunch?" asked Connie eagerly. "I can have the maid whip us up a spinach soufflé."

"I've come here for something much more serious," he said. Connie began to tremble with anticipation. Was he going to propose marriage so quickly? They hadn't even slept together yet.

Eric stood up and began to pace. "As you know, with your permission, the maid let me search your house last week for additional evidence relating to the notes you've been receiving from a stalker. What I've discovered may come as a shock to you."

"But it's just some crazy fan, isn't it?" protested Connie. "One of those autograph hounds who's gone over the line."

"I only wish it were," said Eric softly.

"Is it someone I know?" gulped Connie.

"Someone you know all too well."

Connie felt a chill run through her as her mind raced toward the outer shores of paranoia. Could it be Morty, poor, farting Morty, trying to strike back for years of mistreatment? It didn't seem possible.

"It's someone very, very close to you," said Eric ominously.

"Well don't keep me in suspense," begged Connie. "Tell me who the hell it is!"

"It's you," said Eric softly.

"What?!" gasped Connie.

"It's you, Connie," continued Eric. "The typeface in the notes matches the one on the typewriter in your study. And the lab's hair and fiber analysis confirmed it. You've been writing those notes to yourself."

"What are you, crazy?" screeched Connie as she jumped up from the sofa. "Do you expect me to believe this crap?"

"It's possible you may not even realize you've written the notes," said Eric. "They may be a cry for help from a very deep place of denial."

"You're making this up!" howled Connie.

"You may even be suffering from multiple personality disorder," concluded Eric.

"Oh I see," spat Connie, "now I'm fucking Sybil. Well listen to me, Sherlock Holmes, the personality that's here now, Connie Travatano, is telling you to take your lab analysis and get the fuck out of here."

"You can be arrested for this, you know," replied Eric. "It's a felony to fake a crime."

Jesus Christ, thought Connie, I've gone from the wedding chapel to the women's prison in the space of five minutes. Why don't they just lock my heart in a jail cell and be through with me?

"Do you have any recollection of writing these notes?" continued Eric.

"You're talking to me like I'm the Unabomber," whined Connie.

"I can't help you unless you help me," replied Eric. "The notes, do you remember writing them?"

Suddenly all the anger Connie was feeling fell away, only to be replaced by a vast, aching loneliness. Could Eric actually be right? Could she have written these notes in some sort of trance, in a pathetic attempt to win sympathy and attention? Perhaps. Stranger things had happened, she thought, remembering Ethel Merman's infamous *Merman Goes Disco* album.

Connie leaned forward and rested her head on Eric's shoulder. She began to cry into the crisp, blue cotton of his policeman's uniform.

"Mama," she sobbed, "Mama, I'm sorry if I hurt you. I did it for you, Rose. I did it for you."

The woman sitting across from Lori in the hotel room was perfectly composed. Carefully coiffed, dressed in a red Adolfo accessorized with just the right amount of David Webb jewelry, she radiated poise and warmth. Eyes flashing with intelligence, she pursed her tiny lips as she prepared her next question. Everything about her was flawless, Lori concluded.

But then why shouldn't it be? She was, after all, Barbara Walters. And who was Lori? Just the next chunk of movie meat Walters would throw to her ever-hungry audience on her annual Oscar interview show, to be broadcast just a week from today.

Melissa had pleaded with Lori not to go ahead with the interview after she'd been released from the hospital. "She'll chew you up and walk away with you in her alligator bag," she warned her. "I've seen Barbara when she's around a big story, and that's just what your suicide attempt is to her. She'd eat her young to be the first one to break it."

"Call her and make the arrangements," commanded Lori, hanging up in her highly paid publicist's ear. After two days at home, Lori was clear about what she wanted to do. She still couldn't believe the doctor's report on her aborted suicide. It claimed that she had been hallucinating on tequila and thought that Jacqueline Susann had offered her seconals. If the house-keeper hadn't come back for her keys, Lori could have died.

But the brush with death had allowed her to look at her life with a new perspective. Things that once seemed obstacles, now appeared to be challenges. Risks that once seemed to be death-defying, now had become imperatives. It was as if a vital, bubbling spring had erupted within Lori, clearing the clogged arteries that led to her heart. Suicide, it seemed, had proven to be Drano for Lori's soul.

And so she sat in a suite at the Beverly Wilshire waiting for Barbara Walters to fire her next question at her. They had shared barbecued spare ribs from a silver chafing dish provided by room service and swapped stories about their worst inter-view experiences, all under the watchdog eye of Melissa. When the formal interview began, Lori found herself amazed at Wal-ters's charm and compassion. With her uncanny mixture of chicken soup wisdom and Bergdorf Goodman chic, Barbara Walters was truly the Jewish mother of America.

"Now, Lori," said Barbara, signaling a change of topic, "we've talked about the Oscars and your career as a child actor. Now I'd like to move on to something more personal."

Lori steeled herself, noting out of the corner of her eye that a small but succulent band of perspiration had appeared on Melissa's upper lip.

"I'm a mother," continued Barbara, "and like every mother

in America, I wonder if my little girl—who'd kill me for saying this, but I'm going to say it anyway—I wonder if my little girl is going to get married. And when. Does your mother ever ask you those questions?"

"Not really," replied Lori with a small smile.

"Well then," Barbara pressed on with an equally small smile, "let me be your mother. Lori, do you have any plans to marry?"

"What do you mean by marry?" asked Lori, warily.

"Oh you know," grinned Barbara. "To settle in with someone, set up housekeeping, make a garden and adopt a couple of dogs."

"You mean a partnership?"

"Of course. Someone to rub your feet at night when you come home tired."

"Well that I could definitely use," said Lori with a laugh.

"You see," chimed in Barbara, "Mom isn't such a snoop after all."

"Guess not," said Lori, who saw that Melissa had stopped chewing her knuckles.

"Still," continued Barbara, "I wouldn't be a good mother if I didn't ask you if you had somebody in mind."

"I did," said Lori softly, "but that's over now."

"Could you tell us who that was?" asked Barbara, the tiniest glint of a teardrop beginning to shine in the corner of her right eye.

"Yes," said Lori. "Her name was Maria."

There was a moment of silence as Barbara Walters gazed at Lori with an infinite compassion and understanding that, prior to this moment, she had only lavished upon Golda Meir and Eddie Murphy. Then Melissa spoke up sharply.

"Barbara, you know this is just the hugest joke ever. I have been out on double dates with Lori and let me tell you there is no more man-crazy a female . . ."

"Shut up!" snapped Lori to Melissa. "I'll tell my own story."

"But Lori," protested Melissa, retreating in fear, "I just want Barbara to know that you were kidding."

"Was I?" challenged Lori, whose gaze forced Melissa to take two more steps backward.

"Well of course you were. Everyone knows you can't keep your hands off a good man," cooed Melissa as she took just one more step. Alas, it was the one that put her right up against the room service chafing dish. Almost instantly the gas flame from the dish jumped to the seat of Melissa's pantsuit, setting it aflame.

"Oh my God!" shrieked Melissa, turning to inspect the smoke and flame rising from her ass.

"Liar, liar, pants on fire," spat Lori.

"I'm burning up," cried Melissa.

"You're also fired," said Lori.

Melissa ran from the room, slamming the door behind her. Barbara Walters turned to Lori with an urgent expression.

"Shouldn't we help her?" she asked.

"Don't worry about Melissa," replied Lori. "Nobody can take care of herself better."

"But what will she tell people, running down a hotel corridor with the seat of her pants on fire?"

"She'll think of something. Melissa's good at making up stories. Now shall we return to the interview?"

"If you insist," replied Barbara. "I just hate to think of Melissa with a burned ass." But, ever the trouper, Barbara rallied and pushed on. "You said that there was someone you cared about, someone you dreamed of sharing a life with, and her name was Maria. Can you tell us any more about her?"

"Only that I loved her and now she's gone," replied Lori.

"And why is that?" asked Barbara, the single, jewel-like tear returning to her right eye.

"Because I lied and tried to make the public believe I was in love with a man," replied Lori. "I thought it might help me win the Oscar. Instead it lost me the only person I ever cared about."

"Lori," said Barbara softly, oozing a sincerity so real it could have been exchanged for gold at the U.S. Mint, "are you aware that you're the first person to ever come out on one of my specials?"

"What about Elton John?" asked Lori.

"Oh darling," murmured Barbara, "by the time I got to him he was practically wearing a dress. No, this is a first for me."

"Me too," said Lori.

"I'm glad," whispered Barbara, leaning over and squeezing Lori's hand.

"I just wish I had done it sooner," sighed Lori.

"My dear, it's never too late," said Barbara, as tears began to plunk down her cheeks. "Oh my!" she exclaimed, dabbing at her face with a Kleenex, "you've made me cry. That's what I was supposed to do to you."

"Does it feel good, Barbara?" asked Lori with an impish grin.

"It feels great," bawled Barbara, whose mascara had formed two thick, sticky trails down her rouged cheeks.

Lori decided to go for it. "And if you were a tree, Barbara, what kind of a tree would you like to be?"

"Oh hell," sobbed Barbara, blowing her nose and wiping futilely at her eyes, "you know the answer to that one. I'd like to be a goddamned weeping willow."

===

This year's Best Actress race has turned into a full-blown public relations nightmare for the Board of Governors of the Academy. Normally the high glam event of the evening, the category features a group of actresses who might be more at home in a police line-up than an acting competition. Adding fuel to the flame is the late rumor that nominee Lori Seefer comes out as a gay woman on the Barbara Walters Oscar special.

Unless new indictments are handed down in the forty-eight hours before the big night, the nominees for this year's Best Actress Oscar currently include a rumored suicide attempt (Seefer), an alleged murderess (Fiona Covington), an alcoholic shoplifter (Connie Travatano), a drug addict (Amber Lyons) and a sex symbol picked up for lewd conduct (Karen Kroll). In this field, which has older Academy members thinking fondly of the days of Sacheen Littlefeather and Marlon Brando, Greer Garson, who died almost two years ago, is seen as even money.

—*USA Today*
April 2

36

"Harder, harder . . . that's right, push in . . . now softer . . . keep pushing in . . . more, more . . . Oh God, do I ever need this . . . harder, harder . . ."

Connie moaned and moved fitfully under the careful kneading her flesh was receiving from Helga's hands. The fumes of the rubbing alcohol filled her nostrils, reminding her fleetingly of the joys of one hundred proof vodka, a pleasure she had sworn off for life. She certainly could have used some now, with the Oscar ceremony only six hours away.

"Would Madam like some cold oatmeal applied to the soles of her feet?" inquired Helga.

"What for?" asked Connie. "I already had a bagel for breakfast."

"You're wearing open-toe shoes tonight," said Helga. "We don't want the bottoms of your feet to look dry and scaly."

"Maybe I'll wear pumps," mused Connie. "Skip the oatmeal."

"Bjork says Ingmar Bergman wore open-toe shoes," confided Helga. "When he used to get dressed up as a woman."

"Ingmar Bergman was a cross-dresser?" asked Connie, secretly fascinated.

"Well, not really," admitted Helga as she worked her hands up and down Connie's inner thighs. "But Bjork's putting it in his book anyway. He says it will help it become a best-seller. Makes it spicier."

"You'd better tell Bjork to check the Swedish libel laws. He may wind up making meatballs on a prison assembly line."

"They don't make meatballs in Swedish prisons, Madam. That's where all of Ikea's furniture is produced."

Connie sighed as Helga continued massaging her. She was as nervous this afternoon as she'd been three decades ago when she made her debut in *Moscow or Bust!* In just a few hours she'd know whether she'd won the Oscar and become Hollywood's flavor of the month or lost it and been reduced to a sound bite on *ET*.

At least her outfit hadn't been a burden. She'd decided to wear the blue dress she'd planned to wear at Ford's Theatre, an Armani that never went out of style. It would look perfect, accessorized with a few diamonds and a simple Chanel purse.

Helga's hands, firmer than ever before, moved up to her buttocks, first caressing them, then squeezing them in a curiously erotic fashion. Connie moaned softly. Then she felt the hands moving lower, still squeezing, until suddenly a finger moved inside her, probing her, opening her most private parts.

"Helga!" shrieked Connie, whipping her head around.

"I gave Helga the rest of the afternoon off," said Eric, who was standing behind her, clad in a beach towel and sly grin. "I told her I'd finish your massage."

"Did you now," said Connie, who found herself feeling warm and tingly all over.

"How am I doing so far?" he asked, rhythmically moving his fingers in and out of Connie.

"Not bad," she murmured as she collapsed softly on the massage table.

"Not bad?" he whispered. "Only not bad?"

Connie began to moan spastically.

"This is no better than not bad?"

"Harder, harder . . . that's right, push in . . . now softer . . . keep pushing in . . . more, more . . . Oh God, do I ever need this . . ."

"**A**re you almost ready, love?" asked Colin.

"One second, dearest," shouted Fiona from the bedroom. "I'm simply trying to rearrange Hardy Amies's revenge upon womankind so that it doesn't make my hips appear to be wider than the English Channel."

Colin poured himself a scotch and took a large sip. The liquor relaxed him, but he was strangely calm to begin with. He and Fiona had forgiven each other their indiscretions at once, spending the last week doing the things they loved most: going to the theater, reading good books and dining on endless, indigestible portions of bangers and mash. They had promised not to ask each other the details of their affairs, a sensible vow that frustrated Colin terribly since he was wildly titillated by the idea of Fiona with another woman. As for Ted Gavin's murder, Colin was certain of Fiona's innocence, despite the fact that no further suspects had emerged.

It occurred to Colin that his present circumstances—living with an alleged bisexual murderess—were enough to make him the envy of several Hollywood production heads and hack screenwriters.

"Does it please you?" inquired Fiona as she entered the room. Her dress, designed by the Queen's designer, Hardy Amies, was a bold concoction of purple taffeta, tight in the hips, draped sarong-style over one shoulder and cinched at the waist with a large black velvet sash. Dramatic as it was, the dress had nothing on the hat Fiona had chosen to wear with it. A large bowler of black straw, it was fashioned in the shape of a Venetian gondola, with a red ribbon tricked up to resemble a gondolier.

"I'd lose the hat," said Colin warily.

"But it's the very hat Sarah Ferguson wore to Churchill Downs last year," protested Fiona.

"There you are," responded Colin. "Her horse lost."

"I suppose I do look a bit like the *Titanic* is going down on my head," admitted Fiona. She removed the hat and played with her shimmering auburn hair.

"There's my redheaded girl," said Colin as he embraced her and planted a kiss on her neck. "The limousine awaits us."

"And what of our police escort?" asked Fiona. Detective Ysplanski had established surveillance outside Colin and Fiona's house, following them on their daily excursions, even to the laundry and the grocery. "Have we got a third ticket for him?"

"I spoke with the good detective this morning," said Colin. "He conceded that since we would be on national television there was little chance we'd try to flee the country. We're on our own tonight."

"I wonder how he'd feel being followed all day by an overweight flatfoot," sighed Fiona as she took a last glance at herself in the mirror.

"He has no other leads," reminded Colin. "If you could just tell him how that pipe wound up in that poor chap's pocket."

"It's as great a mystery to me as the raves Kenneth Branagh received for *Hamlet*."

"You've no idea at all who's behind this?"

"It was Colonel Mustard. In the library with a candlestick." Fiona snapped her Chanel purse shut. "And now shall we proceed to an even greater trial than the one I may face for the murder of Ted Gavin?"

Karen grabbed a Marlboro Light from the pack in her Chanel purse, lit it and inhaled deeply. The long plume of smoke she exhaled flew directly into Lars's face.

"What do you think about Fiona Covington being booked as a suspect for murder?" she asked as Lars, fanning away the smoke, continued to work on her hairdo.

"She hasn't actually been booked, has she?" said Lars.

"They're probably just waiting until after the Oscars."

"What I don't understand is why she chose to murder a magazine writer," said Lars, "when there are so many other bad writers out here she could have killed first."

"Rumor is she was screwing him," said Karen, taking another drag on her cigarette.

"But she told Jay Leno she was sleeping with a woman," protested Lars as he quickly worked his way through Karen's white-blond hair. It was two o'clock and he still had to get home and change into his tux.

"Could've been part of a cover-up," shrugged Karen. She loved misleading Lars, knowing full well that the gossip she passed on would be spread all over one of Beverly Hills's best hair salons tomorrow morning. And she couldn't believe it when the papers reported that Fiona was a suspect in Ted's murder. Finally she was getting lucky.

"I think it's time for the main event," said Lars, holding up a magnificent, formfitting evening gown Karen had borrowed from Valentino for the ceremony.

"If I can get into this, I can get into anything," sighed Karen as she rose from the vanity table and dropped her robe. Nude, save for a pair of panties, she walked over to Lars.

"Do you think Fiona's involvement with this murder will affect how the Academy votes?" asked Lars as he helped Karen shimmy into the gown.

"I don't know," she replied, hoisting the dress up over her breasts. "Is O. J. Simpson still a member?"

"Why do you have to wear black?" whined Tatianna as she held up the chic Richard Tyler cocktail dress Amber had picked out for the Oscars.

"I'm supposed to be in mourning," replied this year's youngest nominee for the Academy Award for Best Actress.

"For the late Mr. Personality?" asked Brianna.

"Nooo," cooed Amber, a smile flickering across her face as she applied the last of her eyeliner. "I'm in mourning for my life. Like Nina in *The Seagull.*"

"Is that a new rock group?" said Tatianna.

"No, silly," replied Amber. "It's a play by Chekhov. Ever hear of him?"

"Hmm, Check-off," said Brianna phonetically. "Is he any relation to jerk off?"

The Beavis and Butt-Head of Beverly Hills broke into peals of laughter while Amber put on her dress. Keep laughing, kids, she thought; if I win tonight I'll be doing Chekhov with Daniel Day Lewis while you two are still doing failed rock stars in the backseats of your BMWs.

"How do I look?" asked Amber, slipping into a pair of black pumps and grabbing her purse.

"You're sooo black!" exclaimed Tatianna.

"Way Morticia," grumbled Brianna. "Even the purse."

"Like it?" beamed Amber. "It's Connie Travatano's, the one she copped at Barneys. I swiped it from her at Betty Ford."

Lori looked herself over in the mirror. The aqua silk Donna Karan gown clung to her breasts, offering a tantalizing hint of cleavage, before descending in a series of concentric swirls down her legs. It was the most feminine thing she'd ever worn in her life.

It struck her as ironic to look this femme after coming out as a gay woman on American television, but then why should she cop to stereotypes? Did her conversation with Barbara Walters condemn her to appearing at award shows in a woman's tux and sneakers? Hell, all the Hollywood dykes did that.

No, the gown looked fine and she would stick with it. Reaching for her red leather Coach purse, she took a final glimpse at herself. I look good, she thought.

And she felt good too. Although she had purposely avoided reading or watching the news since she came out, Lori had been heartened by the people in the industry who had contacted her. Elizabeth Taylor had sent a note praising her courage; Cher left a message of support on her answering machine. Rosie O'Donnell and Jodie Foster had each sent huge bouquets. Lori's house was such a mess that she didn't know where to put them. Finally she just put them in her closet. Oddly enough, they thrived there.

Best of all, she had reconciled with Maria.

It was Maria who had made the first move. Her displeasure with Fiona's letter requesting a break in their relationship had been offset by an item in Liz Smith's column hinting that Lori came out as a gay woman on Barbara Walters's annual Oscar show.

"Baby," breathed Maria when Lori picked up the phone, "I hear you're coming out."

"Maria," gasped Lori. "It's you?"

"Yes. Now tell me the truth: you're coming out on national television?"

"I am. I really am."

"Then I'm really proud of you."

There was a pause, and then Lori spoke in a small voice. "Maria, I'm scared to death."

"Everybody's always scared to death to do the right thing," replied Maria. "What counts is that you're doing it."

"Maria?"

"Yes?"

"Could we have dinner tonight?"

"On one condition."

"What's that?"

"You gotta take me to the Oscars."

And it hadn't been that hard a decision for Lori to make. After all, with Claudio out of the picture, she didn't have a date to begin with.

"Ready?" asked Maria, who was now standing in the bedroom doorway watching Lori inspect herself.

"Yes," replied Lori, turning to look at her. "What do you think?"

"You look beautiful, baby," said Maria, coming over to her and planting a passionate kiss on Lori's lips.

"Thanks."

"Just one thing," added Maria, stepping back to inspect Lori's outfit.

"What's that?"

"That red purse clashes with the aqua dress."

"You think so?"

"I know so," replied Maria confidently. "Why don't you grab that black Chanel purse Melissa sent over to you instead."

"Hey, great idea," smiled Lori. "After all, we don't want Mr. and Mrs. America thinking that dykes have no style."

OSCAR NIGHT 6:30 P.M.

The show was only half an hour old and already she was bored. This endless stream of cleavage, capped teeth and platitudes could put anyone to sleep, she thought to herself.

Idly she opened her Chanel purse and rechecked its contents: Tic-Tacs, a vibrator and a revolver. She smiled wickedly, secure in the knowledge that she would have cause to use one of them before the night was over.

The mob outside the theater had been unbelievable. Security guards held the fans in check while television newscasters battled with each other for the attention of the stars. The red carpet that stretched from the street to the entrance of the Shrine was a veritable celebrity gauntlet: the death of a thousand sound bites. And the outfits! Raquel Welch had worn a chartreuse gown with a bodice so tight it made her breasts appear to be twin boiled hams on display in a butcher shop window. And Tori Spelling, under the mistaken impression she was attending the Emmys, had arrived with a TV antenna woven into her upswept hairdo.

And when the big stars began to arrive the crowd really lost it. "Jack! Jack!" they screamed as Nicholson flashed by, a blur of teeth and sunglasses. She couldn't help wondering what kind of a fuck he was.

And then it was "Cher! Cher!" Not her, she groaned. But it was, draped in sequins and on the arm of a seventeen-year-old. The rumor was she had met him skydiving.

But the biggest chant came near the end. "Liz! Liz! Liz!" the crowd roared as a tiny, teased head made its way through the mob. Boy, she thought, they had really pulled out the old guard tonight.

Jack and Cher and Liz. You could joke about them all you wanted, but you had to hand it to them: they were *real* stars.

Built to endure. Through good movies and bad, marriages and divorces, plastic surgery and drug abuse, designer perfumes and blow jobs, they went the distance. They had gone beyond mere celebrity and into legend.

Which was where she was determined to land tonight, as either an Academy Award winner or a murderess.

The strange thing was she wasn't nervous at all, despite the fact that she was considering assassinating someone in front of an international television audience of over one hundred million people. So what if everyone saw her do it? She'd take all her money and get herself the best goddamned defense attorney in the world. She was sure she'd get off.

After all, she thought, this is Los Angeles. No one's guilty of murder out here unless they've been tried for it at least twice.

37

Charlton Heston belched mournfully.

The former film star, who now largely occupied himself by writing angry letters to the *Los Angeles Times*, was waiting backstage at the Shrine Auditorium where he was to introduce the fourth nominee for Best Song, "Baby You Blow Me Away" from *L.A. Tornado*, sung by Bryan Adams. But his eating habits of the past two days had come back to haunt him. He had eaten roast ham for last night's dinner, a pound of bacon for today's breakfast and a double ham sandwich with mayo for lunch. Now Heston had a terrible case of indigestion and he felt like a big, old ham.

Despite Ben Hur's stomachache, the Oscars were proceeding at a frenetic pace. The logjam of limousines threading their way to the entrance of the Shrine Auditorium was over a half mile long.

Fiona snuggled deep in the backseat as Colin poured two flutes of champagne from the mini-bar. His mind slipped back to the last time he'd been in a limousine, when Karen Kroll had iced her nipples and then gotten them arrested for lewd conduct. What a nattering fool I've been, he thought.

"For you, dearest," he said as he passed Fiona her drink. "May you be the winner this evening."

"Ah, Collie," purred Fiona, "if I have you in my life once again, there is no greater trophy."

It warmed Fiona to contemplate how quickly she and Colin had reconciled. The past few days had gone by as quickly as the second act of a Pinter play. It was strange, mused Fiona, how a potential murder rap could bring old friends together.

"Collie," said Fiona, a wicked gleam in her eye, "I want you to know that I have yearned for you in every way."

"In every way?" replied Colin with an eyebrow arched high enough to qualify him for a Noel Coward play. "But what of Maria Von Trapp?"

"Bugger Maria Von Trapp," murmured Fiona.

She leaned forward and kissed Colin, forcing her tongue into his mouth. He quickly responded by placing his hands on her breasts, which seethed against the bodice of her purple taffeta dress.

"Dear one," groaned Colin, sinking down and covering her cleavage with kisses, "there is one thing I've always dreamed of doing with you."

"Yes, my love," whispered Fiona huskily.

"Don't think me kinky," he said, "but, now that you've dabbled in lesbianism, well, dearest, I've always wanted to do a threesome with you."

"Would that turn you on, Collie?"

"More than an offer of knighthood from the Queen herself," he mumbled from deep within the valley between her breasts.

"Then why don't we try it tonight?" proposed Fiona.

"Do you mean it?" asked Colin, shocked at his good fortune.

"Absolutely," responded Fiona. "Should I win tonight, let us retire to our bed: you, me and the Oscar. After all, who in Hollywood wouldn't want to go down on that little golden fellow?"

Lori was considerably more reserved in her rented car, settling for merely holding Maria's hand. She'd been holed up in her house for the past four days, emerging only for groceries and to pick up her aqua Donna Karan gown. She'd ignored all newspapers and kept the television off. If the world was talking about her coming out, she didn't want to know about it. She also screened all her calls through her answering machine, which relieved her of the chore of talking to Melissa. At first she had called twice a day, each message more desperate than the one before. The capper had come on Saturday morning, a final wail from the cave of hypocrisy and manipulation that Melissa had dwelled in for close to forty years.

"Lori, you must pick up," she exclaimed. "I can get Barbara to pull the segment. I have secret information on her and Tony Bennett in the sixties. You must pick up!"

But Lori didn't, deciding to attend the Awards on the arm of Maria rather than the tides of public opinion. She was still frightened of what might happen when the two of them stepped out of the limousine. She didn't think there would be boos, but she had prepared herself for a stony, self-conscious silence. There would probably be hostile looks from the fans, maybe even a few nasty posters. She was ready for the worst.

The car drew up to the curb and Lori and Maria alighted. She held on to Maria's hand, the perspiration from her hand almost soaking through her white velvet glove. Cameras were flashing in her face and she smiled gamely as she and Maria made their way through them and onto the red carpet that led into the Shrine.

Suddenly a roar began to build, starting like a low growl and growing into what sounded for all the world like a football cheer.

"Lori! Lori! Lori!"

She looked up into the bleachers to see hundreds and hundreds of fans standing and chanting her name. They were holding signs that said "We Love You!" and giving her a thumbs-up motion.

Just then a glamorous woman came up behind her and squeezed her around the waist. It was Susan Sarandon, on the arm of Tim Robbins.

"Honey," whispered Susan in her ear, "I am so proud of you. Don't you ever apologize for being as fabulous as you are!"

Maria leaned over and smiled at Lori. "Wave to your fans, baby," she said. "They've been waiting all day to see you."

Lori lifted her arm and waved to the bleachers as the chant grew in volume and intensity. She spotted a young girl in overalls and a T-shirt who was holding a sign. It said "Thank you."

I can't believe I waited all this time to do the simplest thing in the world, thought Lori. She tried to look at the girl again, but her tears blurred her vision.

"Karen Kroll," said Roger Ebert, placing his mike right above her magnificent breasts, "you're nominated for *Sacrilege*, the first film in which you've kept your clothes on. How does that make you feel?"

"Warm all over," replied Karen as she shot Roger a meaningful glance. She was hand-in-hand with Lars, having kept her promise to bring him to the Awards.

"Any predictions about tonight's show?"

"It'll run too long and I'll have a drink when it's over," said Karen with a wink.

"That was Karen Kroll," continued Roger Ebert, "and now I see Connie Travatano, a nominee for *Tomatoes and Diamonds*, approaching us. How are you, Connie?"

"Fine, Roger," said Connie, who was holding on to Eric's hand for dear life.

"This is your first nomination in quite some time," said Roger. "How does it feel?"

"I'm taking it a day at a time," smiled Connie, heading to the entrance doors.

"I think we have Fiona Covington and Colin Tromans heading toward us," said Roger to the camera. "Let's see if we can get their attention. Fiona, Fiona, over here."

"Yes, Master Ebert," replied Fiona with a smile. "What do you require of me?"

"Your impressions of this evening so far?"

"Well it's quite the little melodrama, isn't it," she replied. "But then my life hasn't lacked for that of late, has it?"

"This has been a hectic time for you," replied Roger. "Any plans for the future?"

"Like Portia," smiled Fiona, "I shall defend myself." With that she clasped Colin's hand and headed up the carpet.

"I see we have Lori Seefer next to us," continued Roger. "Lori, how do you feel tonight?"

"Like a winner, Roger," said Lori, circling her arm around Maria's waist.

"Well that's nice," he replied. "But I should point out that we're about three hours away from the Best Actress Award for which you've been nominated."

"Doesn't matter," said Lori. "I still feel like a winner."

"Well that was Lori Seefer, obviously in very high spirits. And now I think I see the final nominee for Best Actress, Amber

Lyons, whose performance in *As if . . . Chillin'* was one of the surprises of last year."

Amber was walking solemnly next to Billy Walsh, who had thoughtfully removed his nose ring for the evening. She approached the Chicago film critic stoically.

"Hello, Mr. Ebert," she said.

"Is this a tense time for you?" he asked.

"No," replied Amber dolefully. "Just a sad one. I recently lost someone very close to me."

"I imagine you're referring to Ted Gavin, the writer for *Personality*," said Roger, feeling somewhat uncomfortable.

"That's right," said Amber.

"Nevertheless, I want to take this opportunity to wish you the best tonight. And of course, the best to your fellow nominees as well."

"That's rather hard to accept, Mr. Ebert," said Amber with an angelic stare, "considering that one of them may be his murderer."

"Well I'm sure we'll all be looking forward to that on Court TV," said Roger, moving down the red carpet. "One interesting thing about the five nominees for Best Actress," he continued, trying to change the topic as quickly as possible, "is that they all seem to be carrying the same small black purse. Now I'm no fashion maven, but I can tell you that whoever designed that purse is going to be one busy person tomorrow."

"It's Chanel, sweetheart," said Anjelica Huston as she passed him on the carpet. "And she's been dead longer than you've known Gene Siskel."

Connie was in the ladies' room touching up her lipstick, one hour into the show, when she spotted Amber. Her long red hair spilled over her shoulders, and Connie couldn't help but notice how striking it looked.

"I love your hair," said Connie. "It looks so natural."

"It *is* natural," replied Amber, eyeing Connie suspiciously. "You should try wearing yours the same way."

"Not at my age," grinned Connie, snapping her compact shut. "Long hair on an older woman is a no-no."

"They say you're as young as you feel," said Amber, applying a thick coat of lipstick while staring at her reflection in the mirror.

"They say a lot of things," mused Connie. "They also say that after forty a woman must choose to preserve her face or her ass."

"I see you've chosen your ass," said Amber, blotting her freshly painted lips.

Connie thought instantly of the fight scene between Susan Hayward and Patty Duke in *Valley of the Dolls*. She contemplated the possibility of thrusting Amber's head down a toilet bowl and flushing it until her long red hairs turned up in the sewers of Pasadena. Then she took a deep breath and thought of Eric, who was waiting for her back at their seats in the third row. And she made her decision.

"Have a nice life, kid," she said, heading for the door. "But remember, it's lonely at the middle."

"I just saw you on the monitor outside the men's room," said Lars to Karen as he slid back into his seat. "Your nipples are bigger than Sylvester Stallone's thumbs."

"Thanks," murmured Karen, squeezing his arm. She had spent weeks getting ready for this night: virtually fasting on a high-protein, low-carb diet, daily workouts, a $750 hair color job. All to set off the skintight crimson Valentino gown that rustled ominously every time she took a deep breath. Karen looked wonderful and she knew it.

Lauren Bacall, stunning in a black Armani and a pearl choker, walked swiftly from her dressing room to the backstage waiting area. In the distance she spied Charlton Heston. A lifelong liberal, Bacall was not anxious to trade banal pleasantries with an actor who had become a shill for the handgun industry. Still, she believed in professional courtesy.

"How are you, Chuck?" she volunteered.

"Betty," he groaned as he clutched his stomach, "I've got indigestion. And now I'm afraid I'm constipated."

"Pity." She smiled and walked onstage to hand out the Best Actor Award.

She had been waiting all night, and now the moment had almost arrived. The endless parade of stars, has-beens, wannabes and probably-never-would-bes was almost at an end.

The Awards had provided few surprises: Dianne Wiest had won Best Supporting Actress (again!) and James Woods Best Supporting Actor (never again!). A Chinese designer had taken the Best Costume Award for *Larva,* a modern-day prequel to *Madame Butterfly.* A sound editor had thanked his wife, an animator had thanked God and a vegetarian documentary filmmaker had thanked tofu, "through which all things are possible." Best Song had gone to "Let's Boogie S'More!" from *Can't Stop the Music II.*

Now it was time for Best Actor, and the winner is . . . Robert De Niro. She'd look wonderful next to him in the pictures in tomorrow's papers, she thought to herself. And yet what if she lost? It was a possibility.

Alternating between anxiety and a deadly calm, she was still certain of only one thing: it would be her or a dead woman up there onstage in the next two minutes.

Lauren Bacall escorted Robert De Niro offstage as Al Pacino entered from the left. Hair flopping in his eyes, his bowtie askew, he still radiated the street sexuality that made most college-educated women want to sleep with their garage mechanics.

"The five women nominated for this year's Best Actress Oscar have presented us with five distinctly different portraits of the eternal female," said Pacino, dutifully reading the Tele-PrompTer prose that made appearing on the broadcast such a potentially embarrassing situation.

"Fiona Covington offered us a Mary Poppins who was part Baby Snooks, part Baby Jane Hudson in *Mary*."

Fiona rubbed her knee against Colin, visions of Dunkirk flooding her mind.

"Karen Kroll enthralled us with her performance as a nun whose habits were irregular in *Sacrilege*."

Karen clutched her purse in both hands, leaving Lars to fend for himself.

"Amber Lyons demonstrated that surfing and racial injustice are twin social evils in *As if . . . Chillin'*."

Amber chomped down on her Juicy Fruit, her molars grinding it into a sodden mass.

"Lori Seefer in *Losing Sofia* gave us a stunning portrayal of a woman who must lose her faculties to regain her soul."

Lori wound her hand around Maria's, letting her purse slip to the floor.

"And Connie Travatano reminded us that the secret's in the sauce in *Tomatoes and Diamonds*."

Connie absentmindedly handed her purse to Eric as she began to hyperventilate.

Al Pacino raised the envelope he had been holding to midwaist level and began to open it. He pulled out the card and looked at it before he spoke.

"And the Oscar goes to Karen Kroll," he said.

"Oh my God!" gasped Karen as Lars put his arm around her and helped her up. The applause swelled as she stepped shakily into the aisle and began to make her way up to the podium. Tears began to form in her eyes, yet her face was bathed in joy.

So this is what it's like, she thought. Well, world, you can kiss my ass now!

Karen mounted the steps to the stage and walked over to Al Pacino. He handed her the Oscar which she accepted with an iron grasp. Had it been Johnny Dante's dick, it would have broken in half.

"I don't know how to express the gratitude, the joy, I mean, there are so many people to thank, so many people I owe so much to. I just hope I don't leave anyone . . ."

A shot rang out with a single loud clap. Karen yelped in pain and threw her hand on her breast. Blood poured through her fingers. She swayed dizzily as Al Pacino, frozen with fear, watched in horror. As she crumpled to the floor, she dropped the Oscar, breaking it into dozens of pieces.

The audience turned and stared in shock at Amber, who had risen from her seat and was holding a pistol in her hand. It was Colin, unfazed by death scenes from all his Shakespearean work, who leapt to action. He vaulted across the aisle, grabbed Amber's arm and wrestled her to the floor. People around them screamed in fear and began to stampede toward the exits.

Arnold Schwarzenegger elbowed Tom Hanks aside and stepped on Julia Roberts's hand. Jodie Foster jumped over Tom Cruise and held on to the train of Jessica Lange's gown. Jack Nicholson leaned back and lit up a joint.

The chaos that ensued was broadcast worldwide and wound up on the front page of every newspaper from Burbank to Beijing. But there was one person who missed it. Walking down a corridor backstage, Charlton Heston found the Shrine to be strangely deserted.

"Where's everybody?" he asked a lone stagehand who was sweeping up.

"Mr. Heston, didn't you hear?" asked the man. "There's been a terrible tragedy. Karen Kroll won the Oscar and Amber Lyons shot her onstage."

"I didn't hear a damn thing," grunted Heston. "I've been in the can for the last hour and a half."

===

BOARD OF GOVERNORS HOPING FOR CALMER CEREMONY

Object Is to Restore Dignity to the Academy Awards

In the wake of an awards ceremony that turned into the first live broadcast of a murder, the Board of Governors of the Academy of Motion Picture Arts and Sciences is hoping for a calm, dignified evening next Monday when the annual Academy Awards will be held at the Dorothy Chandler Pavilion.

The millions who watched last year's Awards are unlikely to ever forget the shock of seeing young actress Amber Lyons assassinate Karen Kroll after Kroll had been announced the winner of the Best Actress Award and gone to the stage of the Shrine Auditorium to accept it.

The impact of the tragedy and the bizarre details uncovered in its aftermath still echo in the halls of the Academy and the plushly decorated living rooms of the mansions that line the streets of Beverly Hills. "Darling," comments actress Zsa Zsa Gabor, "it was a complete panic after that happened. I haven't seen that many frightened people out here since that crazy rumor in the seventies that Warren Beatty had herpes."

In the year since the shooting, the lives of the actresses nominated for last year's Oscar have undergone some major changes.

Connie Travatano announced her retirement from acting and married Beverly Hills policeman Eric Collins. She is currently scheduled to headline at the Save Our Streets fundraiser for the LAPD at the Wiltern Theater next month.

Lori Seefer flew to Hawaii to wed her female lover Maria Caldone. After accepting an honorary award from the Los Angeles chapter of GLAAD last week, Seefer departed for Paris to star in Franco Zeffirelli's remake of the classic love story *Tristan and Isolde.* Mel Gibson is set to appear opposite her.

Fiona Covington was cleared of all charges in the death of *Personality Magazine* writer Ted Gavin and reconciled with her estranged husband Colin Tromans. The pair are planning a remake of the Julie Andrews vehicle *Thoroughly Modern Millie,* in which the title character will be portrayed as a lesbian feminist.

Karen Kroll, even in death, provided some of the most shocking revelations of all. A search of late writer Ted Gavin's office unearthed tapes in which he alleged that Kroll had borne and deserted an illegitimate child whose funeral she refused to attend. When an investigation proved this to be true, the Los Angeles Police Department exhumed Gavin's corpse for a battery of tests. Hair and fiber samples from the corpse matched those of the late Kroll, leading police to believe her responsible for the writer's death.

It was this last fact that may have provided the motive for Amber Lyons's seemingly senseless crime. This was the argument presented by her defense attorney, Johnny Cochran, at her murder trial in January. The trial resulted in a hung jury, and Lyons remains in custody, awaiting her second trial.

Academy officials feel confident that this year's nominees for the Best Actress Award will produce no further scandals. The nominees are Meryl Streep for *Foreign Accents,* Sharon Stone for *Guts and Beauty,* Geena Davis for *I Need a Hit,* Michelle Pfeiffer for *Goddess Descending* and Diane Keaton for *Strange Garments.*

One final irony about last year's Best Actress race is the fate of the Oscar statuette itself, reconstructed after Kroll dropped it when she was shot. An only child whose parents are dead, Kroll left only a one-page will made out when she was a college stu-